Iron
Doves

Compiled by Nikki Yager

Edited by Fox Emm

IRON DOVES

ISBN: 978-1-945468-08-7

DEDICATION

Dedicated to everyone who has been harmed by another. You are not alone. You are not forgotten.

IRON DOVES

CONTENTS

IRON DOVES

FOREWORD

This anthology was put together to help support The DOVES
Program provides services for victims of Domestic Violence,
Dating Violence, Sexual Assault, and Stalking. They help serve
women, men, teens, and children. All proceeds of this anthology
will be donated to the Doves Program and the stories, edits,
formatting, and cover art has been donated for this cause.
If you are ever worried about your safety please check out the
website www.dovesprogram.com or call the 24-Hour Helplines
at 866-95-DOVES or 308-436-HELP (Español) to speak to an
advocate.

IRON DOVES

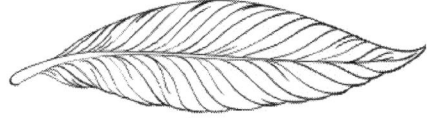

SECOND SLAVERY by Stephanie Barr

When the light of day finally found her, Xana woke, stiff and cold, with the smell of freshly turned earth in her nostrils. The clean scent of earth—not mildew and sweat—made her startle awake as she realized she wasn't in the room they had confined her to. She jerked up, wary of pursuit, and bit down on a gasp as her caned back protested. Hopefully, they couldn't hear her.

She'd slept in the lee of a large stone that had shielded her from the sun all morning and, only now, saw it was a grave marker. When she'd crawled through that fence last night and had come to rest, she'd had no idea she'd found a graveyard.

She bowed her head in respect to the fallen—whose name she could not read—but made no sign against evil nor even felt her heart quicken in fear. She'd lived with enough real terrors that superstition was no more than a possible means to keep her pursuers at bay, though she had never expected a full morning's respite. They couldn't be far behind her, now. She'd best make her escape while she could.

She shifted her stiff shoulders. Sleeping on the ground never got more comfortable and her bed had been rocky indeed. Her back protested again, the welts still fresh on her skin. The manacles on her arms and one leg remained, the skin raw beneath. Her best attempts at picking them had yielded nothing, but a farm implement had helped her pry open a link of chain so she could escape.

But to where? And where would she go now? It would do her no good if she ran in the direction of those that pursued her.

"I figured you were tired," a voice said. Xana nearly leaped to run, but the voice was old and female. And kind. She'd heard old and female voices before, but they had been every bit as cruel as the men's. She'd never heard one that was kind.

"Who are you?" Xana's eyes latched on to an old woman perched on a low stone. She wore a mishmash of faded clothing but looked so natural that Xana hadn't noticed her before.

Between the shawl, the apron, the dress, and the coat she wore over it the woman could be of nearly any girth though she was not tall. Her face was ancient, but she still had her teeth and a smile that showed them off. Her hair, silver streaked with a darker gray, was pulled to the top of her head in a messy bun that left much of it free to move when she moved.

The woman heaved to her feet with a grunt of discomfort. "Normally," she said in that kind voice that disarmed Xana against her will. "The trespasser would be the one explaining herself." The old black eyes, lost in a seamed landscape of a face, regarded Xana's manacles with sympathy. "But I'm guessing you might not be ready for that. I'm Corna the Witch."

Somehow, Corna had moved right next to Xana and brushed her cheek with a gnarled digit. "I will do you no harm, child."

And Xana believed her. Why, was a mystery.

Corna took her hand, the one without the broken finger as if it were perfectly reasonable, and led her through shrubs and clumps of plants. They were scattered as haphazardly as the many stone and wooden markers. "Where am I?" Xana asked, trying to summon distrust, then braced for the blow that usually followed her queries. The inevitable punishment had not, to date, curbed her curiosity, however.

Corna cackled and Xana was charmed. "'Tis my backyard, little one."

"What does a witch need with a graveyard?" Xana didn't recognize many of the plants, some pungent enough to sting her nostrils.

The old woman did not turn around. "Some plants are more powerful if they grow in a graveyard."

Xana gave the woman's hand a little tug. "Really?"

The old woman paused just long enough to turn and give her a wink. "As far as you know."

A breeze blew past that raised the hairs on Xana's neck. She started, then flinched as her wounded back brushed against her blood-stiffened shift.

Corna turned back at once, her face concerned. But she stared past Xana to where the touch of breeze seemed to play with a green plant that smelled strongly of mint. "Why didn't you tell me earlier?" Corna demanded with some disgust.

Xana felt bewildered. Tell her what?

But the old woman went on as if Xana had answered. "That's no excuse. Look at her wrists. She'd never have told me. And Kalor has been here and back again. You had plenty of time to return."

The crazy hair escaping her bun twisted in the breeze as if in apology but Corna did not appear mollified. "Flirt! I hope you at least thanked him and sent thanks back to Morsus. He gets little enough appreciation as it is, and it was kind of him to spare us his pet."

Corna blinked then turned her attention back to Xana. "I'm sorry, my dear. Alona says you have other wounds."

"Who is Alona?" Xana interrupted. "Is she a ghost?" The breeze that had been tugging at Corna's hair whipped Xana's short locks in irritation.

"Ghost? I guess some might call her that, but she's a good bit more. Think of her as a capable spirit that occasionally drinks blood."

"Drinks blood?"

Corna smiled and Xana's fear evaporated inexplicably. "She won't hurt you, child. You've been hurt enough. Do you want me to treat your wounds first or remove your shackles?"

It was as if the question awakened every hurt on her body. Suddenly her back stung unbearably, her broken finger throbbed, scratches and blisters complained, and the dull ache from where her master's son had pounded himself into her mourned. But, she did not hesitate. "The shackles."

"Yes, I thought so. Perhaps we can do both if Hildr remains about."

In the distance, a dog bayed and Xana remembered her

3

pursuers and their cruelty. "I have to go! I shouldn't be here."

"Of course, you should," Corna said, with no loosening of her grip on Xana's hand. "Else you would not be here."

"They'll find me and if I'm with you..." Xana twisted and yanked desperately, but Corna was amazingly strong. The thought of what the master and his men would do to the kind woman turned Xana's stomach. It was made all the worse because it would be her fault.

"It would not be your fault, little one," Corna said, "And that is not your former master's dog. Nor are they chasing you. They are gone."

"Gone?" The notion seemed impossible, but she *wanted* to believe. Plus, there was something in her that trusted Corna.

"Gone. Destroyed." She pulled and Xana followed. "Dead. That was Kalor's doing. Nor will there be bodies to lead others to you."

"And who is Kalor?" Xana asked, attempting again to tug her hand free.

"Kalor is Morsus' familiar, a phoenix. Kalor's protected by Morsus' spells from all but ensorcelled weapons." She regarded Xana closely. "Those who once owned you are charred to ash from Kalor's fire."

Xana tried to summon sorrow or even satisfaction, but could only feel relief. Corna seemed pleased at that response and pulled again at the girl's hand. "You are free of your shackles in all but the literal sense and those will go soon enough." She led Xana through a gap in the fence toward a sprawling cottage, "*If* that's what you want."

"If? How could it not be?"

"You'd be surprised. But, yes, I can see that you are different." The top of the door was open and Corna called through it. "Hildr, are you still here?"

"Someone," an irritated voice growled from within the shadows, "had to be, else my hero could have died again while you were off who knows where."

"Yes, yes," Corna responded with no sign of remorse as she opened the lower half of the door with her free hand.

"That is not an apology!"

"Nor will you get one," Corna said, rifling through baskets

4

near the door, which blocked Xana from following her through for a moment. "You are not my only responsibility. And, if he had died, what's one more revival? You should have taken him to Valhalla long since and well you know it."

"Better, I'm thinking, to take him to Fólkvangr when he has completed his quest," a dark figure said, looking out a window. The figure was cloaked and hooded, and the voice low. "I have promised him enough life to finish his quest, and he has promised me his afterlife."

Xana regarded the inside of the cottage in some surprise. It was large, as expected, but stuffed with baskets and cupboards, bottles and jars crowding shelves and nearly every other flat surface. On the far side of the room, beneath an open window, a man lay asleep, bathed in the afternoon sun beneath a blanket. Near his shoulder, a huge raven eyed her with suspicion, flapped its wings, and cawed.

"You're soft on him," Corna said. "How many times can you fail to bring him as commanded without paying a price?' 'Tis your job, is it not?"

"I am not without influence," The voice was diffident.

"You can't fool me, Hildr. Why else would you bring your hero to me to heal his wounds when you could take him to Eir? Has she refused you or offered to inform your leaders?"

The figure turned and Xana gasped. Despite the low voice, she was obviously female in stylized armor that ensured her gender was a given. Cloth, like metal scales, covered her long legs and her arms set akimbo on her hips. She was tall, far taller than either of them and her hair, long and curly, tumbled like molten copper from her helmet. She flicked her green hood back with a "tch" and regarded Xana with amazing grass-green eyes from the most beautiful face Xana had ever seen. The face also glowed—actually emitted light—as if she were…

"Are you immortal?" Xana asked, then gasped as the raven flew across the room to perch on the armored shoulder.

"I am." Hildr strode forward and grabbed Xana's chin, perhaps to see it better in her own glow. Most would turn away if Xana looked at them directly, but Hildr was not among them. "Pretty cheeky for a mortal pipsqueak, aren't you? Unusual eyes and, an aura… Is this the reason you wandered off and left my hero with a half-healed belly wound?"

"Aye," Corna said, examining bottles in a crowded cupboard. "Something, isn't she?"

Xana had not understood any of their conversation, but it was more frustrating now that she was the subject. She lifted the chin Hildr gripped defiantly. "I know I'm not much to look at."

"How wrong you are, child," Hildr said, her voice warmer. She released the chin gently, her touch lingering like a caress. Hildr's eyes traveled down the soiled and scrawny length of Xana then latched onto a manacle. With a light touch, she stroked the one on Xana's wrist as her eyes narrowed and her voice hardened. "Who did this to you, child?"

"My parents, I was told. They found my sight too frightening and sold me to a slave trader when I was nigh an infant." Xana closed her eyes. "I do not remember them. As I grew older, the slaver could not find a buyer, so loaned me out to clean a chimney or a henhouse. He was harsh but rarely cruel. I was fed, and treated fairly if I did as he directed."

She shrugged, embarrassed by what she knew she looked like in the face of such glorious beauty. She scrubbed a bit of blood between her fingers and wondered how many bruises there were on her pointed face with its wide brow, narrow chin, and large yellow-green eyes. Her short hair was matted with sweat and mud and blood, while her filthy shift was torn and bloody, equally discolored. Her scratched legs were muddy and bruised.

"Perhaps things might have been different if I had grown up a beauty as the slaver hoped. But I was short and slim, with no sign of womanliness at all. My face was ugly, my gaze disturbing. Since I could never serve men in the brothel, he finally sold me to a prosperous farm in need of extra hands." Her teeth gritted at the memory. "They needed far more than mine, yet, though I did the work of three hands they needn't hire, I was still beaten for dropping a single squash or my way of laying hay or if I was caught looking at them. They hated my eyes.

"So, I ran away. What they wouldn't spend on hands for the fields, they spent on guards to pursue me and the few other slaves. When they caught me the first time, I was sure that beating would kill me, but I lived. So I ran away again. First, they locked me in, then ropes, but those can be defeated. So, finally, the chains."

Xana couldn't read Hildr's face, or Corna, for her mind had turned inward. "I would have worked, a trade of my labor for a chance to live. I would not have left—I had nowhere to go. But they delighted in hurting me, and that was not a bargain I would accept. After I ran away the first time, I refused to work and devoted all my attention to escaping. But this last time, when they brought out the chains, they used them to hold me back as Brill—the farmer's son—used my body, the one he had always found so ugly." She swallowed against the memory but refused to flinch from it. "I fought against him, against the chains. I lost but I *never* stopped. And, when he had finished, I found a pick and pried the links open."

"How do you get them to bare their soul like that?" Corna said, wiping away a tear.

"We all have gifts," Hildr said.

"Hildr, can you use your magic to open the shackles while I attend her hurts? As a favor?"

"I will do it gladly," Hildr said and touched the manacles in turn, which fell away instantly. "Then I will deal with your pursuers."

"Kalor has dealt with them," Corna said, offering a quilt of surprising softness to Xana. "Why don't you cover yourself, little one? I'm going to cut off your shift to treat your back."

Xana took it, held it to her chest then said, "My name is Xana, though I know not if my parents named me or the slaver."

With deft skill, Corna sliced through the shift, and behind each shoulder so the garment could fall away without taking scabs with it. Hildr, looking over Corna's shoulder, hissed her irritation at the sight. "Even Kalor's end was too good a fate for such monsters. That's going to be painful to clean. Let me help."

Hildr slid back around to where she was facing Xana. Ignoring the blanket, she grasped both Xana's hands in hers and tapped her forehead to Xana's. "Imagine Valhalla..."

Xana had no idea what Valhalla was, but she felt transported to a huge hall, beyond what kings might have in even her dreams. The beams that curved overhead to hold the roof were enormous and blackened with smoke from the fireplaces at either end. Tables, closely packed, filled the void between fireplaces with a warrior at every place setting. Before her was metal cutlery and a plate and, within easy reach, a roast pig, a haunch of beef and sea of dishes with foods she could only guess at as to contents. A metal tankard, foaming with some golden liquid, was at her right. Her body felt painless and light, snuggled into a padded seat of some kind rather than perched on a wooden stool in Corna's cottage. She picked up the plate, clean and smooth enough to reflect her image, and she saw her face—hers—with the same short hair but clean and neat, the same pointed face, but with the skin free from bruises and scars. The eyes that stared back at her were fearsome and powerful. Seeing them stare her down from her own face made her feel fearsome and powerful as well. Not beautiful, but glowing with a sense of her own worth.

She returned the plate and reached for the tankard. She was so thirsty…

With a jerk that set her mind spinning, she was back in the charmingly cluttered cottage, her back on fire before Corna smeared it with an unguent of delicious coolness.

Hildr regarded her with sympathy and offered her a ladle of water. "Sorry, small one, but best you not taste the mead nor viands of Valhalla lest you rush to return in earnest."

"What is Valhalla?"

"A place not of your world or of my hero's, where valiant souls can find rest before the last great battles."

"And why would I go there? I'm a slave and a peasant, not a soldier or a king."

Hildr waved away Xana's protest. "Many a soldier or king will ne'er know Valhalla, my child. But you?" Corna had quietly moved to treating Xana's broken finger. Hildr took the other hand, her finger sliding to the raw flesh left by her manacle. "No armor, no sword, no axe, and yet you stood up to those who would destroy you. Believe me, child, you are a hero."

Corna emphasized the point by setting the bone, then wrapped it against its neighbor with a tiny board and cloth strips. Xana flinched but made no sound, just held the blanket to her chest with the free hand that Hildr had relinquished.

"Corna! Healer Corna!" They all turned to the voice from without, a voice just short of screaming with the edge of hysteria already pushing her voice to high register. "Help me!"

Corna exchanged a glance with Hildr. "Will you take over?" Hildr sneered. "I'm no healer, woman!" But she took the jar and smeared the soothing ointment on the raw wounds where Corna had left off.

Corna scurried out the open door and returned, almost immediately, her arm draped around a richly dressed woman cradling what appeared to be a ten-year-old boy in her arms. "He doesn't move!" the woman cried, her face stained with tears and paint. "I cannot see him breathing! You must help him, Corna! He's all I have!"

Bruised and dirty, Xana refused to move or bow. The woman spared Xana a single withering glance as she went by, then hobbled past to lay the child on a padded bench with the rattle of her gold bracelets.

"Lady Wense, you must let me examine him," Corna said, pushing the woman back gently.

Xana was no healer, but the way his head flopped as he was set down, argued his neck was broken. Xana had killed many a chicken and knew it was a bad sign for the boy.

Corna primmed her lips after touching the boy's cheek, then laid her hand on his forehead. "I'm sorry, Lady Wense, he is beyond my care. He is gone."

The woman collapsed in a puddle of vibrant silks. "He can't be! He can't be! When he fell, I wanted to bring him then, but he wouldn't let— And then I was unconscious, locked in my room and only just managed to escape. If only I had broken out earlier! Loba! Loba! You can't be dead!"

"It would make no difference, Lady Wense, for his neck was broken and I cannot heal that."

"No!" the woman wailed, then said nothing else coherently as she wept with abandon into her hands with Corna crouched beside her.

Xana found herself confused. She could see this woman was high-born, beautiful, despite the ravage of tears on her face paint. She was richly clothed, gems winking from bracelets and rings and neck chains. But her arms were bruised, angry finger marks firmly imprinted in a way Xana could not mistake, having worn those marks herself many times. She could see the shadow of a bruise near the ear on the woman's cheek, something fresh. And there was blood in her hair. But there was another bruise near the opposite temple that was yellow with age. Her fingernails were bloody and torn, though the remaining paint argued they were generally well-cared for.

Xana couldn't reconcile the woman's obvious wealth and power with her injuries. Obviously, she had been beaten. Obviously as well, it had not been the first time. She had had to escape, but she was wealthy! Xana could not make sense of it. And to wail as if she had nothing but her son?

"Your face reveals everything, little one," Hildr said softly, for Xana's ears only. "But I see no compassion."

"I don't understand her," Xana said. "She has money. She's not a slave. Why would she take abuse? Why would she stay with one who would abuse her son?"

"And if she leaves, who will protect her son? Do you think a man who would kill his own child—would injure his wife as you see here—would let her take him? She felt she had no choice and likely accepted the beatings thinking it would protect her son."

"Corna said you revived him, that man back there. Did she mean, from the dead?"

Hildr's eyes widened in surprise, but her voice became softer still. "You are surprisingly observant. Yes, but do not ask if I can save this boy; his soul has already flown and could not be returned to a body with a broken spine. Nor should you fret for his soul, child. He died a warrior, defending his mother from his own sire. All honor to him."

"Why does she say she has nothing now?"

Hildr's eyes were moist and the sympathy she showed was for more than the woman sobbing on the floor. "Not every mother is as callous as yours. When you have a child, if you have a child, you will understand a love that is larger than yourself."

"Like yours for the man under the window?"

Hildr's brows lifted again. A sad smile touched her lips. "Indeed, all real love is greater than the person who loves. It can go too far, if you lose yourself in it and refuse to care for yourself, as likely happened here. Or it can be less than love, just a reflection of the love one has for oneself."

"Like a man who would beat his wife, slay his son?"

"Yes, or sell one's child."

10

Outside, the sound of horses, riding hard and close enough to be heard over the woman's keening, caused Hildr to look up in some alarm. She flipped her cloak off and swung it around Xana, "Stand behind me. Others come!"

The woman's sobbing stopped as if she'd been gagged. She huddled on the floor, in the arms of Corna, staring at the open door with terror. Perhaps it was seconds, perhaps minutes, but the time from the woman's silence to the time the horses came to a halt outside the cottage door seemed interminable, marked only by the rhythmic sound of galloping hoofs and the throb of their own heartbeats.

There was the jingle of reins, a soft neighing, and the sounds of spurred boots on the hard soil. Hildr blocked her view of the door, but Xana peeped carefully around her to see the large room crowded with men. They were massive, well dressed, and, except for their leader, bristling with weapons. The leader was as pale and beautiful in his own way as Hildr. He was beardless, and his eyes were blue, not green and his hair was gold, not copper. His beauty was marred by the ugly look of disdain on his face for the cottage, the sneer on his sculpted lips for its clutter and relative poverty to his beringed and braceleted person, and the rage he wore for the silent wreck of a woman cowering before him.

"You stole my son, woman! How dare you think you could do so! And to bring him to this *hovel*? I should lash you as I would my dogs."

"I had to try to save him, Petral! He would not answer me nor move! And now I find that he is dead!" The tears, never really abated even if they had been silent, flooded her cheeks as her voice caught. "How could you kill him? He was just a boy!"

"I? *I*? Kill my son? It was you that killed him, with your puling weakness and coddling ways so that, when I would treat you as any honorable husband would, he interfered, standing against *his own* father! It was not *I* that killed him, but you, for putting your needs above his own as well as mine. And now I have lost my son because of *you!*"

"No! No! Petral!"

But he ignored her pleading, turning aside as if she meant nothing. "Take the boy and my wife. The boy gently. My wife as

11

harshly as necessary. Then put this useless place to the torch so
she does not escape here again."

The wind that Xana remembered from before—Alona—
swirled around the room, lifting dust and powders in its
agitation, but the men ignored it. One man lifted the boy's body
up with care, while the other grabbed the woman's arm and
yanked her to her knees, despite Corna's gasp of protest.

Xana was moving before she thought about it. With a kick to
the soldier's elbow, she forced him to release his grip on the
weeping woman. Then, draped in a cloak that dragged the
ground, she stood between. "You will not take her."

Petral was livid. "Who are you? And where did you come
from? How dare you stand between a man and his lawful
consort!"

"How dare you slay your child and harm your wife, sir! What
kind of husband and father is that? How dare you demand your
wife return for more pain at your hands!"

She glared at him with her yellow-green eyes, the ones that
had scared so many. He stared back for a moment then looked
away. "Kill it."

The man Xana kicked reached for his sword with his off arm
and slid out a curved blade with an ugly grin. "You're dead,
cockroach."

He stepped in and slashed, though Xana did not move, only
closing her eyes for the final blow. Then, she opened them again
at the clang of metal striking metal. Hildr stood beside her, the
henchman's curved blade trapped on her straight one.

"Who are these people interfering?" Petral said. "Where are
they coming from? This is your doing, witch!" The raven took
wing, screeching raucously, and slashing at faces with its claws.

Corna stood to Xana's other side, completing the wall of
women protecting Petral's wife. "I've never made a secret of my
witchcraft." She waved and Alona became a whirlwind, working
in concert with the angry bird, picking up dust and flinging it in
the men's—and only the men's—eyes. Then, when that had little
effect, small bottles and other items were chosen and tossed with
considerable force from nearly every direction.

"Enough!" Petral shouted as a bottle bounced off his
shoulder.

"There goes my belladonna," muttered Corna. "Do be careful, Alona."

"Did I not order you to kill them?" Petral demanded of the man confronting Hildr. "How long am I to be kept waiting?" His henchman swallowed. Perhaps Corna and Xana did not look threatening, but anyone gazing without fear at the tall and powerful form of Hildr, sword unsheathed, was a fool indeed. With a shout he perhaps hoped would cow her, he leaped forward again, sword at the ready. Xana—eyes open this time—never even saw her move. One moment the man was screaming and lunging, the next he was surprisingly still, a look of shock on his face before his body slid apart at the diagonal slice through his body.

Hildr's patience appeared to be at an end. "This house and all in it are under my protection. The next one to die will be you, Petral." And there was a rush of power as she spoke his name.

Petral stepped back, paling, but his words were still brave, "Give me back my wife."

"If she wills it, she may go with you. You will not take her by force."

To Xana's surprise, Petral laughed, transforming his face, for the moment, into the vision of beauty it might have been. "Oh, she'll come with me. I need only tell her to."

Corna gripped Xana's arm through the cloak. "We will not stop her if that is her choice."

Petral waved back his remaining men, sent them out the door with his son's body, humor gone. "Come, wife. You have shamed me enough this day. Come with me now or never show your face at my door again."

If Xana was surprised at his laughter, she was shocked as Petral's wife, quiet now, tears quenched, her face wiped of the worst of her paint and tears, rose to her feet with a quiet dignity. She walked around Corna without sparing a glance for the woman she'd begged for help, or for her other defenders. The raven, perched on a ledge, cawed at her as she passed.

Xana moved to stop them—again without thought—but Corna's grip stopped her. "Why would you go back with him?" Xana asked.

Petral's wife stopped but did not turn. "He has my son."

"He has the corpse of your son. The son he killed!"

Petral's wife sighed and then continued forward. "You do not understand."

"No!" Xana said. "No, I don't."

"Xana!" Corna hissed, her grip like iron.

Petral, his face transformed again with a smile that was anything but beautiful, would have turned to follow his wife's form, but was stopped as Hildr was at his side in an eye-blink. "Know this, Petral, if you harm anyone of this cottage or cause it harm, either through your agency, a hired agency or even rude talk in the town, I *will* find you. And your end will not be glorious."

That killed Petral's smile. He paused as if debating with himself if he should argue, but there was no give in the eyes that stared back at him. "I give you my word," he sighed at last.

"Your word is not worth spit. But I believe you will do as I say because my word is sacrosanct and you're just smart enough to figure that out."

If he stumbled as he walked to where the men held his horse in waiting, his men were careful to make no comment. Seconds later, they were riding away.

Hildr sheathed her sword. "Sorry about the mess, Corna."

"Alona will dispose of the body—I will not defile my graveyard with it—and the blood. Should make a nice repellant with the proper treatment."

"Why did he seem surprised to see us?" Xana asked.

"Because no one sees a Valkyrie unless she chooses to be seen, so you were protected as long as you were behind me." Hildr punctuated her words with a smack on the back of Xana's head. "And what was that foolish stunt you pulled? You could have and should have been killed."

"I couldn't do nothing!"

"Of course, you could. But you probably should have acted *if* you'd had the slightest means to protect yourself and her. But you didn't. And getting yourself needlessly killed when there are other choices is foolish indeed. Were we not here as well?"

"Would you have stopped him?"

"If she had chosen not to go with them?" Corna said, examining the work Hildr had done on Xana's wounds. "Yes.

But she didn't. Hildr, you did fine work. Perhaps you could hold your own against Eir in healing."

"Yeah, no thanks. Care to check on my hero?"

"I'm going," Corna said, shuffling to the recumbent man.

"Why don't you use your hero's name?" Xana asked.

"Damn, you see everything. Because, little one, if I call his name three times, his life is over and I will have no choice but to take his soul to the proper realm. That is why I have not named you nor the witch either."

"You named Petral," Xana said.

"Aye, twice, and he felt my power both times. That is the protection I promised. How is he, witch?"

"Healing with alacrity. You can likely take him tomorrow so he can get himself killed again for his glory."

Xana had to know. "Why? Why did she go with him? Won't he hurt her again? Won't he be as much a threat for the next child as he was with this one?"

"Yes," said Corna, washing her hands in a basin.

Corna sat on the bench where the dead boy had been before and patted the seat next to her. Hildr forestalled her with a hand and offered her a clean shift. The cloak! With care for her hurts, though they were far less painful than they had been, she donned the shift and handed the long cloak back to Hildr, who swept it around herself with a sigh of contentment.

Gingerly, Xana sat next to Corna and stared at her without flinching, "So, why?"

Corna returned her gaze calmly. "Women of this world and many others are often doubly enslaved. One means is the direct threat and power of her husband or father, and a society that backs them so that her options for escape are few if any. No matter how harshly she may be treated, where is there to go where she will find better?"

Xana shook her head. "That was true for me as a slave, but these are free women. Don't they have families? Friends?"

"Families can sell their daughters as easily to a husband as you were sold to a slaver. To accept a daughter's return is an insult to many," said Hildr. "Friends will often not stand between a husband and his wife."

Corna shook her head. "There are sometimes places for

15

protection or escape, but, if you're unaware of them, they might as well not exist. And if you have children to protect or fear for your life—or theirs—if you should try, even knowledge of a safe haven can't help you. And even safe havens may not provide for you indefinitely. If you have no skills to support yourself or your children, like as not, you will end up in the same situation."

"But she chose to go back! She had a safe haven and she chose to go back."

"That is the second slavery, the one in her own mind, the one that tells her she belongs to men, that ties her sense of self-worth to her roles as wife and mother and nothing else."

Xana felt bewildered and glared at Hildr. "Did *you* not say that love was greater than oneself for a mother or a lover? Which is it?"

"There is nothing wrong with being a wife and mother," Hildr said, perching on Xana's abandoned stool, her raven preening on her helm. "Unless you relinquish your sense of self to them or lose sight of yourself and your own worth as a human being. You heard him blame her for the slaying of his own son. Before the week is out, she will believe it herself, if she doesn't now."

Xana sighed, rubbing her temples. "I don't understand. How could she possibly think that? How can she feel responsible for her husband's violence?"

"They are taught from birth that their worth is in the eyes of a man, that his treatment of her reflects on her worth, that her ability to produce offspring is the culmination of her life. You heard him. He has blamed her for the child's bravery as if protecting another were a sign of weakness." Corna sighed. "Men are taught, too, to expect that devotion and never relinquish that power. Some, even with education and examples, can't escape the conditioning. Some never get those examples or education."

"Everyone does this? Everyone believes this?"

"There are some," Hildr said, "who do use those examples and education to break free, to respect themselves, though their path—society being relatively unchanged—is generally a hard one. Some, like you, without education or example, find self-respect on your own."

Hildr shook her head. "Your world really is horrible in so

many ways."

Corna, narrowed her eyes. "And is the world of your hero much better?"

Hildr laughed. "Not yet, but I expect it will be."

"Will this world always be thus?" Xana asked, feeling the dark maw of hopelessness open above her.

"Perhaps not," Corna said. "People can change their fate if they've will enough."

Xana's frustration at the woman's return ate at her. "Women like that won't change it."

"No," said Corna. "She is a victim, trapped in two prisons. But even she can inspire change in the son who hates his mother's mistreatment, in a daughter that refuses that fate, even in a man who wants no part of a woman cowering before him."

"People like you of innate power and determination and many others who become enlightened through education, both men and women, can make the world a different place. Not only for yourselves by freeing yourselves from your slavery, but by providing examples and safe havens for those who will need them in future generations. Every soul you free from both slaveries becomes another example, potentially another safe haven, another lesson in the collective society." Hildr reached over and brushed Xana's cheek. "You give me hope for this realm, child, you and that witch beside you."

The wind in the room swirled in protest. The body was gone and there was a large flagon of dark fluid Xana feared might be blood. There was no blood left on the stone floor. Hildr winked at Corna. "Yes, yes, you give me hope as well, you sprite."

"So, Xana, what will you do now?" Corna asked.

Until she was asked, Xana had literally never thought of "what's next?" It was about getting away and then adjusting to the loss of her pursuers. What would she do? Where would she go? Penniless and homeless, she was no prize as a bride, even without her lack of appeal. Any employ she attempted would likely leave her in a situation not unlike that she left behind. What *could* she do?

Her stomach chose that moment to rumble. It had been more than a day since last she ate.

Corna and Hildr laughed. Corna heaved to her feet. "Best get you some lunch then, young one." She hobbled to the fireplace and stirred a cauldron simmering near the fire.

"That is *food*, isn't it?"

Corna laughed again, her body shaking and her eyes leaking tears. "It is, child. It is." She spooned out a bowl of what appeared to be a savory stew with actual meat in it and offered it to her. Xana didn't hesitate to dive in and relished the first bite with something approaching ecstasy. Nor did she flinch when Corna added after the second bite, "As far as you know."

"You've a mean sense of humor, healer," Hildr noted. "Has it occurred to you, she may not know what to do? For instance, she may not know you'd be willing to teach her your trade."

At that, Xana choked. When she finished coughing, she asked, "Would you? Really?"

"Aye," Corna said without hesitation, "but you best be understanding that it would not solve all your problems. I will not live forever, or even much longer, and the path ahead, if you choose to follow me, will be hard. Though, I fear there is no path for you that isn't difficult."

"I am not afraid of hardship. I would like to learn. I would like to repay your kindness to me."

"You pay the next one, the next child that needs you, the next one who needs a haven, the next one that calls you. That's what my calling is about. It has no less sorrow than any other calling, but I sleep well knowing I did my best."

Xana finished her stew. "I would like that. I would like a calling where I made a difference, even if I cannot change everything."

Corna nodded and fetched another bowl of stew.

"You're thinking of the woman today. Smart girl. Too observant by half, you are," Hildr said. "Such a valiant spirit, I've little doubt that someday I shall collect your remarkable soul when you finally fall."

"Yeah? Well, you'd best not be too hasty about it. I've a quest of my own now."

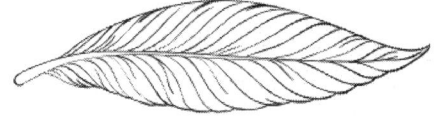

FADE by Timothy Callahan

Eniko peeked through the space between the bushes hoping her younger self didn't see her. In a few minutes Mitch would show up in his black Camaro and the two of them would head off into the night where they would go to the movies, eat a cheap meal at a pizza shop, and then not go home. Instead, they'd make out in the backseat of the car for hours until the cops showed up to see them both naked and minutes away from having sex. It was a funny story. They would both tell it hundreds of times, and each time it would end with her saying, "That's how I knew I would marry this guy." He would squeeze her hand when she finished. It was a nice memory, one that sustained her for years even after she discovered his mistress, a memory she needed to obliterate. The strange woman who showed up at her door offered her the chance to erase Mitch from her life.

Eniko had no idea who the woman was or what she was saying. She kept pacing around the living room talking about changing the future, about being drawn to Eniko's pain, about how God gave her the power to send people back in time to change their personal history. She rambled on like that for a good ten minutes before Eniko slowly closed the door, only to have the woman's foot stop it. Eniko vividly remembered the chill she got when the strange woman looked deep into the eyes and said, "You have to believe me."

Of course, Eniko didn't believe her. But this woman, with her too short dark hair, her strange speaking style, and her old school stubbornness, eventually wore Eniko's will down. She realized she had nothing to lose, a lot to gain, and didn't really have any other plans for the day anyway. So, why not play along with the strange woman and see what would happen?

After one crazy dance that involved several of Eniko's clocks, a few chicken eggs, a magnifying glass, and sounds no human throat should ever be able to make, Eniko found herself behind a bush looking at her younger self. It took a few minutes for her to realize what day this was and when she did she whispered, "Holy shit. I'm actually in the past." All she had to do was walk out from behind the bushes, talk to her younger self, let her know how horrible Mitch is then—

"Eniko?"

The voice came from behind her and she spun around quickly, her heart leaped to her throat and she felt her skin both turn hot, then cold, at the same time.

"What the hell are you doing here?" Mitch asked.

It was older Mitch. His hair was gray, almost white, and he still had that stupid goatee he thought made him look younger. A pair of what he thought were trendy glasses sat on top of his nose. She could tell they didn't have real lenses in them, just glass. He wore a pair of black dress pants and a casual shirt, the kind of clothes you'd wear on a casual Friday. His arms were on his hips and his eyes were on her.

She stammered. "Um, what-what are—?" *Compose yourself, Eniko, get your head in the game.* "Hey, what's up?" She finally got it out in a way that she hoped sounded casual even though she know, deep in her heart, it was not.

"What are you doing here?" He looked over her shoulder and over at the bush. "Is that a younger you? What the hell, what are you doing? "

"Um, well," she said, hating how awkward he made her feel. Her mind numbed as she tried to think of something say to her ex-husband. "I-um…"

"My god," he said looking back at her. "Are you here to make sure we don't get together? Are you here to—?"

"Hey," she finally said as a thought passed through the storm raging inside her head. "What the hell are you doing here?"

"That's not important."

"How did you get here?"

"Well, um." It was nice to see him squirm.

He couldn't make eye contact with her. He shifted on his feet as if wanting to leave his own skin.

"Oh my god!" She yelled, "You're here to make sure we never get together too, aren't you?"

"No," He said like a little boy who was caught red handed with his hands in the cookie jar.

She crossed her arms and lowered her head so all he could see were her eyes glaring at him. He was always powerless against this look. It always brought down all his defenses.

Dropping his arms from his hips he spat. "Fine, yeah. I'm here to tell my younger self to not make the biggest mistake of his life, okay?"

"Why didn't you just say so?" Eniko asked. "Just like you. Your first thought was to make me feel bad. Well, I'm not going to feel bad, I'm not—"

Mitch held his hand up to stop her talking, "Shhh. Listen."

She turned when she heard the growl of the Camaro. The sound of it made her heart speed up. She knew that sound so well, reminding of her times when Mitch would drive up to her house. She could always hear the finely tuned engine coming from several blocks away. When she heard it she would grab her coat, kiss her dad, scowl at her mom, and run out of the door to wait for him.

"I forgot how beautiful that sounded," Mitch said closing his eyes as if in orgasm. "God, I miss that sound."

Eniko shook her head. "Idiot. That means you're close. Unless you can think of a way to stop my younger self in ten seconds, we'll have failed. "

"Don't call me an idiot!" Mitch yelled. "Look, we know how this night plays out. We'll have plenty of chances to stop us from falling in love, right? "

"What was your plan?" She asked listening as the car turned the corner.

"I was going to find my younger self and talk to him. But that stupid woman put me here and not at my old house. I walked around a bit and found you. "

"Was she a short woman? Kind of weird? Talked about how God gave her the power to send people back in time to stop their pain? "

"Yeah," he replied. "What do you think that was all about? And why did she send up both back to the same time? "

Eniko shrugged her shoulders. "I don't know. She was kind of weird. "

"Okay," Mitch said looking over Eniko's head. "That's a good enough answer for me." He pointed. "I just picked you up. Do you remember what you were thinking about when I picked you up?"

"I thought guys with Camaros had small dicks," Eniko replied. It was a lie and she was sure he knew that from the grin she was trying to hide.

"Screw you," he replied walking past her and toward the street. "Come on, let's flag down a taxi and go to the movie theater. See if can do something to stop them there."

Eniko's stomach tightened and she felt a wave of nausea. With sickening resignation she asked, "We're not going to have to watch The Phantom Menace again, are we?"

Mitch flinched as if he were hit in the knees with a baseball bat. "I don't think there's any way we can avoid it."

"Ugh!" Eniko said throwing up her hands. "I always hated that movie."

*

"God, this Podracing scene goes on forever," Eniko whispered to Mitch. The two sat next to each and as far away as possible in the uncomfortable movie theater chairs. Older Mitch munched on a bag of popcorn and sipped a soda. He refused to share either. The younger versions of themselves were in front of them, five rows down. Eniko noticed the younger Mitch also had a bag of popcorn and a soda which he shared freely with her younger self. She tried not to smile, not wanting her Mitch to see it. He really was a sweet kid and did treat her well at the start.

"I have a plan," Mitch whispered over the THX sound effects of the pod race. "When this scene is over I'm going to leave to go to the bathroom. When I do I want you to go out there and seduce me. "

"What?" Eniko yelled. It was quickly followed by several

22

shushes. "I don't want to seduce a 16-year-old boy."

"I'm not asking you to sleep with me. Just be nice to me in a sexy way. Look, at this time in my life I wasn't sure I wanted a steady girlfriend. Maybe if someone had shown me some unsolicited interest I'd have second thoughts and I'd take you home after dinner instead of making out. "

"Why don't you seduce me?" She asked.

Mitch looked at her and raised his right eyebrow just enough to force her to pause and think about what she had said.

She folded her arms across her chest. "Fine, okay, I get it. It's creepy for a 46-year-old man to flirt with a 16-year-old girl." She rolled her eyes and said as sarcastically as she could muster, "But I guess it's okay in this society for a 46-year-old woman to seduce a 16-year-old boy!"

Mitch smiled, took a loud sip of his soda through a straw and said, "Don't hate the player, hate the game."

"Lord oh mighty I hate that you still say that."

Mitch pointed to his younger self. "There I go. Get going. "

"Fine!" Eniko muttered standing from her seat. She stomped down the steps and followed the young boy out from the theater. She watched as he went into lobby then made a quick beeline to the bathroom.

She leaned her left side against the wall and folded her arms across her chest. She looked down and wished she had worn a top that showed some cleavage and not a gray tee shirt with the picture of a yellow flower on it. Checking her legs she decided to cross her right foot over her left foot. She stood there hoping she looked sexy.

This was stupid, she thought. *No way this is going to work. No way. But*, she countered, *Mitch always did have a wandering eye. That eye would eventually become flirting, which eventually became cheating, which eventually became me leaving him. Wouldn't it be ironic if I started that by flirting with him now?*

She saw the young Mitch walk out of the bathroom rubbing his hands on his pants to dry them. She suppressed the urge to yell at him to go dry his hand properly, something she had to do thousands of times while they were together. She saw his head turn when a pretty girl walked past. His eyes glanced at her ass. He continued to walk as he watched. He walked toward her.

When he looked up they made eye contact. Eniko gave him the best smile she could muster and said in a soft, seductive voice, "Hey cutie, having a hard time with the hand dryer?" *Oh crap, what the hell am I talking about?*

"Um, excuse me?" Young Mitch asked. His voice was so small, like a child.

Her hands began to sweat and she resisted the urge to wipe them on her pants. She was committed now, no turning back. If this worked her life would be so much better so she pushed on. "I noticed you were wiping your hands on your pants. Was there a problem with the hand drier? Couldn't use it or something? "

"Um, no, the dryer is fine. Are you a friend of my mom's?" Mitch asked. His body language was something Eniko knew well. His right fist was clenched, his body tense and tight, and his eyes kept looking behind her as if willing himself past her body. "I just- I want to get back to the movie, is that okay?"

Shit, I think I'm scaring him. Eniko said with a flighty laugh, "I just want to talk."

"Miss, I'm sorry, but my girlfriend is waiting for me."

She resisted the compulsion to say 'aww'. He actually called her his girlfriend even though this was still the middle of the third date. She never knew he thought of her that way this early in the relationship. It warmed her heart just a bit. But, she had a job to do and she was going to seduce this boy whether he liked it nor not. "What's her name?"

"I don't think I should tell you," Mitch replied.

"No, you shouldn't," Eniko replied placing her hand on Mitch's shoulder. "I don't want to know the name of the girl whose boyfriend I want to steal. "

A look of panicked terror crossed Mitch's face and he ran. Eniko hesitated, unsure if she should block his path. He looked behind his shoulder one last time before entering the theater.

Well, she thought, *that didn't work at all.* She waited another few moments before re-entering the darkened theater.

She walked up the steps, past her younger self and the young Mitch doing her best not to make eye contact with him, and sat next to old, asshole Mitch. "Didn't work."

"I know," he replied with a smirk on his face. "It's funny, while you were out I tried to remember this date, tried to remember if some hot older woman tried to talk to me and you know something strange? I actually do remember it."

She snapped her head to look at him. "What?"

"Yeah, I remember it. I don't know why I didn't remember it before, but I remember it now. God, you scared the shit out of me with that 'steal you away from your girlfriend line.' Might have been your age. I mean, geez, you were older than my mom and you were hitting on me. That was just weird. "

She punched his shoulder as hard she could. "I'm not that old!"

"Old to a 16-year-old me."

"Fine," she huffed. "Why do you think you remember it now?"

He shrugged. "Maybe it's because the memory wasn't created until now. Maybe I just forgot. I don't know." He stood from his seat. "Come on, this movie has like another 45 minutes and I don't want to watch it again. We'll go to the pizza place where they go after the movie and wait for them. Hopefully, we'll come up with another plan by then."

She followed him and caught a glance at her younger self. Young Mitch had his arm around her and they were sharing popcorn. She tried to remember if he told her about the strange, older woman in the lobby but nothing came to mind. *So, even this early you were keeping secrets from me. Typical.*

*

"So, what do we do now?" Eniko asked as the two waited in line for some pizza.

"Well, since you can't seem to seduce me I guess we just wait here until we arrive. We have some time so we're going to just have to figure this out."

"Ugh!" Eniko said in a low growl. "Don't think we've spent time together doing nothing in, what? Five years?"

"We never were the sit down and talk kind of couple, where we?" Mitch replied just as he was asked what he wanted by the pizza maker. "Two plain for me and the lady will have pepperoni and plain."

"The lady?" Eniko raised her eyebrows to an alarming level. "Why are you ordering for me?"

"I'm paying for it and I know what you like. Am I wrong?"

She folded her arms across her chest, wondering if she should change the order. But, a pepperoni and plain is exactly what she was going to order and it was nice of him to pay. But still— "No, I want a mushroom and a pepperoni. No plain."

Mitch looked at her, a stupid grin she learned to hate on his lips. "Give the lady what she wants."

"What's with all this 'lady' crap?"

"Just trying to lighten the mood."

"Well stop it. If you hadn't shown up this wouldn't be a problem."

"Really?" he asked pulling out a credit card from his wallet. "What was your plan?"

The cashier looked at the card, then up at the two. "We don't do credit cards."

"Oh, right," Mitch said pulling out a twenty from his wallet. "1999, forgot."

The man looked at the twenty, crumpled it out and threw it back at Mitch who flinched at the attack.

"What's wrong with my 20?"

Eniko looked that bill which lay on the ground. Andrew Jackson's portrait looked back at her. She didn't know much about currency but knew enough to recognize this as one of the newer 20 dollar bills with a very large portrait of Jackson, not the one inside the circle. She leaned into Mitch and whispered, "You're a dumbass. That's a new 20. Got any older ones?"

Mitch reached back into his wallet and looked around. He found another 20, this one looking old, and pulled it out. "Here you go."

"None of you or your wife's money is good here. Get out of my store and don't come back. "

"But—"

"Get out or I'll call the police on you!"

"Fine, fine," Mitch said holding his hands up. "Geez, can't believe I used to love this place."

Eniko shook her head as she followed Mitch to the door. She turned to the guy behind the counter, "I'm so sorry. I told him about this and he never listens to me. Ever. He's a real asshole so, again, I'm sorry.

She let the door close behind her and nearly bumped into

Mitch who simply stood there with his hands on his hips looking at the sky. He let out a long sigh. "I really thought this was going to be easy. Just go up to myself, talk, let him know not to cheat but- no, guess that's not going to happen."

"Not to cheat?" Eniko repeated. "I thought you came here to break us up?"

He turned to face her. When he did he looked into her eyes. She knew that look as well. It was one of the looks she fell in love with. "I came here to stop him from making a huge mistake. That's what I said."

"Come here," she said pulling him away from the front of the store and to the side. She needed some privacy. This wasn't much, but it would do if they talked in a low voice. "What's going on?"

Closing his eyes and shaking his head he said, "It doesn't matter. I am who I am, not even I can change me I guess."

"What?"

He looked at her again then gently places both his hands on her shoulders. "Eniko, I made a huge mistake cheating on you. I know that, hell I knew it when I was doing it but—well I have no excuse really. I was a jerk. "

She felt something she had kept inside for a long time break. She had waited such a long time to hear him say that. He'd never admitted he was a jerk; never told her he was at fault. It was always something she did, something she pushed him to. "Wow. Thank you for admitting that."

"You're welcome."

She resisted the urge to give him a hug. The moment passed and he took his hands off her shoulders. Pursing her lips, she asked, "So, what now? Do you have a plan? Should we just go back? "

"No. We should wait out here and confront our younger selves. Just get it out into the open. I'll talk to my guy about not cheating, you tell your girl not to be such a naggy bitch and we'll—"

Before he could even finish the sentence and before Eniko even knew what was happening her hand was moving, her palm flat, her aim true. She slapped Mitch so hard his whole body was pushed to the left.

He looked up at her, his hand on his deeply reddened cheek, his eyes wide in surprise. For one brief moment she thought he was going to slap her back. Instead, he stood there looking at her shocked. "What the hell?"

"Naggy bitch? Really?"

"It was figure of speech! God, that hurt."

She pushed him as hard as she could. He barely moved. "How dare you. You still think I had something to do with you cheating?"

"It takes three to cheat."

She raised her hand and he flinched. She slowly lowered it, but kept the weapon cocked and loaded just in case she needed it again. "No, it takes two, you and the real bitch, not me."

"Can I talk to you honestly without you slapping me in the face?"

"Not if you're going to insult me or my intelligence."

"Fine, I won't." He paused, then continued. "Okay, I'll try. Look, just—no violence okay? I've had enough of that."

"No promises," Eniko replied. "Just tell me what you have to say."

He took a deep breath, then let it out. "When we first started dating it was great. You let me do everything I wanted, both with you and with my friends."

She opened her mouth to talk, then closed it deciding to let him make enough rope to hang himself with.

He continued as if he hadn't noticed. "Even after we got married it was great. Remember when I went to Vegas with the guys? You hardly batted an eye. I was so happy I found a woman that I thought 'got it'. I didn't even go to the strip club with the guys."

She didn't believe that, but let him continue.

"After we were married for a few years, you changed. I wasn't allowed to go out with the guys. Then I had to go with you everywhere. We did everything together. If I even mentioned going out you'd whine and cry and tell me not to."

"Yeah," she said. "Cause I knew what you were doing out there. I knew you were hooking up with a woman!"

"Not at first," he said, then blushed. "Okay, that sounded horrible. But, it's true. I mean, do you remember that? You

28

changed and I never understood why."

"I matured," she replied. "You didn't. There was no need to spend time with your friends every weekend. Maybe if it was once a month sure, I get that. But, come on, every Saturday night? Sometimes Friday and Saturday? That's too much."

"No, no, it didn't start out that way." He said, his voice raised for a bit as if trying to keep his own temper under control. "It was once a month, maybe twice."

"I don't remember that," she said and she didn't. She remembered him telling her he's going out, not asking, telling her. He never invited her to tag along, never asked if she wanted to come. It was just the guys, he told her, just the guys. "But please, keep talking, keep trying to rationalize what you did. Is this what you tell yourself or anyone who asks?"

"Yeah, it is." He snapped, then calmed down and said in a much more controlled voice, "It is. And most agree that neither one of us was in the right, so there's that."

"Yeah, there's that," she said. "Have you reached your point yet?"

"No," he replied. "It wasn't just me going out with my friends. It was everything. Every move I made was criticized. Every thought I had was rejected. Every opinion I had was mocked. After a while—well, after a while when a pretty girl talked to me and listened- it was something I had missed."

"There you go," she said replied bitterly. "Blaming me again."

"No, I don't blame you. I blame me for not telling you to stop. For not letting you know how you were making me feel. I kept all that inside."

She felt a small hint of sympathy for him. What he said was bullshit, but what he felt- that was real, even if the reasoning for it was thin. "Why? Why didn't you talk to me?"

He shrugged. "I tried. I told you how I was feeling a few times but you ignored it, or you reacted poorly."

"What? When did you talk to me about this and how did I react? "

"Remember when I asked you to control your temper? Told you it made me uncomfortable when you yelled at people, or children, or dogs?"

She nodded. The memory was there, but just barely. It was at the moment the hand she slapped him with started to sting again, as if an example of what he was talking about. "I don't really remember it, just you asking me."

"Well, I remember. For the next month when you got mad you didn't try to calm down, instead you yelled at me, 'Oh, sorry, guess I should learn to 'control' my anger.'"

"Oh," she smiled. "I thought I was trying to be funny. Using humor to defuse my anger."

"Well, it made me feel as if my opinion didn't mean a damn thing to you so, guess I stopped trying."

She thought about that for a moment, letting it sink in. "You know. You should have just left me if you weren't happy."

"I was so happy," he replied looking over her shoulder. His eyes squinted. "So happy for so long. I thought we could just have that back if I waited."

"We grew apart," she said. "I should have left you when I started nagging. I wasn't happy either you know. Guess my way to express that was to boss you around."

"Yeah, you became the alpha male," he laughed. "Or the queen bee, or whatever."

"Guess so," she sighed and turned to see what he was looking at.

The growl of the Camaro engine was easy to hear as it pulled into the parking lot. She gasped, and pointed. "They're here now? They shouldn't be here for another twenty minutes. The movie doesn't end for a while. Why are they here now?"

Then, she remembered. Mitch coming back to her, telling her about the strange woman talking to him. How he panicked when she walked past him to sit in a seat behind them. How nervous he was when he looked back and didn't see her anymore. Begging her to leave before the movie ended.

She looked at Mitch who opened his eyes, and smiled. "Did you remember it at the same time?"

"Your movie freak out?"

"Yeah, my movie freak out. Very odd, isn't it? Us remembering it at the same time an hour later."

"Time travel fucks with your mind," she replied. "What happens next? Do we hide?"

"Should we?"

She saw the door open and watched as her younger self got out, followed by a young Mitch. "If we talk to them we'll change time."

"We were going to do that anyway. The only issue is, what do we tell them?"

She thought about it for a moment. He was right, it would be a mixed message that neither would understand, or believe. But, she had an idea. "You talk to a young me, tell me what happens, and I'll talk to a young you, tell you what happens. We'll let them draw their own conclusions."

He nodded his head. "Yeah, that sounds like a good idea. Here they come, you ready?"

"As I'll ever be."

They both turned around just at their younger selves approached the door. Young Mitch turned when he saw them, then grabbed Young Eniko's arm and pulled, "Shit, oh shit, that's her. That's her!"

Young Eniko stepped up to the older one, rolling her sleeves up, her face red with anger. "What's the big idea stepping up to my man and asking him if he wants to go home with you? Huh? What makes you think—?"

"Go home with me?" Eniko said. "I never said that," she looked over at her Mitch who simply shrugged. Eniko turned to the Younger Mitch, "What I did say was that I wanted to steal him away from you. But, that was wrong of me and you'll understand what's going on in a few minutes."

Young Eniko looked over at her Mitch, who simply shrugged. It was like looking into a mirror as the two Mitches matched the expression almost exactly. Young Eniko noticed that too. She folded her arms across her chest and said, "Let me guess? Are you Mitch's mom and dad or something?"

"No," Eniko said.

"Those two look a lot alike, like father and son and you," she looked at Eniko who simply stared back. A look of confused recognition passed across her face and she stumbled back as if she had lost her balance. "You look like my mom, sort of."

"No, hon. I look like you because—well I am you. From thirty years into the future. And this is Mitch, the man you marry, from the same time. We came back in time to talk to you guys."

"What?" Young Mitch asked looking at his future self. "How did that happen? Do they have like, time machines in the future? That would be really cool, you know?"

"Not like that," Old Mitch replied. It was so strange hearing the same vocal inflections coming from them. "That's a long story we don't have much time for."

"Look, we just want to talk to you guys. Mitch, I want to talk to you, and Eniko, you talk to my Mitch. We won't be long; we won't take up much of your time. We'll let you finish the date then we'll go and you won't see us again for another 30 years, when you look at yourself in the mirror."

"This is so strange," Young Eniko said walking up to Old Mitch.

"I think it's kind of neat," Young Mitch said walking up to Eniko.

Eniko gave a glance at her Mitch who winked. She smiled then lightly grabbed Young Mitch by the arm and led him few yards away from the pizza shop. "I know this is weird, trust me, I know."

"Weird in a good way. I can't wait to tell everyone." He looked back at her Mitch. "Wow, I really went gray though, didn't I?"

"Yeah, a bit." She looked over his shoulder to see her Mitch having an animated discussion with her younger self. She reached into her memory, trying to recall what he said. Nothing came to mind. Maybe it takes some time for the memories to come? "Look, Mitch, listen to me, okay? You're a good kid, a very funny and sweet teen but things change. We change. I changed." She placed her hand on his shoulder. "When I met you in the movie theater my goal was to get you to think about other women. To get you to maybe look at a younger me and wonder if you really wanted to be with one person. You didn't take the bait, which, by the way, good for you. But—"

"That's not always going to be the case, is it?" He asked, his eyes deep with concern.

She shook her head no. "I'm afraid not. That's where the change comes in."

"I'm sorry?" He asked. "I mean, I know it doesn't happen for a while but, I'm sorry."

"You don't need to be sorry, he does. Or, your future self does anyway." She sighed. "Look, I came here to break you and a younger me up. I didn't want to feel the pain of knowing you had betrayed me. But, now that I look at you. I remember what it was that made me fall in love with you."

"You really did?" He asked looking back at his Eniko.

"I did," she replied watching as her younger self listened with great intensity at her Mitch. "You guys will have so much fun, see so many things. Things I don't think I'd change. A few hours ago all I wanted to do was remove you from my memory. That was wrong. Without you in my life I wouldn't be me. "

"So, I should stay with her? With you? I shouldn't try to get with other girls?"

She nodded, "You do whatever it is you want to do. All I ask is for you to accept that life will change, you'll change, she'll change, the world will change. Try to change together and try to be nice when things go wrong. Okay?"

He nodded his head yes. "Is that all?"

"Yeah. Now, go back to her and have a really nice date. Okay?"

He turned and walked back to his Eniko who was finishing up her talk with her Mitch. As he did the memories came flooding into her mind. He didn't have much to say, and she was only really half-listening, unable to believe what she was hearing. But, he did tell her that he was sorry for what was going to happen and that all he could do was ask that she forgive him.

The memories didn't stop there as a younger version of herself talked to her date, how they had a deep conversation about what they wanted for the future. How he told her that—

"Oh god," she said as a fresh set of tears formed in her eyes. "No, that's not what—no. "

Her Mitch walked back to her, his own eyes starting to mist up. "Damn, my younger self did not understand what you told him."

"He broke up with me. You broke up with me."

"Yeah. All I can say is the prospect of being with other woman was too much for my younger self. I was never really confident with the ladies and a big part of me at 16 didn't think I could be with anyone else. But, when you told me that I could meet other women—well it got my younger self to thinking that anything was possible and I didn't' want to be tied down with you." He said, wiping his own tear away from his eye. "I am so sorry about that."

She reached back trying to remember their wedding, their vacations, anything from the life they had together. "It's all gone. It's like our life together is fading away from my mind."

"I-I hardly know who you are now. I can't remember anything," he said shaking his head. "When we get back to our time we'll have a new set of memories. A new life."

She hugged herself tightly. The door from the pizza place flung open and a young Eniko ran out crying. "I hope the new memories are as good as the old."

"Me too, " he said. They both stood there on the corner in a strange silence. He reached out and grabbed her hand and squeezed it hard. She returned the squeeze then relaxed and let old memories fade away.

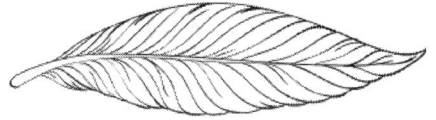

LADY MARIE by Eli Dawson

Someone once told her: "Lady Marie, sometimes you don't have to chase so hard after something. It seeks you out eventually. "

Slather. Who had ever heard of such a name? Well, many since she arrived on earth. The name was her earthbound alias, and it tricked many into thinking not an ounce of danger was upon them. With a name like that, you'd probably imagine some old lady making cookies or humming in her garden. Not an all-powerful titan of her race who was known to consume enemies whole. Yes, she had an abundant proportion, and she was aware of that. Those who remarked about it were eaten. Aside from her size, her resume as a leader was more impressive: She became the first queen of her people; the first to conquer other worlds through space travel; with a list of numerous honors and asterisk-worthy accomplishments. Unfortunately, many thought she had become paranoid and unfit to rule any kingdom or race. Ever since her belief in a prophecy from a fortuneteller, she had grown increasingly odd in her behavior and untrustworthy as a leader, eating enemies on sight rather than questioning them first and following protocol and such. She even went so far as to start a cult and lived and traveled only with her followers. Many believed her era of power had passed. She had become known as an eccentric warlord. Nevertheless, she continued to kill off many and was considered a great threat.

Lady Marie, who went by Lady now, admired Slather for her accomplishments and bluntness. And for no recognizable reason, Lady also feared her more than anything else.

There did not appear to be any rational reasoning for it, but according to her therapist Gilda, she had to look deeper. "Penetrate the surface and go further," she often said. Lady had never met the alien queen and the fact Slather was so malicious by reputation appealed to Lady. You might say that in some strange way Lady held Slather up as a role model, a heroine of special magnificence. But why? Gilda told her there was something primal at the heart of this. Indeed, there was. There was something so intrinsically ghastly that even the mention of Slather's name used to trigger panic attacks for Lady. She overcame these eventually, but hearing the name was different than actually seeing her, and who knew what might occur if that happened?

Lady's therapy lasted for roughly a year. It was not her idea. She had promised her team leader Stephen she would try it, and she did. As far as finding out the reason why Slather was such a profound presence within her, she knew only she would be able to figure that out. Her stubbornness was an immovable object according to Stephen. She was mostly happy on the ship, but she would backslide into old habits and become trapped all over again. Signs of this were obvious: dirty laundry everywhere, dirty dishes in her room and under her bed, moping, not showering, failure to achieve missions, etc. Stephen always said Slather had her under some sort of dark spell. And for the most part, he seemed to be right.

When Lady and Stephen argued about the dirty dishes or clothes scattered about or other telltale signs of the spell, he sometimes pulled out his trump card: "I love you, but you are a stubborn fool. God's own special train wreck." It was a joke Stephen used on her and one Lady got in on as she learned to mouth it with him eventually, but underneath he really meant it.

Lady always smiled in reply to this and hugged him and told him things would be fine. He would say, "I know, I am just a worrier." They were just really good friends and cared a great deal about one another. They had both lost so much and knew a lot about each other. After they picked her up on the ship, Lady and Stephen talked late at night about whatever was on their minds, whatever eased them into sleep. Stephen told her about when Leroy proposed to him while Lady talked about how she often dreamt of spiders.

Their talk did her some good, but her breakdowns and depression needed professional attention. Not only was the therapy best for her, but it was for him as well. So he introduced her to Gilda, who happened to be his therapist after Leroy died. While she was in therapy, she seemed better and kept clean and completed her missions and did not cause any fights. When she finished therapy, though, the fights between them grew more frequent and more intense.

David, Stephen's son, turned his music up louder wherever he went to combat the fury. Mal, Stephen's android daughter, could fix anything on the ship. Though she spoke very little, she hummed as she heard everything said on board. The swearing and crying intensified with every fight.

Finally, during one momentous fight, Stephen laid out his trump card, but not as a joke. With the utmost cruelty, he yelled the bittersweet truth: "I love you, you stubborn fool! God's own special train wreck! Please don't let me let you go!"

Lady was not exactly sure what happened next. All she knew was that her vision went black. She found herself standing over Stephen's unconscious body on the kitchen floor. Blood oozed from his wounds and Lady, upset and traumatized by her actions, panicked and knew she must leave. Other team members were on missions, so they could not help him, and there was no way to stop or land the ship. She grabbed her leather jacket from her room and clutched it with trembling fear as David and Mal tried to wake their father. Worried he might be dead, she pressed a few buttons to summon a swirling gray smoke portal at the front of the ship. This was the "runway," where travelers entered and exited different gateways in time. Lady looked solemnly down at both of Stephen's children, knowing she had broken them and done them wrong. Their shared expression was one she knew all too well. She saw the tears in those sad, sullen eyes that asked her 'why?' with deep melancholy and confusion.

Initially, David was sad when he saw his father on the floor, then shifted to confused as to how this could have happened.

Everything was gray. As he regained focus, the realization of events becoming clearer, he blamed her. He'd glared at Lady. He wanted to yell at her and hit her. He wanted to bruise her and cut her open like she had done to his father. He wanted to tell her how selfish she was, how ugly, and how ungrateful she was, but he never did. He couldn't. He realized after looking at her remorseful face that, no matter what had occurred, she had done what she did because she was unwell. She had been through a lot. What exactly it was, he didn't know. One day, maybe he would be told when he could stomach it. The realization that she hadn't hurt his father out of malice meant the anger in him didn't last. It couldn't. All he felt for her was pity.

"I am sorry…for everything," Lady said timidly before jumping into the smoke. Mal jumped and tried to grab Lady's arm. She missed and once Lady was gone, she clicked a few buttons to close the gateway. David wiped his eyes, oddly thankful for Lady's apology. Despite her actions, he knew she had meant it.

Within seconds, the gateway closed. Lady had become a ghost. She remembered at some point she'd had a dream of becoming one, and for that moment her dream had come true. David started doing CPR to revive his father. Mal retrieved a damp hand towel from the kitchen and began soaking up their father's blood.

The ship was roughly the same size as a house, and it was an empty environment where David somehow still couldn't seem to get his father's attention. Stephen seemed preoccupied with the missions or the loss of Leroy or both. Before, he was always a ball of energy. At one time it seemed as though Stephen never stopped talking. Following Leroy's murder by an alien soldier, he hardly spoke. And when he did speak, it had seemed monotone and uninspired.

That was until they rescued Lady. When she first arrived she began as a student. Stephen taught her all about the business; time-travel and changing the world. He gave some speech, explaining how what they were doing was great for the universe and prevented much turmoil. Lady felt inspired, or she at least acted like she was. She was mostly quiet and seemed very distant and melancholic at first. She went on to graduate to runway supervisor, and eventually progressed up to time-traveler. It seemed to be the happiest she'd been in a long time. Stephen certainly seemed to be the happiest he'd been in a long while. Those days were long gone. David used to like Lady, especially because she brought him gifts. When Stephen started paying her more attention and even after he began fighting with her more, David felt like the distant one. He knew they were fighting, but he still saw it as time they were spending together. David hadn't fought with his father for years it seemed. They didn't do much of anything together anymore.

After David revived his father, Stephen grabbed them both and hugged them tightly.

"Thank you, David. You're a lifesaver." He coughed and chuckled. So did David and Mal.

"Horrible joke, sorry. Where is Lady?"

"Back," David replied.

"Back?" He questioned with concern. "Are you sure?"

"Yes," Mal said. "We saw the date and time on the screen."

"Mal, you remember how to…"

Mal sat in the driver's seat and punched in some numbers and clicked a button. She turned and smiled.

"Okay then," David replied.

Lady looked over the fields of Bergman Manor. The land was as dead as it was when she had last been there. Historically, it was a time of much fire and death. The fields were charred and burnt after the fire had spread, as black as the night sky. The mansion had collapsed under the massive red flames. She remembered the twilight; as purple as she had ever seen. It was so beautiful and so tragic, such strength and ferocity amidst such violence. Lady remembered seeing from a distance her adopted family hanging in the doorway of the now-dilapidated barn.

Then, it seemed so abstract and surreal, like she had dreamt the entire thing. She felt the memory should have had more meaning, but it didn't. She blamed herself for the incident. The family told her to hide and she did. Gilda told her it was the robbers, not her. The robbers killed the Bergman family. The more she repeated it, the more it did work. She felt a breeze whisper over the field as it bounced her black hair about. She sneered at the black doorway of the derelict barn. There was nothing, and she moved on.

She crunched over the dry, dirt field, encroaching upon the forest where she had lived before. This was where it all began. Her journey started here. It was what Gilda told her to seek out. She didn't know her original parents. It had been brought up in therapy. She stood for many wind gusts and lost track of how much time had passed. It felt like an invisible wall that had stopped her in her tracks. She trembled and breathed harder. She felt like if she went any further she might panic, her heart might gallop like the horses Mother Bergman used to ride. It was Gilda who taught her to associate her racing heart during moments of panic with positive memories. Lady blinked and saw Mother Bergman on the horse. Lady then breathed and entered the forest.

The forest blanketed Lady in shadow right away. She remembered the thick quilt she used to sew with Mother Bergman. A generational quilt with symbols of love and change women in her family had been adding to for nearly two centuries. Lady had added a spider, but it remained unfinished and burned along with the mansion.

Lady brushed a branch and a twig snapped. The sound penetrated the black tunnels and winding paths of the forest. It awoke something. As Lady stood still, she swore she felt breathing. The woods had come alive, and in a second she was knocked out on the forest floor.

Stephen joined Mal at the front of the ship after resting and visiting with David.

"You tried the runway, right?"

"Yeah, she coded the access. We've got to get there manually. All ship from here on out. So, how'd it go?"

"Planted the seed. Done and done."

"I hope you're kidding. You do know he has learned from Marie. You can't make up with him that easily."

He sighed and pondered this. "Crap."

"Yeeeaaahhh," Mal replied knowingly.

"Wait, are we calling her by her actual name again?"

Mal shrugged. "She lets me."

"How long?"

"Oh, just only a month or so," She lied.

"Still. I should know these things."

"You getting a bit upset, Stephen?"

"No." Stephen replied stubbornly. "Just fine."

"Stephen, I love you, but you are a stubborn fool. God's own special trainwreck."

"Okay okay. Enough. I get it. I liked you before you got so..."

"Adept? Sensible?"

"I was going to say human." He let out a frustrated sigh. "Tell me when we get there."

Mal smiled as she kept the ship on course through black space and stars, various portals and gateways opening and closing like exits off a highway. This was Mal's favorite job on the ship Leroy.

Lady awoke to pitch black. She dug her fingers into the dirt all around her. She didn't know where she was. Confused and anxious, she sprung up and fell backward into a dirt wall. She reached her hands out and walked to her left...dirt. To her right...more dirt. It was a hole she had been tossed in; quite possibly a dungeon or jail. She walked forward with her arms outstretched.

She felt something fuzzy, prickly, and then something else that felt like a huge eyeball. It was silky and far too big. Frightened, she backed away and fell into the wall again. She collapsed and felt tiny dirt stones hit her head and break apart. She heard deep, heavy breathing a moment before she felt the rancid breath cover her. It was unbearable. She coughed and pulled her jacket collar over her mouth and nose.

"Dear lord. Are you kidding me?" She slid and pushed herself into the corner. She covered her entire head with her jacket as she felt the giant breathing thing creep nearer. She then felt a sharp limb prod her. It then nudged her; pushing her into further the dirt wall. As it crushed her more dirt crumbled from the wall and fell on top of her.

Lady grew irritated and impatient. "I am already as far back as I can go! What do you want you territorial jackass!? You toddler!" It then tickled her, and she started to giggle. Within moments she was heartily chuckling aloud in the dark. It was so strange, but she couldn't help it. What was this thing? She felt a

41

connection with this moment. It had occurred before. She recalled a time in the forest with an almost unnaturally massive spider crawling along her arm and then under her tiny shirt, poking at her and tickling her skin. It was her earliest memory. It was her first memory, the fondest memory of all her recollections.

The enormous spider spoke deeply, gently: "Marie."

"Alexis!" Lady screamed. "Your breath is horrible!" She laughed giddily. "I'm sorry." The spider's legs tickled her body and tossed her in the air like she was nothing, and then caught her.

"Okay. Down girl."

The spider set her down. "I cannot see you, but you've grown so much! I can't believe you're still here! I nearly forgot, but you remembered. Thank you for that." Lady laughed and cried and hugged its big eyeballs. "Where are we Alexis?"

A soft, paralyzed voice shook from the creature's mouth. "Deep...in...Slather's barn."

"You sound so...hurt. What happened Alexis?"

"Slather...took...my family. Just...like...she did...to you. They...wanted...me...to...eat you."

Lady clutched one of Alexis' trunk-like legs. "Alexis. I don't remember."

"You do," Alexis uttered. Her breath was not as overwhelming anymore, but it was still fairly wretched. Lady kept her mouth and nose covered as she thought. She pictured their time in the forest when Lady couldn't have been but four years old, and even then maybe just turning.

"Remember," Alexis said.

Lady recalled a ship and many robed figures circled around a giant woman. Lady could remember her fierce red eyes. Such dreadful, evil little things. She knew them...at least she thought she did. They were tiny dots she often saw after her dreams faded to black. The woman spoke with such an eruptive force, her voice boomed like thunder in the sky. Lady watched Slather open her greedy, cavernous mouth, with those razor-sharp teeth and a slimy, flopping tongue. She swallowed Lady's parents and baby sister whole before she cackled like an evil witch. The laughter made her sound like the most unnatural, monstrous being to ever live. Lady's heart began to race. Her skin grew clammy, her limbs weak, her mind raced. She had come face-to-face with her fear, with the memory of her original family being killed. Slather had killed them all.

Lady couldn't fight it. She screamed and from the deep chasm within the barn in the forest the scream echoed and Slather and her followers knew that the one they wanted gone was dead. She almost was, anyway. The panic ended when she felt Alexis' leg on her back. Alexis picked her up and they climbed out of the hole. Alexis carried Lady through the barn and out the back door so the guards could not see them. She carried her into the woods. Lady felt the cool breeze along her face. She thought of the times she and Alexis would race through the forest. Alexis always won. Lady had always said, "You're quicker than the devil, Lex."

As Alexis placed Lady on the soft grass floor, Lady looked up with tears in her eyes and an exhausted smile. She whispered to her old friend, "You're quicker than the devil Lex." Lady fell asleep and dreamt about all of those horrible things from the dark...

Lady awoke to Alexis standing over her. She was startled at first, forgetting over the course of her sleep what her friend had looked like and how gargantuan she was.

"Good lord Lex. Back up some, huh? Please?"

Lex obeyed and Lady scratched and itched her eyes. "How long was I out?"

"A...half...hour."

"Are you okay?"

"Just...old. You?"

"Ah. I heard some words I swear I've heard before Lex. 'Sometimes you don't have to chase after something so hard. It seeks you out eventually.' You want to help me kill some aliens?"

Lex sprung in place, and Lady smiled. "Alright. Mind if I hop on?"

Lex lowered her body so Lady could climb on her back. "I, um seemed to have forgotten a weapon. You happen to know where my stash is?"

Lex raced off and Lady nearly fell off and had to contain her giddiness. She held on as Lex sped along their racing trail to a private brook where water surprisingly still flowed.

"Wow. Lex, this is still amazing." Lady grew chilly and her arms formed goosebumps. It was only from the cold, though; she was infused with courage beyond what she had felt since the old days. It was the playful recharge she needed. She dug into the dirt on the narrow bank and pulled out a wooden chest with spears, knives, and a homemade fishing net. She took as much as she could, and they were off.

Within minutes, they were on the outskirts of the forest, at the edge of a field where Slather and her followers stood. Slather was easy to distinguish; she was the massive, orange skinned alien inside a circle of tiny, robed ones. The aliens stood about thirty yards from them. Slather resembled a slug, but was definably human in her aesthetic. She wore a robe that was more than likely ten robes sewn into one. Lady squinted and looked closely at what Slather wore. It was the family quilt from the Bergman mansion. Lady knew it as soon as she spotted her spider. Lady pointed and whispered to Lex.

"Can you go for that husky alien there?"

"Indeed."

"How are you with fire? They will have weapons. As for her (she pointed), she is wearing your quilt I made for you."

"Good." The spider seethed and snarled at this reveal, its energy restored, and they shot out of the trees.

The robed beings hadn't noticed them yet, so they picked up speed. Finally, the creatures noticed and some ran. Others grabbed for weapons under their robes. This movement exposed some naked alien bodies, which was very upsetting to gander upon. Slather yelled at them to shoot, unfazed by the ghastly sight. Slather retreated to her ship. A few shots were fired, but missed. Lex was incredibly agile. She kept up her speed as the shots continued to fire at them. Once they were close enough, Lex started running over aliens while Lady stabbed them with her spears. Lex could kill ten, even twelve at a time with her fangs, front legs, and body.

Slather, seeing her underlings fall, emerged from the ship with a massive gun and shot a humongous fireball their way. Lex dodged it and the blazing projectile ended up hitting a group of Slather's own alien followers. Lex leapt at Slather and knocked her over with a huge thud. Slather got up. Lady tried stabbing her, but missed and fell off her perch. Slather, seeing the opportunity, ran at Lex and knocked her over with a thunderous shove. Slather opened her mouth wide and prepared to take a bite out of Lex's midsection, but Lady stabbed her in the back before she had the chance to close her mighty jaws. Orange ooze started to flow out of the vile alien slug. Slather turned and struck Lady several feet away. The wounded alien came at her, eyes like pools of blood. Lady reached for the knife at her ankle, but she couldn't get it out of her boot in time. Despite what seemed like an inevitable victory, Slather's followers ran into the trees. Slather followed Lady's gaze to where her subordinates fled and spat at them.

"You think this is over Marie?" Slather grumbled loudly. "I will eat you. Do you remember me? Do you remember what I did?"

Lady panicked. She felt her heart going a mile a minute, but then she saw a horse galloping in her mind. She thought of her true family. Stephen, David, and Mal. She noticed her spears were still by her side, and she felt courage and hope fill her. "I remember what you did. Do you go by Slather or Gilda now? "

"Good for you. You know, you wouldn't be here had I not helped you. It was meant to be. You were always my curse, and I yours. Imagine if we were friends? What fun we would have had. How many lands we would have conquered. Worlds. Galaxies. But that's not the way it was meant to be. You were always my curse."

Lady had edged closer to the spears. "Your red eyes. They never left my dreams. Neither did those words."

"Yeah, I have that effect on some," Slather grumbled proudly. "What were those words I said? Please, if you will indulge me? I've been around for a long time and have uttered so many memorable lines."

Lady sneered and decided she'd indulge Slather for another few seconds. She imagined her spears piercing through the center of the alien slug. "'*Sometimes you don't have to chase so hard after something. It seeks you out eventually.*' I have to say. Those words have haunted my entire life up 'til now."

"Oh honey. You think you had it bad? I couldn't sleep for

weeks. I still can't sleep right, dreaming every night you'd be there to do me in. Living in fear bleeds us dry. It slowly kills us, doesn't it, Lady Marie? "

Lady sensed vulnerability in Slather for the first time ever. She found herself nodding, agreeing with Slather. She didn't know she had been causing her so much fear and dread all along.

"These worlds. They are hard on the underdogs. I still see myself as one after all these years. What does that mean?"

Lady found herself at odds with battling Slather. She felt a connection with her. There was an understanding she never would have guessed could be there.

"One of us has to go. Don't go down without a fight. You're an underdog. You know that."

Lady rolled and grabbed her spears. She stuck them through Slather's chest as her mouth hung open ready to feast. Lady lay back and watched Slather fall backward, orange ooze bleeding from her wound. It was done. The greatest fear of her life was dead. Lady smiled and laughed with her entire heart, pounding with cheerful relief. She felt her heart as she began to cry also. The dark spell was lifted, disappeared in the breeze as it whispered over the field. Followers lay in the dirt, still, as dead as Slather. Lady felt proud but not finished. She looked to her friends coming for her. Things would get better. There was time to heal the wounds. There was always time.

The team boarded the ship Leroy after trekking along to the other side of the estate. Lex boarded comfortably, and since other team members who hadn't returned had been killed by Slather, there was more than enough room and weight allowance available. Stephen let Lady fly on out of there. Without hesitation they lifted, hovered, and took off.

Lady breathed a fresh breath of air. Well, nearly. Lex was right behind her. She couldn't help but think of what Slather revealed to her. She knew it was somewhat sad, but her hope was restored nonetheless. It had to be either her or Slather, and it felt great to be alive. She exhaled and felt the dreams float out, along with her deep, primal fear of Slather and the dark spell she had over her all her life. It all disappeared as Lady looked down at the orange blob that lay in the field, shrinking as they drifted away.

"Lady."

Lady turned and saw Stephen smiling. "So, everyone says you have been letting them call you Marie. Is this for everyone? I mean..."

"Especially you Stephen. In fact, only you from now on." She smiled and gulped, wiping a tear from her cheek. "I am sorry."

"So am I Marie. We'll be okay."

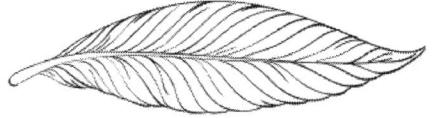

FAVORS by J.Z. Belexes

For someone who made a living hunting down vampires and rogue 'thropes *and enjoying it*, Reilly Austin felt her palms growing damp as she pulled into her uncle and aunt's ranch. The entire pack—minus one—stood outside waiting for her as she parked her rental car by the fleet of weathered pickups, a mix of human and canine faces staring expectantly. Right. No pressure.

Audience aside, it was good to be home. And she did think of this forest as "home" more than her parents' vineyards. Her parents' pack had been formed in the 60s, and sometimes felt more like a commune of ex-hippies than a "proper" werewolf pack. Proud Argo had a heritage older than the country, its original members having immigrated to the New World before the Revolutionary War, and migrating into Montana over a century ago. The Ranch House in the territory's southwest corner was almost as old. Cattle gave the pack food and money, but also a façade for the outside world's benefit. Few humans looked twice at a community if they thought the people lived together to work, but all the while, they roamed freely throughout the woods in their fur coats, reining supreme over the land as as apex predators.

She barely had a chance to stand up before she was almost knocked back into the car by her exuberant kid sister Madison screaming her name. Uncle Nicholas, or Odysseus as he preferred to be called, was the next to greet her, placing a large, furry hand on her shoulder and sniffing the top of her head when she bowed it down, the traditional greeting of an Alpha welcoming a packmember back home. Then the rest of Argo converged upon her, family and friends alike. They were even joined by a face she didn't recognize but was quickly introduced to, a shy young woman who introduced herself as Clara.

"But around here we call her Ironclad," Odysseus said. Her uncle was something of a traditionalist who preferred to hail his fellows by their Pack Names. It made sense, since he had named most of the werewolves present. He had even given Reilly her Pack Name, "Fortune."

"Oh, yes. I forgot," Clara said.

"How was your trip?" asked her cousin Liam.

"Did you bring any cool weapons? I wanna see!" said Madison.

Somehow the wordless gaze of Hatchet, a veteran of two world wars who didn't look a day over fifty, added to the clamor.

"I made you something," Aunt Ruth pressed closer, pushing a large white box into Reilly's hands.

"What? Oh!" Reilly cracked open the box and gasped. "Aunt Night Sky, you didn't…!" She pulled out a twelve foot, multicolored scarf.

"Well, I know how much you like that show, so I figured you could wear it to your science fiction conventions."

"Oh, you guys!" Reilly wrapped the impractical article of clothing around herself and surveyed the loving gazes around her. As the pack passed her around for hugs, it was just as she expected, overwhelming and comforting at the same time. Homecoming. She had always preferred Argo to her father's pack back in California, and this was why. Everyone here was so close. There was only one face missing... Sammy's absence was one of the first things she noticed, if only because the six-foot-six-inch giant stood head and shoulders above the rest. But given their history, she didn't expect him to be here.

*

When his dilapidated pickup pulled up a few hours later, Reilly excused herself from the family revelry. It was just as well; Liam had recently decided to focus his creative energy into learning the flute, and when he broke it out after dinner, she decided that was as good a time to get some fresh air as any. Plus, there really was some air to clear between her and the tall, muscular man stretching his limbs as he pried himself free of his truck.

The last time Reilly had seen Sammy, he had been a scrawny, almost loathsome-looking sixteen-year-old whom her uncle had recently rescued from some organization experimenting on 'thropes. But even back then, he had looked older, with a hollow look in his green eyes that made one wonder if he had *ever* been a child. The scar above his left eyebrow didn't help that effect. It took a *lot* to scar a werewolf; their ability to heal rapidly meant a wound had to be serious to leave a memento. Reilly didn't know much about Sammy's history, it wasn't her place to know, but before being rescued by Argo, he had apparently been through some shit.

And Reilly, a stupid, impulsive eighteen-year-old, had been completely freaked out by him and broke his arm when he tried to offer her a flower. Of course, thanks to a werewolf's inbuilt ability to heal, a broken arm was merely one or two days' inconvenience, but still. There really was no excuse for that, and the guilt of it caused her stomach to knot anew as soon as she laid eyes on him.

As soon as he saw her, she saw suspicion and smelled nervousness. Despite his physical maturity—having grown even taller, filled out, and no longer carrying himself with a slight hunch or his hoodie drawn over his face all the time—his posture shifted into an overtly defensive stance. She considered shifting back into her human form in the hopes of seeming less intimidating, but she had left her clothing inside, and she doubted bare skin would put him at ease.

"Got bored with your fan club already?" He sneered as she approached. The best defense was a good offense.

"Well hello to you too," she said, eschewing offense for bravado. "It's been, what, six years?"

"Just about. I was hoping for ten."

Reilly gave an obviously-forced "Hah," and punched him on the arm. He flinched. *Damnit!*

She withdrew her hand and gave him a bubble of personal space. "Really, Sammy? Still mad at me?"

"It's Samson, now. Or Phoenix. Only my friends call me 'Sammy.'"

"Samson. Well," Her sister had started calling him that a few years back and apparently he had taken it as his own. It certainly suited him. She began to circle him, sizing him up more closely. "You *have* grown up. You even have a girlfriend now! Congratulations. But you didn't answer my question." She stopped in front of him and looked him square in the eye.

This time, Sammy maintained eye contact, though he wavered. "I'm not mad atcha. I just don't like you."

Wow. For some reason, that hurt more than she expected.

With the wind knocked from her sails, she found herself adrift. "Look. I'm really *sorry* for what I did. You were right at the time. What happened to me as a kid didn't justify treating you with such hostility. And I'm willing to apologize as many times as it takes for you to believe me."

Sammy threw his hands into the air. "What do you care whether I believe you or not?"

"Because of Maddy! She's always calling me up, telling me about this or that adventure you take her on, or the things you do for her!" In some ways, Reilly was jealous. As much as she believed in the work she did, reveled in the life she led... she did miss spending time with her sister. A mischievous half-smile formed across her muzzle. "She even showed me a video she took of you singing 'Baker Street' at a karaoke bar."

Sammy shut his eyes. "I am going to kill her."

"My point is; she loves you like a brother. I thought..." Wait, what did she think? Where was she going with this? *Why hadn't she planned this out beforehand?* "I dunno, maybe..."

"You thought what?" Sammy scoffed.

"I guess... I've kinda been vicariously enjoying your friendship through her. I'm gonna be here for about a month, I was thinking I could treat you both to a night out?"

"Stop right there," Sammy raised a hand. "Just stop, will you? What is this, really?"

"What do you mean?"

"You got a whole pack in there that... treats you like royalty. You're *Fortune*, niece of Argo's Alpha and daughter of California's. You're the freakin' princess of *two* packs. Even *Hatchet* likes you. What is it—what is it, you see one peasant who isn't bowing to you and it's drivin' you nuts? S-sorry to be the pea in your bed, but we ain't friends. And we never will be. Now, if you'll, if you'll excuse me, your highness, I'm going to spend some time with a girl who actually *cares* about me!"

He gave her a melodramatic bow and marched inside, right past the revel-makers, faltering only as Liam's rendition of Let It Go assaulted his ears. But then he was out of sight, leaving Reilly wondering... Was he *right*? Why did she care so much about *him*?

*

"That was *really* rude." Clara said.

Sammy hung his head and curled up on his bed. "I know. I don't know what it is about Reilly. I know I was a huge dick to her. She just brings out the worst in me."

"You've been cranky since yesterday."

"That's when it sunk in that I would be face to face with her again."

"I met her. I think she's pretty awesome."

"You *would* think that. In the two years we've been together, you've never taken my side."

"I'm your girlfriend, not your enabler."

Sammy grunted.

"Maddy told me the whole story, including what happened when she was a kid. You don't expect me to hear that story and *not* sympathize with her, do you?"

"Problem is, she condemned all guys for one asshole's behavior and became just as violent herself. Sure, you have a psycho ex-boyfriend, but you didn't condemn *me* for it."

"Sammy, I can't possibly make you understand. You have no idea what it's like to be a woman in a man's world and can't even walk down the street without fearing for your…innocence."

"Can't I?" Sammy said, leaning forward. He was growing aggravated now. "Can't a lone, packless kid werewolf living in a humans' world, scrounging food out of *dumpsters* for fear of being caught by humans, who ended up *getting* caught and experimented on, understand what it's like to live in fear of…of violation? You think just because I'm not a woman, I can't understand what happened to *me*?"

Clara just sighed. "How do you manage to bring that up *every* time we have a fight?"

"I do not bring that up *every* time," Sammy spat. He took a deep breath and counted to ten, then got up. He had never worked up the nerve to kick her out of his room, and that trend wasn't likely to change soon. "I'm going for a run. If you think Reilly's so awesome, you can go talk to her about how all men suck or something, I don't care."

"It's snowing out!"

"I know."

*

Sammy trudged his way through the foot-high layer of snow. The retreating sun was casting its final lingering alizarin glow over the horizon, but visibility that was no concern for someone who could navigate home by smell. He ducked into a secret recess in the earth, where trees surrounded a small rock outcropping that formed, not so much a cave as it was a Phoenix-sized cubby hole. He kept a few personal belongings stashed here, such as an archery set, a waterproof case where he kept a few scraps of art, a magazine of questionable content, and currently, Clara's Valentine's day gift. It was a leather jacket he'd found at a thrift store, on the back of which he'd had Madison draw the outline of a wolf's head. He was still filling in her work with leather paints to make the likeness of Clara's wolf-face, and was halfway satisfied with the result so far. It would never be mistaken for the work of a professional, but it was recognizable. He would probably keep working on it through the two and a half weeks left till Valentine's. With the latest layer of highlights dry, he put the jacket away and set back out into the forest.

Looking over his handiwork had helped relieve his bad mood somewhat. It was nice having something to be proud of, as well as remind himself of how much he loved this girl. After all, a few years back he didn't think he would *ever* find someone who could see past his problems. So they fought sometimes. No couple was perfect, except maybe for Odysseus and Night Sky. He really was *lucky* to have Clara in his life.

*

"I'm not interrupting anything, am I?"

Reilly released her hold of a gleefully-squealing

Madison and quickly wiped the fur off her tongue. "No, no,
not at all. Come on in." Reilly got off her sister and rubbed
her tussled belly fur until it was straight again. "I was just
reestablishing the pecking order. Do you have any
siblings?"

"No, not that I know of."

"Ah." Reilly dropped the subject before it got
awkward. "So what can I do for you?"

Clara sat down on her own bed. There was a stark
difference between her side of the room and Madison's.
Clara didn't seem to own much in the way of earthly
possessions. But what she did have was neatly organized.
Madison's side, on the other hand, looked like Lisa Frank
had had an orgy.

"I was hoping for some girl talk. It's nice to have
another girl here my age. No offense, Maddy."

Madison shrugged. "None taken. Where's Phoenix?"

"He went out for a run."

"I think I'm gonna join him." She bumped muzzles
with Reilly and primed herself to escape through the
window.

"Wait!" Reilly called out. "Did you do your
homework?"

"Ugh. Fine."

Once Madison had slumped away, Reilly turned her
attention to her newest pack-sister. "My girl talk might be a
little rusty," Reilly warned. "I've spend the last six years
talking about little else besides weapons, vampires,
criminals, that sort of stuff." She tried not to sound like she
was bragging.

"Must be an exciting life," Clara said as she sat down
on the edge of the bed, hands on her knees. "It must
feel…empowering to fight the bogeymen."

Reilly tilted her head. "I never really thought about it
like that. But I like it. It's definitely gratifying, making the
world a safer place. Not just for our kind, but for

everybody."

"I wish I was that brave," Clara said with a rueful smile. "Me, when I run into a problem, my answer is to just run away."

"Well, there's valor in discretion," Reilly tried to be diplomatic. Unfortunately, as she had been reminded earlier tonight, diplomacy was not her specialty. "Besides, no one messes with Argo, not even Sippe Wiegand. No one's—"

"Sorry, Seep what?"

"Wait, you never heard of the German pack?"

Clara shrugged. "I was bitten, not born. Still new to all this, and I've only heard of a few other packs."

"Oh. Well to give my analogy effect, Sippe Wiegand is a eugenics pack. In the final months of World War Two, Nazis found out about our kind and tried making werewolves of their own. The Order liberated them and helped them establish their own pack with their own identity. These days, some of the Order's best warriors come from The Kennel, but…" she leaned closer and winked, "never call them *that* to their faces."

"Huh. How many packs are there in the world?"

"A lot. Anyway, my point is you have an alpha who's an ex-Order agent, not to mention Hatchet the Living Legend. And Sammy… I mean, *Samson,* has been training under Hatchett since he was sixteen, so in a fight against most agents, I'd bet my money on him."

"Really? Sixteen?"

Clara's obvious surprise surprised Reilly. "Well, yeah. You did not know that about your own boyfriend?"

She screwed her eyes shut. "I hate watching them train. It's so brutal. Sometimes Sam comes out of it caked in dried blood, and I just…"

Reilly nodded her head. Clara was definitely a Bitten. Rapid healing was an advantageous side-effect of the shifting process, and those born with it saw most injuries as a minor inconvenience not worth concern; a bullet wound was no more severe than stubbing a toe. And blood was a fact of life for predators, as elemental as water. Those adopted into the lifestyle could master their lycanthropy as well as anyone born into it, but there would always be a gap in philosophies.

"You should be proud of Samson. Hatchet doesn't train just anybody these days," Reilly shifted the topic slightly, but the words stirred a flash of jealousy. *She* was supposed to have been Hatchet's protégé. Instead, he had passed her over in favor of Samson, a decision that had baffled her at first. Samson had shown no interest in joining the Order, or even in fighting. So what had prompted Hatchet's choice? Up until today, she had always believed it was pity. But now that she had what he had grown into… Hatchet must have seen that potential all those years ago. Once again, the old warrior had proven why he was the master.

But Clara only shrugged. "You're right. He has kept me safe all these years, so who am I to judge?"

"Kept you safe?" Reilly quoted. "What do you mean?"

"I have an…ex-boyfriend who won't accept the 'ex' part. He thought because he turned me, that meant he owned me. I was nothing more than 'his bitch.'" She shut her eyes and shuddered. "He was possessive and controlling and one day, after a particularly nasty beating, I looked in the mirror and reminded myself that I was nobody's possession. So when he and his drinking buddies went out for a ride, I packed a suitcase and ran."

"That's terrible!" Reilly cried, and crawled up beside her. "So what happened next?"

"Well, Argo was the only other pack I knew about back then, but I had no idea what they were like. But I figured whether they gave me asylum or death, I'd be free of Ray. Fortunately, they weren't the monsters he was. Unfortunately, he tracked me down.

"A few days after my initiation, he and a couple of his thugs jumped me near the border. But Sammy came and singlehandedly fended off the three of them off. Ray hasn't bothered me since, but every now and then he rides into town and leaves his mark on our borders. Reminding me he's out there."

Reilly struggled to imagine Samson fending off three invaders. Her training allowed her certain insight; he could tell the difference between genuine aggression and fear-based bravado. Samson's behavior around her didn't fool her for a second. He didn't have a mean bone in his body. But still, it sounded like when his loved ones were in genuine danger, he could be a force to be reckoned with. She could see how Clara would fall in love with a guy after that.

"I'm sorry to hear that," she said. "But at least you have Samson, right?"

Clara snorted. "Yeah, the only way to get away from one boyfriend was to get another."

The awkwardness became palpable. "Oh… That's not what I…nevermind."

Clara stood up. "Anyway, it's been nice talking to you. No really, it has. But I don't want to overstay my welcome. I'll see you around."

"Yeah. I'll see you," Reilly said, but she was busy replaying the conversation in her head. She couldn't put her finger on it, but something about that conversation had not been right…

*

Reilly didn't let it ruin her vacation. She barely caught more than a glimpse of Samson outside of family meals. For such a prodigious figure, he was quite skilled at disappearing into the backdrop. Skilled, but he was not infallible, as they almost walked into each other on his way out of and her way into the kitchen. He mumbled a halfhearted "excuse me" and headed for the bedrooms with a plate of steaming oatmeal cookies in hand. This did not surprise Reilly, as it was the smell of applesauce-infused cinnamon, nutmeg and grains which had drawn her from halfway across the pack's territory.

She found a glass of almond milk already awaiting her on the table as Aunt Ruth (who always seemed to know) pulled another batch fresh from the oven, momentarily causing Reilly's sense of smell to override all other senses. She didn't even remember sitting down as the hot, crispy delights were transferred to a cooling rack beside the previous batch, though she was more or less back in control of herself when she reached for one of the cooled treats and bit into it.

"How do you do it?" she choked out. "Everything you cook is two hundred percent better. Not even my mom can match you."

Her aunt grinned and kissed her on her forehead. Reilly had a feeling she would never be too old for that.

"There's a reason a black woman's cooking is called 'soul food,' hon."

Reilly nodded and cooled her mouth with a drink. She sometimes forgot what it meant in human culture that her aunt was black. Thropes considered themselves a race unto themselves. Pink, brown and black didn't matter when it all got covered up by fur. Aunt Ruth was Aunt Ruth—or Night Sky, to her husband and the nonrelated members of the pack.

"Do you need any help?" she offered, eyeballing the large bowl of still-uncooked cookie dough. Feeding a pack of werewolves even a 'light snack' could be a monumental undertaking.

"You just sit and enjoy your cookies for now, Fortune. Once you finish that milk, you can give me a hand."

"I bumped into Sam on my way in here. It looked like he took half the cookies you made with him."

"Big boys with their big appetites," her aunt responded.

"Hey, I've been known to pack down food with the best

of 'em," she responded out of a knee-jerk reaction. She didn't like being shown up by a man in anything, even the stupid things.

"So I've heard. I have a friend in the Order, not going to say who, who keeps me updated on you."

"Yeah, I kinda figured you did. No one escapes the 'Eye of Night Sky.'" Certainly, it was a minor intrusion, but Reilly had learned a long time ago to roll with her aunt's machinations. Night Sky was a force of nature that looked out for everybody. The most aggravating thing about it was that she always knew best.

"And honestly, I mostly just binge eat after a mission goes sour. We all have our coping mechanisms; you know? I've had some friends who deal in worse ways. But there are times—not often—when things don't go right in the field, and like a whole strudel gets my mind off things."

"That's perfectly reasonable, in moderation."

Reilly helped herself to more cookies and remembered an incident she had been meaning to tell her aunt about. "Like this one time, me and two other agents were deployed to wipe out this basement full of vamps. Pretty standard op, none of them were higher than level ones, so we mowed them down." She thought back on the moment. Vampires were nothing like in the movies, suave, seductive immortals. Instead, they were walking corpses, needing human blood to sustain their own failing bodies as their organs slowly necrotized. Their brain chemistry was the first thing to go askew, creating a similar effect as being drunk. Vampires were degenerate, uninhibited piles of rotting flesh, and destroying them was considered a mercy to the people they used to be.

"But one of the guys, he gets bored, right? Starts showing off, thinking he's a damn action movie star. So Van Damme decides to stuff a thumb-sized grenade down one's throat and toss them into a cluster of their friends."

"Oh, no…"

"'Oh no' doesn't even describe it. We all get *splattered* by pulped vampire. It gets everywhere. In our ears, in our mouth, soaked into our *fur*. Getting blood in your fur is one thing, but to get bathed in vampire puree—just *ugh*. I know my other partner had a therapy session the very next day. Anyway, the helicopter comes to extract us, and none of us want to shift to human form and get that stuff on our bare skin. And y'know, they tell you your body doesn't absorb any filth that's on your fur when it sucks it back in, but when it comes to vampire you don't even want to take the *chance*. So the three of us squeeze into the back of the chopper, and by this point it's all starting to coagulate and get sticky. That was without a doubt the most uncomfortable hour of my entire life."

"Well, I'm sure you made your partner regret his showboating afterwards."

"Oh, he wasn't even done pissing me off. So we get back to the safehouse, and draw lots for the shower. Guess who came in last? Yeah, me. By the time those two guys were done working all the crap out of their fur, they had used up all the hot water *and* the shampoo."

"Well, now I just feel sorry for your partner for whatever revenge you got."

"Oh, I left it to the other guy to mete out his punishment. I didn't trust myself after that, so I ran into the kitchen and polished off a whole box of donuts. Which is the point I was ultimately trying to make."

Aunt Ruth turned around and beamed. "That's good, Fortune! I'm so proud of you!"

"For… binge eating?"

"No. You were angry, weren't you?"

"Oh, I was absolutely livid," she conceded.

"The old you would have probably ripped off your partner's ears. But you identified your rage and controlled it. That shows growth on your part."

"Huh." Reilly tilted her head. "Yeah…yeah, I suppose

so."

She earned another hug and plate of cookies from her aunt, a rather ironic, but welcome, reward for being a grown-up.

*

But being a grown-up didn't mean Reilly was devoid of anger. She just channeled it in less destructive ways, and every now and then it was healthy to blow off some steam. She had been keeping an eye on Hatchet and Samson's training regimen since her arrival, waiting for the right moment to step in and get a chance with the Master. She watched from a perch in the barn rafters above as her idol stabbed Samson multiple times. The tumbling mats had been stacked into the barn's corner so they wouldn't be stained by the copious amounts of blood raining down from both mens' bodies. Of course, their wounds were sealing up almost as fast as the knives could be pulled out, but Hatchet could stab like lightning.

She could feel Samson ignoring her. He was positively *radiating* non-acknowledgment, rather than merely focusing on the knife in his gut. Even Reilly winced as he yanked Hatchet's blade out of his body, head-butting his mentor to make him relax his own grip on the blade. Now, Samson had both knives.

"Good, good," Hatchet said, wiping the blood dripping from his nose away. "Caught me off-guard. First time you've ever done that. Now what're you going to do about it?"

Samson took a deep breath and charged forward, bringing one knife down and stabbing upwards with the other, but Hatchet became a blur of motion that left Samson on the ground, both knives in his gut.

"That's the thing about being disarmed. It leaves your hands free," Hatchet stated. There was no gloat in his voice, nor compassion. He wasn't dispassionate about it, either. To him, the Fight was simply Life. It was matter of fact. He could have just as easily been teaching Samson how to read.

Samson picked himself up and groaned as he un-stabbed himself. "Yessir. If I'm ever in a knife fight, I'll remember that. Can we take a break now?"

Hatchett nodded and strode over to the cooler where he pulled out a pair of bottles. Reilly could smell the freshly-squeezed orange juice from three stories up, and suddenly felt very thirsty herself.

"Give yourself a minute to replenish your blood. Then you're going to try something new."

"What's that?" He knew better than to protest. Hatchet did not tolerate whining.

Reilly found herself the target of Hatchet's pointing figure. "Her."

"Me?"

"Her?" Samson said, after spraying his drink. So spit takes actually *did* happen in real life.

Reilly jumped from the rafters, rebounded off the second story, grabbed one of the chains hanging from the ceiling and swung down to ground level. "You're serious?" she asked as she handed Hatchett a towel.

"First of all, ugh. Secondly, have you ever known me to joke? I wanna see what they're teaching you kids in the Order these days. You trained under Niklaus and Vadik, right? I trained them both."

She nodded. When she could not be Hatchet's pupil, training under his former protégées had been a major consolation.

"Then why don't you fight her?" Samson protested.

Hatchet folded his hands behind his back. "Because these sessions are about improving *you*, and *you* need to get over your fear of her."

"What?" Samson's voice rose a pitch. "I'm not-"

"Yes," Hatchet spoke in a tone that was indubitably truthful. He could say the sky was green in that tone and everyone would glance upward with self-doubt. "You are. Now, finish drinking your juice and I want you both to shift for this."

"Uh," they both said in unison. Reilly glanced at Samson and for the first time today, he looked right back at her. She could see his face was as red as hers felt.

Hatchet just snarled. "Oh you pups! If you're really so concerned about modesty, *turn around.*"

Reilly spun and began to strip. Behind her, she could hear the shuffle of Samson shedding his exercise shorts, then his bones quietly popping as his legs transferred from plantigrade to digitigrade. Reilly neatly folded her shirt, unbuckled her belt and pulled her shorts off before she, too, joined him in the fur and performed a few stretches. "Okay," she said, and turned around. Reilly's fur was just as ginger as her hair, an uncommon-enough trait that she was more than a little proud of, but for the first time ever, she felt self-conscious about herself. Samson had transformed into more of a mountain than a werewolf. His fur was the color of coffee, with his braid stemming out from somewhere in his mane. She tried very hard not to spare a glance at his genitals, but even werewolves had that peculiar streak of self-defiance common to human nature. What she saw made her bite her lip. It was at that point she noticed he was looking in every direction *but* hers.

"Okay, let's get this over with," he said.

Reilly spared a glance at the stack of tumbler mats, but if Hatchett wasn't going to suggest them, then she wouldn't either. She wasn't going to *blow it* in front of a living legend.

"Whenever you two are ready." Hatchet stepped back, still with his arms behind his back.

Samson's eyes suddenly snapped her way, green eyes filled with concentration. Reilly gave him a respectful bow before assuming her favorite stance.

Samson closed the distance between them with a single

step and surged his fist forward. Reilly grabbed it, spun around, and tried to elbow him in the gut. He had anticipated that, though, and caught her arm to entrap her into a chokehold. Reilly wrapped her leg around his, pushed her butt back, and levered him over herself, throwing him onto the floor. Samson rolled and tried to sweep-kick Reilly down, a maneuver she barely managed to leap over.

"Reilly, keep your left guard up!" Hatchet snapped, then muttered, "Just like Vadik."

Reilly snapped a nod. Her nostrils flared, her ears flattened. Yes! This was what she wanted, this was the challenge she had wanted-

Samson lunged for her again, and Reilly spun, practically dancing in a move she had embedded into her muscle memory, getting behind him, using her momentum to propel her fist into the small of his back…

Samson screamed and went down. His legs flopped uselessly underneath him, and Reilly went wide-eyed in horror at what she had done. No! This was supposed to be training, she was supposed to hold back…

"I'm sorry I'm sorry I'm sorry!" She drew back as if she was poisonous. Maybe she was. It seemed like she could never stop hurting Samson.

Behind her, she could hear Hatchet swearing, and the old man pushed her aside to check his protégée. After a few prods to the whimpering giant, he looked up at her with relief in his eyes. "You just hit the nerve cluster, he'll be all right in a few seconds."

Reilly's head hung. "That wasn't supposed to happen," she said. "I'm sorry, I should have held back…"

"Yes, you should have," Hatchet said, in the same damnably calm voice he had used on Samson. "You and I will work on your self-control later. I think Samson's had enough for today."

His assurances failed to make her feel better. And that

surprised her.

"I think you two need a moment," he suggested. "I'll go get Samson something for his... discomfort."

"Wait, Hatchet, don't go-" Samson pleaded lamely, but Hatchet was already out the door.

Reilly sighed and sat down beside the prone figure, bringing up her knees and wrapping her arms around them. It looked like she would have to be the adult here.

"Hey," she tried to say, but it came out as a mumble. She cleared her throat and tried again, and this time the attempt was more acceptable. "You're probably sick of hearing this by now, but I'm sorry. And I mean for everything. I was shitty to you when we were kids. It knots my stomach to think back on it. And I hate seeing you on the ground like this. I didn't mean it, I swear."

She was answered only with steady breathing. He didn't even turn his head to look at her.

Irritation started to bubble, but she swallowed it down. "God, just say something, will you?" she snapped. "Right now *you're* being the immature one."

Finally he stirred, pivoting his head towards her. She made eye contact with him and refused to flinch at the sight of his seething suspicion. "I just... don't know how to respond, okay?"

"You're not ready to forgive me. I get it. I didn't expect that. Something I learned from my therapy sessions, anger's a parasite. And once it gets its bite in you, it's hard to shake loose."

For a moment, she saw him grow downcast. "Yeah," he mumbled.

"Look. You don't have to forgive me till you're ready. But you're Madison's big brother just as much as I'm her sister now. And my aunt and uncle have all but adopted you. I see the way they look at you and then look at Liam. You can practically read 'Why can't you be more like Phoenix?' in their eyes. They love you. You know what that makes you and me?"

"What?"

"Family." It was a big, heavy word, and felt full in her mouth. Werewolves did not use that word lightly. *Family* was a lifelong thing. And it was meaningful enough to shock Samson into looking right at her. She had never seen his eyes that wide before... those big, soulful seafoam eyes.

"So please... can't we just get along? For Odysseus and Night Sky? For Maddy?"

"S-sure," he said, and slowly pushed himself up into a sitting position. "For Maddy."

Reilly grinned in triumph. "For Maddy."

"I guess... I guess I owe her, anyway. I promised to take her skiing this weekend but this morning I had to cancel those plans. She's pretty upset about it right now."

"Why, what happened?"

"Eh, Clara's car broke down and so I had to tap into the ski-trip money to help with the repairs." He looked down at his feet as he spoke and Reilly followed his gaze. He was flexing his toes experimentally, as if testing his ability to feel his feet again.

"Oh. Well why don't I take you guys then? It'll be my treat."

He looked up at her warily. "I dunno... And give you the chance to bury me under an avalanche?"

Reilly stared at him in shock until he started to snicker. A joke. He was making a joke around her. She smiled and stood, offering him a hand. To her delight, he took it and weakly smiled back.

It was a start.

*

Madison, however, was not as optimistic. Reilly found her sister that evening pouting in the second story of the barn. She was eager to share the good news with Madison, but as soon as she reached the second story, she felt herself caught in a tangible cloud of gloom.

"Okay…" Reilly sat down cross-legged beside her sister. "Spill."

"Sammy promised to take me skiing months ago. Today he told me he wouldn't be able to do it because he has to give his *girlfriend* a thousand bucks to get her car fixed."

Reilly was so surprised by the sheer amount of venom in the way her sister pronounced that word that she momentarily forgot she had the means to lift Madison's spirits.. The meter went way past "resentment" and deep into the red "hatred" zone. "You don't like her?"

Now *this* was some girl talk that might be of interest.

"She told him he owes it to her because she was running an errand for him when it broke down. But the gasket would have broken no matter what she was driving for!"

"Well, it's his fault for not saying something to her, isn't it?"

"I guess… but Sammy's too afraid to stand up to her. Ever. And she takes advantage of that. Low self-esteem and romance can be a dangerous mix."

Reilly was impressed."That's an awfully acute observation for a fifteen-year-old."

Despite the dark cloud looming over her, she grinned sheepishly. "Actually, that's what I heard Aunt Ruth saying to Uncle Nicholas once."

"Really." This conversation had just entered a whole new level. It seemed like not all was right in Stepford. "Now *they* don't like her either?"

"Nnnnot really. At least, they don't like the way Sammy won't stand up for himself. I overheard them talking to him about it once. Sammy got all defensive. Started saying some real stupid stuff, like he's lucky to have a girlfriend at all. He's afraid that if he left her, he would be throwing out his one and only chance at love."

"But that's ridiculous!" Reilly protested, and then shut

up before she could say any more.

"Yeah. I think so too, but he won't listen to me either. Got mad with me once and told me I'm too young to understand. But you know what? I'm not too young to know they've never had sex."

Reilly was shocked by what came out of Madison's mouth. Apparently her baby sister wasn't such a baby any more."Wait... how do you know *that*?"

"Well, you know how you can smell it on someone after they do it, right? Even if they shower after. Remember how Mom and Dad used to tell us that was just gas after eating meat that was about to turn? I'm not stupid, I figured it out."

Reilly didn't know whether or not to be impressed with her sister's powers of deduction. She had purposely blocked herself from that realization for as long as she could during her teen years. On a subconscious level she had known, but her conscious mind had denied it for a long, long time. Still, her head was swimming with this news. If Samson was still a virgin, that made him uncommitted, biologically-speaking.

A werewolf's sex drive was different from a human's. More voracious sometimes, yes, but only for the person they had given their virginity to. The first time one of their kind had sex, they developed a hormonal imprint on whoever they were with. They could have sex with other people, certainly, but it was never as fulfilling as when with their mate. That was why so many of their kind preferred to wait until marriage.

"Well, it's really none of your business what Samson's doing in bed. Or the lack thereof. Besides, after the way Clara was treated by her last boyfriend, no one can blame her for holding off."

"I know, I know. I'm just saying it's surprising that Sammy's so loyal to her when he hasn't even imprinted on her. They're not *mates*, and I hope they never will be!"

"Love's a lot more complicated than that, Maddy. If you're gonna criticize someone's relationship, be careful where you tread."

Her sister's face took a red tint, but that was a sure sign that the lesson had been learned. "Okay."

But despite Reilly's discouragement, Madison's scuttlebutt was very thought-provoking. (In all her years as an agent, no network of informants could ever channel more information than teenage girls.) Reilly knew Madison wanted Samson to be happy. If *she* thought his relationship with Clara was a farce, then there had to be a way to test that theory.

Reilly could almost *feel* a light bulb switch on above her head.

"Oh! That's what I came up here to tell you. I worked some things out with Samson. I'll take you skiing. Sisters' day out, how does that sound? I told Samson he's welcome too. He said he'll think about it."

Madison's reaction was just as Reilly expected: lots of squealing and latching on.

Reilly endured it for a moment, but the call to action could not be resisted. She stood up. "But first I'm gonna go on a trip to take care of something. By the way, have you seen my phone?"

*

Tracking down Ray Corbin was easy. He had already earned himself a spot on the Order's watch list for criminal conduct. The last entry into his file had been the complaint filed when he had violated Argo's border to threaten Clara. It took a few calls, but thankfully Reilly had accumulated a few favors in her five years on the field. Before she knew it, she was driving around the back roads of northern Idaho with an open file in the seat beside her. Her time off had turned into a working vacation.

By process of elimination, she found herself in some dinky little congregation of people calling itself

Stevensville." It probably had a quaint charm to the people who found small towns charming, but Reilly had arrived during the off season. Rain and mud put any driver in a bad mood, and it wasn't until that point that she questioned the sanity of what she was doing. However, she had come this far, and wasn't going to cash in those favors for nothing. She pushed a Rammstein CD in her car and decided to just let the hate and anger flow through her. Sometimes the Dark Side could be useful.

It didn't take long to track down the only other werewolf in town by scent. He was predictably within a bar in the seedy outskirts of town. Parking outside, she went into her trunk and traded her sensible jacket with a beat-up leather one and pulled off her top to reveal a less substantial one bearing Lynyrd Skynyrd's logo. She had brought along a wig that bore a resemblance to Clara's dirty blonde hair, which she hoped would make her more this predator's type. With the application of a little too much eyeliner, the look was complete, but as a final touch, she popped open a can of beer and took a few swigs, enough to allow him to smell it on her.

She spotted him hunched over at the counter as soon as she stepped inside. To her surprise, he was quite well-dressed in a pinstripe suit. From his file photos and the stories she'd heard, her mind had constructed the utter cliché of the typical rogue. He had a beard, all right, but it was trimmed and groomed. This guy could pass for an upstanding member of society, in spite of the dive he was currently in. But then, most predators used some form of camouflage. It made sense if he lured girls in with a smooth act before revealing his true, ugly form. Clara hadn't seemed like a sucker for a bad boy. No, she was smarter than that, judging by the way she manipulated Sammy.

Predictably, Reilly found herself swarmed by men as soon as she found a seat, all of whom she had to reject politely so as not to cause a scene and alert the target, though she would have enjoyed driving a few of the more piggish ones' heads through her table. She may have overcome her childhood phobia of strange men, but entitled pricks still made her hackles rise.

She found herself comparing them to Sammy, and each one fell short. He could have wiped the floor with any one of them, but it wasn't in his sweet nature. As a certain clueless neckbeard became more persistent, she considered calling the whole thing a bust so she could rip his balls off and ensure he would not muddy the gene pool, until she realized this was her opportunity. Sliding out of her booth, she "retreated" to the stool beside Corbin. "Mind if I sit down?" she asked in a timid voice, shifting into a Southern drawl. The Order had given her training in disarming opponents in every sense of the word. But still, she hated this part. After tonight, she would deserve an Oscar. "Hard for a girl to have a drink in peace unless she's already got some company, know what I'm sayin'?"

His eyes were on her in an instant, and she could see his nostrils flaring as he took in her scent. An alert werewolf would have detected the smell of another as soon as she walked inside, but this dive's air was polluted with sweat and vomit, anxiety and failure; and, oh yeah, just a hint of alcohol. It didn't help that he had his head up his ass, mouthing off to another guy. But as soon as she wanted it, she had his full attention.

"Well hello," he growled through a wolfish grin and Reilly had to suppress an eyeroll at the cliché. "What brings you into my territory?"

"Your territory? Sorry, um, I didn't realize there was a…a club here." If he was claiming territory, that meant he intended to start a pack, and with his record, an unauthorized pack was something the Order could not abide. "I just left my daddy's estate to drive around the country before I find a new place to settle down."

"Oh, there isn't one yet," Corbin said. (Good. That

meant Reilly would be doing the Order a favor by nipping a problem in the bud.)"But how would you like to be member number one? Get in on the ground floor, so to speak." He leaned in and whispered with repulsive booze breath, "You could be the alpha bitch."

"Oh *really*," Reilly leaned back, feigning shock and catching a breath of the closest thing around to fresh air. "Well, I don't want to just jump into the first new club I come across. I wanted to travel more before I commit, you know?"

His smile only thickened. "I understand," he said. "But don't tell me it's not a tempting offer, at least?"

"Honey, I don't even know you," she said, but with a coy lilt at the end of that sentence, hinting at a willingness to change that.

He, of course, took the hint, reaching forward with a beefy hand. "Ray Corbin."

She hesitated before taking his hand. She couldn't make this too easy for him. "Back home they called me Fate," she said. She hoped he would look back on this moment as the first warning sign.

*

The next day, she felt the glow of self-satisfaction as she drove through the gate into Argo's ranch, though that could have also been the warmth of the extra-spicy chicken wings she had eaten in town for lunch. Either way, it was a good feeling. Rather than driving all the way to the main house, she turned off the main road into the woods, making to hit a few big rocks before coming to a halt.

Clara appeared as Reilly got out. She was shifted in her wolf form but still wearing form-fitting athletic clothes. Reilly thought it was a shame to cover up that lithe body of hers, but those who weren't born and raised into their culture had a harder time adapting to the casual nudity everyone else exhibited in their hirsute forms. It didn't help that those who had gained lycanthropy through bite couldn't grow a full coat such as those who born with it. Her head, arms, legs and tail were furry, but everything else looked like pubic hair on steroids and did little to hide the skin underneath. Considering what Clara had survived, it would probably take her even longer than most to adapt to werewolf lifestyle, though Reilly hoped this would help her take the next step in overcoming her trauma.

"I got your voicemail," she said, voice dripping with intrigue. "Why did you want to meet me out here?"

"Oh, this turned out to be a working vacation," she said, banging on her trunk. As she inserted her keys, she went on, "I'm making a delivery to an Order waystation, but I thought you would want to get a look at what I'm taking them."

Just as she had imagined it, the sound of the trunk popping open was followed by Clara's gasp. Inside was a groggy, bruised Corbin, bound and collared and looking as uncomfortable as one would expect after three hours in a trunk. He looked up dazedly into the sunlight, not recognizing either women. The shift-inhibiting drug she had injected him with often had that side effect.

"It's okay," Reilly said, placing her hands on Clara's shoulders both to reassure her and make sure she didn't split. "He can't hurt you. He's never going to hurt anyone ever again. He put up a struggle, but I've put down tougher than him. It was an invigorating workout, wasn't it Corbin?"

"Cl... Clara?" The man slurred. Recognition seemed to break through the crust of drug-induced stupor, and he struggled to sit up. "Did yhou put this bitch up tuh this, yhou ungrateful c-"

Reilly cut him off. "The handcuffs and collar are reinforced and lined with silver. He struggles too much, they give him some nasty burn scars if they don't strangle him. Now, I'm just gonna mosey on down to the ranch house to grab a bottled water... Maybe hit the bathroom...

Check my email... Y'know, before we get back on the road. Would you mind watching him for me?"

"Me?" Clara squeaked, clearly too petrified to even move.

Reilly pressed a metal object into the palm of her hand. "You'll be *fine*."

"What's this?"

She winked. "It's the Brass Knuckles of Empowerment. And look, I'll be driving down some bumpy roads, so any bruises he *might* have on him when we get to the waystation will just get chalked up to that."

Reilly scurried off until she was out of hearing range, but then placed her hands on her pockets and moseyed the rest of the way to the pack house. Clara, she was sure, had a *lot* of issues to work out.

*

With dinner finished and his portion of the dishes cleaned, Sammy was looking forward to his and Clara's traditional evening walk. More importantly, he was looking forward to getting the unpleasantness of the other day cleared up. He had driven into town and bought her a bouquet of roses. He knocked on the girls' room door and waited.

And waited.

About a minute later, he was about to knock again, Madison opened the door. Her breath was shaky and she stank of nervous energy.

Alarms went off in Sammy's head. "What's wrong, kiddo?"

"Uhm, maybe you should come in."

Sammy stepped through the door and instantly noticed a distinctive emptiness to half of the room. "Where's Clara's stuff?"

"She uhm... she left y—I mean *left this* for *you*... I'm sorry." Maddy held up a folded sheet of paper, hugged him, and then ran off before Sammy could ask any more questions.

Sam,
I'm sorry I wasn't brave enough to do this in person.
You deserved better. I've been living like a coward for so
many years that I need to learn again what it's like to be
brave. But that's what this is about. I have a chance to do
that. Corbin's been put away, hopefully for forever, which
means I'm finally free. And I want to experience that
freedom.
Please don't take this as any personal condemnation.
You were a wonderful boyfriend, and you took such good
care of me. You taught me what it's like to really *be loved.*
But I think we both know this wouldn't have worked out. I
can't give back the love you deserve...

Sammy began trembling too hard to continue reading.
The cursed piece of paper crumpled up in his fist. The
flowers fell to the floor, making no sound. He had almost
expected them to shatter dramatically. This moment, this
twist in his life, felt much too quiet; too anticlimactic. He
had lost his parents in a tumult fire and screams; he had
been rescued and taken in by this pack in similar
circumstances. *Something* needed to break. But ultimately,
what broke was him. He landed on his ass and burst into
tears, weeping quietly.

*

It was midnight when Reilly got home after dropping
off a rather impressively-brutalized Corbin to the Order's
authorities. If some of her packmates hadn't already gone to
bed, she would have whistled. She liked to think she had
made the world a better place today.

She made a beeline to the fridge, knowing her aunt
would have a plate of leftovers waiting for her. Indeed, she
found a veritable feast of chicken fricassee—with
dumplings. But her happy grin was short-lived when she

closed the fridge door and found Sammy looming.

She eyed him up and down. It was a very impressive loom, even for someone in human form.

"Clara moved out," he said in a voice from beyond the grave.

"Wow, that fast?" Reilly blurted out, and then blushed. "I mean. I'm sorry."

"I knew it!" He waved a crumpled piece of paper in his fist in front of her. "I *knew* you were behind this!"

This was not what Reilly had expected. She had not expected gratitude, but then she had thought Clara would at least stick around for a little while before deciding anything.

"Samm--son, look," she set her food down and raised her hands in surrender. "I just arrested Corbin. He was a bad guy who needed to be put away. I didn't tell her to pack her bags and leave you."

He began pacing up and down the room. "Why couldn't you have just minded your own business?" he growled. "But no, you see a girl who's dating me and you instantly assume she's doing it out of desperation. So you help her out because God forbid a girl ever has to settle for me!"

"That is *not* what happened!" she objected. She wanted to be angry, but the man was projecting his own self esteem issues so vividly, it was easier to be mad at a choleric puppy. "I didn't assume anything when I saw you two together! I was *happy* for you, Samson, hand on the Bible! But if she left you at the drop of a hat, then she couldn't really have loved you, and—"

"Of course she didn't!" he shouted. "You think I'm stupid? You think I'm a rube?"

"I…" Reilly was baffled. "What?"

He stopped pacing and looked at her. With the tone of a teacher giving a lesson to a particularly dense child, he spelled it out for her, "I knew she was using me as a bodyguard against her ex. I mean look at me! I'm a Neanderthal!"

He drew himself up to his full height and swept his thumb up and down his burly torso and thickset legs. "I'm not smart or good-looking. I protect people; it's all I have to offer. But I hoped that maybe if I protected her for long enough and if I really worked at it, I could win her love. Now I'll never have that chance, thanks to you!"

He stormed out with the all the grace of a hurricane, leaving Reilly unsettled. She robotically returned her attention to her food, zapped it in the microwave, and sat down. But the appeal was gone; her triumph tarnished.

"That is one hot mess," she finally said out loud. And yet...

And yet...

Oh damn. She *liked* him.

J.Z. BELEXES

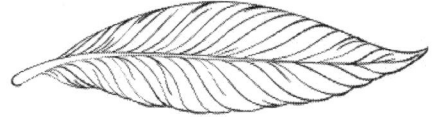

STEPS by Karen Janowsky

Spies don't often have the luxury of committed relationships. Bringing a lover to London, the city of my childhood, was unprecedented for me. Having any preference for company rather than solitude was new to me; willingness to share my secrets and past with a companion was confusing. I felt the need for caution. Imagine that: me, fully aware of my own power and allure and adept at devising any conceivable iteration of the honey trap, cautious of a fellow team member! I am deadly. There is no reason for someone like me to be afraid. With Logan, though, I discovered fear.

Logan was the military attaché to our international team of spies. This man had watched my back so many times as I lured and assassinated enemy targets over the past few months. He'd never once asked, even as we grew close, why I'd chosen this life, what made me so good at seducing and killing. Instead, as if the answer were easier, he asked to see where I'd grown up. He had some daft notion of helping me past the painful memories. His sincerity caught me off guard. We had time off and I acquiesced.

Now at home, with my city peaceful and white with Christmas cheer, my mood vacillated between secretiveness and ridiculous hope. I was torn by the consequences of this next degree of sharing the intensely personal. Nevertheless, there was one thing left to do before our return to duty, and Logan would not leave until his curiosity had been satisfied. The refurbished Tudor stood in contrast to the neighborhood's holiday cheer. It was at the very end of the lane, down a long drive that wound through a series of steep drops. The drive had never been paved and shallow roots jutted out from the ground like gnarled fingers as we descended. Even the smattering of snow, which settled like bright lace on other houses turned dull and translucent as we travelled towards the place where my greatest changes occurred.

"This is a testament to how I feel about you," I told him, as we ascended the walkway to my mother's empty house. According to my intelligence, her acting troupe had been touring on the Continent for four months. As we neared the entrance, it occurred to me that I learned to hide my hideousness the same way she'd adapted her real self: by a series of pretenses. I silently reminded myself that I used my natural talent to eliminate evil from the world. The point was arguable. Her front door was a dark maw set off by the dim, yellow sun that bore down on the grey garden's front steps, making them resemble teeth. Our long shadows expanded, blackening the door as if the house itself sucked light away from us.

We paused in front of the monstrous mouth and Logan shivered. I turned and hugged him tightly to prevent my own shivering fit. This was not a safe place—even all these years later, I knew this fact down to my bones. Sharp little tendrils began to unwind from my center and wind their way to the edges of my ribs. I felt comfortable. Logan's eyes were so pale they brought near-forgotten summers to mind. From the pupils, a starburst of pale yellow and white rays softened to the faded blue rims of his irises. He loves me, I thought. His eyes contradicted the fear furrowed into his brow. I believe even he sensed the malevolent energy of the place from where I'd sprung. I could at least try to get us through this ordeal intact. After all, this house was a part of me. I turned from him and knelt down to retrieve the key from its hiding spot beneath the doormat. "Into the belly of the beast," I half-joked as I stood. I turned the key in its slot.

Inside, I led him up the quiet staircase, one hand resolutely clenched around his, the other grazing the smooth banister. If I glanced down at that hand I would see the honeyed, slick oak exposed in the elongated motion of my palm as it slid up and up and up further, pushing a thin layer of grey dust into the air around us. Upstairs, the corridor itself seemed like a foggy shoreline in the early morning: no end in sight, no horizon. There seemed only a sea of dull light punctuated with white flecks of dusty debris. I loved this place once. It was exactly as I'd remembered it. At the end of the corridor was a window seat where my father used to read "The Hound of the Baskervilles" to me. "Inductive reasoning, my dear," Dad said. "Holmes based his conclusions upon observations, not upon pure premises like deductive reasoning." I remembered going through the text with him, and we pointed out logical flaws together. Reading with my father taught me to read people. Despite the awful circumstances surrounding my metamorphosis, I felt relaxed. A tentacle unwound from the rib just in front of my heart and poked at my skin, begging for release. I resisted, kept it contained. Nevertheless, Logan sensed the change in my demeanor. He grasped my hand a bit tighter and I felt him shiver. "We can turn back," I said to him, trying to sound empathetic. "This place is cold and depressing, and I have no real need to revisit the past." He shook his head, and then leaned over and kissed the back of my hand.

"Let's do this. We need to face your past together," he said. I placed my free hand on the doorknob of the second room to the left and turned it.

The door noiselessly opened, exposing us to its old insides. In front of us was a single bed, its rosy coverlet pulled tight over a mattress where heretofore unspeakable things had happened. Musty light pulsed orange through the room's dark slatted blinds. When I focused, I could see into the past; I could see Charlie and myself alone in the room. I could see his shirt undone and the rough, dark hair of my stepfather's belly curling along his pale skin. I watched my younger self turn from his open zipper in disgust. I saw him take both my small hands into his large, calloused ones. He placed one shaking palm on the soft mass of his belly, and the other he thrust a bit lower down, so I could feel him transform as he grunted approvingly. I heard his voice again: "Cordi, I've come for my goodnight kiss." His voice was unctuous. A smile slithered across his face.

I attempted to pull my hands away, turned my head further

towards the wall, and said, "Please, just go away tonight."

"I can't," he said, clutching my wrists and pressing both of my hands over his thick and damp body. I dug my nails into his skin, but he didn't appear to notice. "It's hard," he growled the sentence up to the ceiling.

All I could hear was the force of the phrase. *It's hard.* And the hard darkness breached everything in the room that was once light. It infiltrated my skin, muscles, and eyes. The darkness, and all the rage it carried through me, seared me from the inside until my body burned. I tightened my fists. White-hot pain and the sharpest of daggers pressed from inside, jabbing from between my ribs. Ropey, clawed tentacles whipped out from my torso. They writhed and parried between my stepfather and me. Of their own accord, my tentacles wrapped themselves around his thighs, forcing him to let go his grip and lurch forward. I raised my right leg high, reared it back knee to chest, and kicked his face so hard he fell to the floor and his nose and mouth seeped bright red.

"*It's hard.*" The words expanded and filled the room, tightening their hold on me like belts. They held me in place just as the tentacles did Charlie. His eyes opened wide, his mouth formed words, but I heard over and over, "*It's hard, it's hard, it's hard.*"

I jumped from the bed and slowly circled him the way I'd seen wild animals assess prey on documentaries. His mouth moved again. More sounds came out. "*It's hard*" filled my brain, crowding out all notions of empathy and humanity. I leapt for the kill. I never knew I possessed such an instinct. I grabbed him by the neck. Another tentacle shot out from between my ribs, struck and slammed him to the floor. I yanked him by the ponytail and then dragged him from the room. It flopped behind me like a ragdoll. In fact, in this moment he was rather like a plaything. He had no power over me. I could have spared him; I didn't want to. The phrase, "*it's hard,*" came shooting out of the room behind us—an animal itself, all predator. I heard a man crying, but the animal words were too loud. "*It's hard.*" I had to end this. Two creatures, the sentence and the man, had to die. This new, unfamiliar thing inside me was certain of this. The sentence flew out at us and with a surge of adrenaline, I jerked us both out of the path of that awful phrase as it flung itself down the staircase. I sent my stepfather hurling downwards after it. His broken body tumbled downwards. His limbs flailed about at impossible angles until he smashed into his last words.

Then it was over. The house was quiet again apart from my mother's protestations. Awakened by the sounds of her husband's destruction, she sobbed, "But it was mine. You've taken what was mine." I looked downstairs at the broken body. Its head twisted over and sagged onto the floor. Only the slightest hint of the magnitude of what had just happened emerged in my periphery. I recalled only little scraps of humanity and remorse. My body was once again that of an adolescent girl. I felt small and constricted. A sense of powerlessness once again crept in, forcing tentacles back to their source. I ran downstairs and kicked Charlie in as many places as I could: rib cage, neck, and especially his mouth, from where that vile sentence had sprung to life. His carcass moved fluidly and slowly, like sludge. No more hardness. Never again.

The memory froze there and I returned to the present. I shuddered, remembering the first discovery of how powerful, monstrous, and afraid I truly am. Why was I not surprised at the changes, I wondered as I watched this memory play out? I never registered how it was done, that a seventeen-year-old girl dragged a two-hundred-pound body. Until I understood the metamorphosis, I'd told myself I'd seen only my hand, that I'd been confused from the fright. I made myself believe that what I witnessed was not real; it was merely my mind making sense of the terrible event. The scene presented itself to me with the clarity of slow motion. There are things which humankind is not meant to understand, nor should persons ever witness, lest they be driven mad. There are horrors in this world that drive people mad with their very existence. I am neither mad nor entirely human.

The fact of my separateness made me an excellent assassin. It revitalized me, watching a victim's eyes go cold and empty. I chose a profession where I could feel the life drain from a person viscerally. It was a calling. The anger and fear built into an exquisite bloodlust. I sated it with impunity. Granted, usually the people I killed were deserving in some way. Logan only killed in combat situations where there were no other options. His job was to protect the rest of the team. I'd always hoped that I'd be more like my human father, who gave of his life energy regularly and willingly to my mother. All of his actions sprung from a deep love for his mate. In a way, he reminded me that I was part human, now more than ever. I fear I am truly evil deep down, however. I felt more vulnerable and less monstrous today, though. After witnessing the memory, I was a broken, frightened girl again. It wasn't just that. For the first time, I'd seen with great clarity the fulfilment of my destiny. I let go my grip on Logan's hand. "I can't be here," I said quietly. "I'm sorry, and I know I promised, but please, let's just go."

He retook my hand and faced me. His brow furrowed and his pupils dilated, making his eyes look like a stormy sky. He was full of concern. I could see that he wanted to ask what just had happened. Before he could speak, my cell phone rang in my pocket. I snatched it from my coat and answered.

I'm not sure whether my voice registered relief or anxiety; I felt both. Christmas was not a time you want Control calling. "We need to get to Heathrow to catch a flight out for a mission," I said after hanging up. "We've got time to get back to my flat, change clothes, and take the Tube to the airport again."

Just as I finished talking, his cell rang as well. His expression showed mostly resignation when he hung up. He kissed me on the forehead. "Guess duty calls," he said unhappily.

We were just in the vestibule and heading for the front door when it opened. Mum hadn't aged all that much. Actually, I'd forgotten that we looked so much alike. Proportionally, she was a bit thicker than I, and a bit shorter. Her arms were more graceful than mine, though: almost like tendrils unfurling from beneath some beautiful and deadly flower. She carried herself with that same elegance and grace that she'd always had. She had the same heart-shaped face and the same dark hair as mine; at the moment, hers was streaked grey with what I knew to be dye. People like Mum and me don't age quickly. We all froze in our tracks and gaped at one another.

"Hullo Mum."

Her face darkened as if night itself had just passed a hand over it. "Why are you here, Cordelia Emily Houghton?"

She knew that invoking my stepfather's surname was a prelude to a fight. I was a Lear, not a Houghton. Charlie Houghton brought out in me what should have lain dormant forever. I was suddenly glad to have to leave England and hopefully get the chance to pummel someone. "It's 'Lear,' Mum," I sighed, "And because it's Christmas, and we happened to be nearby this year."

She looked at the two of us, assessing Logan, who was standing there next to me looking both defensive and unsure of himself. "Mum, this is Logan. Logan, this is my mother, Amelia Houghton." He tentatively put out his hand.

"American," she spat the word as if cursing. She ignored his offered hand and looked at me. "Is that yours then?"

"We're together," I replied blandly.

"Does he know you're a monster?" That was my cue to take Logan's hand.

"I'm no more or less of a monstrosity than you," I replied with as much calm as I could manage. I said to Logan, "Let's go," and began to push past her through the door "It was lovely to visit, Mum. Let's do it again soon, yeh?"

She stepped into our path with a fluidity and economy of motion I'd forgotten about. Solidity only ever barely existed under my mother's feet.

"Does he know all about what you are then, and what you've always been? Does he know you're a murderer?" We stepped around her again and started walking faster. I opened the car passenger door for Logan and then got around to the driver's side, started the ignition.

She yelled after us, "Does he know you'll spread them for anyone, then? Does he care about that?" In my rear view, she was all gaping, screeching mouth and long, waving arms. In truth, I was a bit embarrassed for her. She didn't try to maintain her human form as much as she used to. Perhaps she was mad. The idea amused me, however briefly. Driving away I felt as if those motherly arms, which held me and protected me in childhood, were sucking me backwards. If I'd brought Logan to her as amends, let her destroy my mate as I'd destroyed hers, it would help enormously to heal the rift between us. Never. She will never have him; I will never be like her. I will fight this beastly thing inside me until my last breath, I thought. I pressed on the gas pedal a little harder to break free.

Once we were well on the road, Logan gently put his hand on my thigh and rubbed it a little. "I'm so sorry, Cordi. I can't even tell you." I took one hand off the wheel and picked up his hand, and kissed it.

"It's not your fault. She's been off her head for years." I glanced over at him. He didn't look convinced. "Logan, I'm having the best Christmas ever: I'm with you. I won't let her ruin it. Not for either of us."

The rest of the ride was quiet.

We changed clothes in my flat—we lingered for a while, half dressed; it was good just to be held close, my perpetually cool skin against his warm flesh. I drank in his heat, the pulsing of his life-blood against me. I wished we could have stayed that way for longer until the boundaries between us disappeared. Our skin touching like this always made me very thirsty.

I felt better as we walked to King's Cross station. The cold air and bit of exercise helped revive my spirits. Logan, however, looked pensive. The underground was empty—we had half a compartment to ourselves.

"You are lost in thought," I offered.

He leaned his head back against the window. "Cordi, how much does your mother know about your job? I mean, how much do you talk to her about classified activities?"

"For all she knows I live in Antarctica. I haven't had any contact with her in eight years, almost to the day! What makes you think otherwise?"

He looked unsure. "I just assumed...the things she said about you. Y'know, the killing and the other stuff."

So that was it. This was one of the reasons I should not have agreed to go back to Mum's house. I didn't want to dredge this up. On the other hand, I was almost relieved he suspected me of having supplied my mother with classified information. The memories I relived today were so visceral I was almost sure he knew my deeper secrets. I reminded him of what I'd already said about my past, that my stepfather had died by an aided fall downstairs. I then elaborated: "The last time I was home for holidays, I was seventeen. I'd decided this year was going to be different. I was a university student, I felt like I was an adult—fully hatched and out in the world, and it was time to expose him. So I confronted both him and my mother. Clever beast that he was, he'd already had a story lined up for that eventuality. I listened in disbelief as he explained to Mum that I'd hooked my own claws into him when I was twelve and made him do things to me by threatening to go to the police should he resist. He went so far as to claim that I ran the same con with boys from my school. I was so dumbstruck I didn't know what to do. I opened my mouth to protest, but words didn't come."

I stopped my story to take a couple of breaths. I looked straight ahead and watched the snowy shadows of London swish past the train's large windows. It was as if my life fast forwarded as my mind rewound.

"And your mother believed him?" Logan's voice registered disbelief. "Your own mother chose him over you?"

I explained, "You must understand, Mum blamed me for my father's death. True, it was an accident and I was a child, but he died trying to protect me from an oncoming car. The year prior to that encounter with them, when I was sixteen, things had gotten very tense at home. Mum was away, working in Wales. I told him "no" when he visited me the third night I was home. He came to me anyway. I struggled, kicked and bit, and he hit me so hard the room dimmed and blurred, and he raped me anyway.

"When he left the room, I raided his wallet and ran away. I made it all the way to the city, and I lived on the streets for a while. I learned to defend myself, to fight, out of necessity. I spent nights in and out of hostels, hotels, and jail cells. After about a month, I ran into a Buddhist monk, who offered me shelter and took me in. Apparently his order sends its initiates out in search of lost souls. At the monastery, I learned to channel my rage and through mindfulness training. I learned to keep my most fearful instincts at bay. Even so, I'd earned myself a reputation with the authorities. I didn't lash out and attack men so readily, but I trusted no one, and there were a few incidents. It was April when I left, and I returned to school and passed my exams. Mum already blamed me for my father's death. Given that and my police record, she was ready to believe her husband."

I paused and took another deep breath. I remembered a particular time with a man, the promise of bliss, the quick and deadly swipe of a clawed tentacle. I soaked in the man's life energy as it left his body. I recalled the ambivalence I'd felt about what I'd done, yet how my blood sang with invulnerability afterward.

"To jump ahead a bit," I continued, "My room, which you saw, has apparently not been altered much since I left. Even the sheets look nearly identical to my old ones. Standing there today, I could even imagine where he'd bled...I'd blocked out a lot of what had happened. I couldn't have recalled its details if my life depended on it until today. Today I could remember seeing his silhouette on my door, him at the side of my bed undoing his trousers, and I remembered that I felt numb with fear of the inevitable. I remember seeing white everywhere—no shapes, nothing but pure, white rage. This afternoon I witnessed everything with clarity, and then she showed up."

He was quiet. I waited for him to react. I watched his face cloud and contort slightly as he appeared to mentally revise his image of me as a human being. He offered a scowl but no words. I couldn't read him. It is my job to read a person's reaction to me and act accordingly. It occurred to me, not for the first time, that emotional closeness made me a poor spy.

"I'll tell you if you really want to know all of it, Logan. Just remember it's not easy for me." My voice quavered slightly, my newfound uncertainty plainly evident, I was sure.

He took a deep, slow breath as if steadying himself. He clenched and unclenched his jaw a few times, and then said, "Tell me. If it's part of who you are, I want to know."

I told him what I remembered, and how it felt as if I was watching it happen to some other scared adolescent. I explained how helpless I felt, like some terrified, captive audience, helpless to do anything but watch the violation of a child. Of course, I allowed him to assume the human fight or flight cocktail of adrenaline, cortisol, and norepinephrine accounted for my strength. The events of that night were horrific enough without adding tentacles and claws to the narrative. By the time I was through recounting it, I couldn't hold the tears back anymore. The memories and the admission of my secret were painful. I forced myself to look him directly in the face.

There now," I said, "you've seen one of the biggest, worst skeletons in my closet. Until I got to know you, I'd just as soon have eviscerated you as I would have taken you to bed, and it would have made little difference to me. I do my job by re-enacting that very scene time after time. I care very much for you, you know." I was almost relieved that he knew; that it wasn't a secret anymore. I elaborated, "For more than half my life, I've felt as if the people I trusted the most abandoned or betrayed me. Until I met you, I did not think my own humanity existed anymore. This much truth terrifies me, Logan. Do you understand now why trust is so important to me? Why it doesn't come easily? You probably think I'm as monstrous as my mother asserted."

Logan shifted uncomfortably in his seat, and for an excruciating moment or two, I couldn't read his expression. This was what I was most afraid of—the ugly truth, the first hints of the 'other me:' needy, thirsty, dark, vicious, repulsing him.

He frowned. "Of course I understand. The bastard got what he deserved. In fact, he probably got off too lightly. I don't think he suffered enough, you should have castrated him!" His voice rose to a crescendo, then he fell quiet for another moment. He closed his eyes again, and then opened them and looked directly into mine. Logan had the kindest eyes I'd ever seen. He took up my hand in both of his. I knew he'd been trying to regain control.

"So yeah, Cordi, I understand. And I'm glad he's dead 'cause I'd have done a lot worse to him if he weren't." He picked up my hand and kissed it. The train slowed, then stopped with a jolt. "Jeez, are we at the airport already? I wonder where we're going," he said with that lopsided grin of his.

The cold air in the Tube terminal slapped both of us into a better mood. I felt reinvigorated as we headed to the satellite terminal where the government and Agency aircraft hangar was located. It was a short, brisk walk from the Tube, through a back exit of Heathrow's main building, and then towards the secret exit that led to the Agency's hangars. He kept his arm around my waist. I tamped down the notion that this human man protecting me was ridiculous. Instead, I allowed myself to feel safe and loved.

91

Mid-way, I remembered something and stopped and faced him. "Oh, and another thing, Logan." He stopped short and his posture went rigid. He looked nervous. I smiled up at him. "When we get back to Washington, will you teach me about baseball?"

There was that lovely grin again. He dropped our bags, dipped me down and kissed me. It made me thirsty for him again. Coming here, so close to the place where everything changed, probably had been a poor decision. Human beings make poor decisions when they are in love. Remembering my own humanity, I resisted the Charybdis urge to swallow him whole right here in the cold airport, in front of all these people. He looked down into my eyes, smiled and said, "I thought you'd never ask." From a nearby rack outside a shop, he grabbed a ball cap and slid it onto my head.

Giggling, I returned the purloined hat while he picked up the bags. We proceeded towards the plane. His apparent happiness caused me to crave something else—I couldn't identify the longing. As we walked, I felt wonderfully supported and unjudged. Once again, love made me inattentive. A tentacle wound its way from under my human flesh, through my wrist. It wound past my palms and around Logan's waist, holding him to me. He didn't seem to notice so I clung to him tighter. I rested my head on his shoulder as we made our way up the airstrip. He has seen me kill people in brutal ways. He has seen me toy with the emotions of truly weak, susceptible people in the name of getting something the team needed. He's seen me earn their trust and destroy their lives. Now he also knew that I did these things because it was my nature. Yet, instead of revulsion, this understanding strengthened his commitment to me. With arms and tentacles entwined as we walked, I quietly considered the nature of trust. I wondered how deeply my own trust lay, and what I might one day reveal about my truest self.

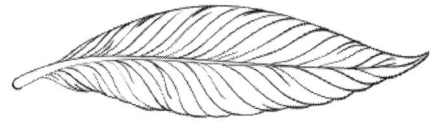

GHOST OUT OF TIME by R.C. Larlham

Elspeth

She awoke dead for the first time, as yet unaware she had died. Something pressed against her everywhere and held her immobile. Something she could not taste or spit out filled her mouth, and her ears were stopped up with it. Horrified, she struggled in desperation to escape and was astonished to find herself floating above a mound of stones that marked a grave. She could see trees moving and hear the wind, but it blew right through her. She could hear, and speak, but she felt nothing and smelled nothing. Like terror in the night, it came to Mirrim that she was dead.

Dead? How could she be dead? She could think. She could speak. She could hear. And she could...float above the ground. She pushed that last thought aside and headed for her parents' cottage. They would know what to do!

None at her family's dwelling could see her, despite her efforts to speak to them and touch them...not even Mirrim's favorite person in all her world, old Gran.

Mirrim left the cottage and went to the one person who was believed to have second-sight, the village seeress. But the old woman was a fraud. She heeded Mirrim's essence no more than had old Gran. Disappointed and angry, Mirrim departed.

In near despair, Mirrim fled through the village. As she passed the cottage of the village Healer, the Healer looked toward the road.

"Mirrim!" Her shriek was muffled by the hand that went to her mouth the instant it began. "Mirrim," she whispered, "you cannot be here. I failed you. You are..." She cleared her throat, "How come you to be here? Whose death do you portend this time?"

"I know naught of deaths save my own."

"Then why are you here? I see spirit-souls only when a death is imminent. The last time was the death of my son. A lonely, keening apparition came to me in midwinter, but spoke no words. In spring, I found my son, who I had apprenticed in another town, dead, along with his master, of hunger and cold. So I ask again, who will I find dead in the near tomorrows?"

Mirrim sighed. "I know not. I know only that I am dead and no one sees or hears me but you. Why," she was suddenly alert, "can you see me and hear me when they cannot?"

"Ah, well, as to that..." The old Healer was suddenly very nervous. "Come inside, Mirrim. I cannot talk to you in the street." She turned and reentered her cottage. Mirrim followed. Inside the darkened dwelling the old woman peered at her. "You have become a spirit-soul; a soul trapped upon the Earth, out of the bounds of time and life."

"You are second-sighted?"

"I am. No one knows. People think it is a great gift but it is not. I am the only such person within leagues of this village. I would have been harassed to an early death had it been discovered."

"Healer, what is your name?"

"People call me naught but Healer, but my name is Elspeth, given me for my mother's mother."

"Elspeth, what happens to spirit-souls?" Mirrim took a breath. "What's to become of me?"

Elspeth looked off into a distance Mirrim could not judge. "Most spirit-souls haunt the places they lived, appearing to the second-sighted as harbingers of great change. They seem to be unable to either speak or hear, but appear and leave at their own choosing." She paused. "My talents tell me that you are more powerful than that. There is a class of spirit-souls that takes the bodies of the dead and makes them live again. Of course, the bodies are only hosts for the spirit-souls. The person they were has gone on to whatever next life awaits."

"And you believe I am one of those?" Mirrim shuddered within herself. "I don't know that I could live within the body of someone dead."

"That may be true now, but I am certain that you will. You are destined to see wonders and do great things. As a spirit-soul you will live beyond my ability to see."

"What do you see?" Mirrim began to feel excitement...leavened by some trepidation. "Is there a way I can return to life?"

The Healer looked sorrowfully at Mirrim."No child, I fear that is not possible. I could not save you." Mirrim suddenly realized the Healer was weeping. "I tried so hard to save you, but you died, and there is no recovery from that."

"However," she continued before Mirrim could interject another question, "I see you inhabiting hundreds of bodies. I see you in wars and in peaceful lands. I see you in great cities of unimaginable size and population, and in isolation with no one to speak with or to rescue you. I see you with many different swords in your hand, often as a man. Beyond that I see nothing specific, except that at some time I see you as a Healer."

Mirrim wasn't sure what to think about that. "A healer? How can that be? I know nothing of the Healer's arts. When did you become the Healer? Were you of a Healer's clan? I am not. How will I learn?"

As Elspeth told her story, Mirrim watched the Healer's life unfold through her mind's eye.

Elspeth stood, tall and spare, by the Healer's grave. A terrible illness was punishing the village, had been since snowmelt. Nearly a quarter of the villagers had died. Now it had taken the Healer. Despair for the survivors filled her heart, and fears for those not yet ill. Most of the stricken had died. Survivors had withered limbs, some also other complaints. Although she had often helped the Healer once the scope of the illness became apparent, she could not imagine that she could replace him. She was but seventeen summers. Her closest friends were gone. Three siblings had died as well...her older brothers Brian, always teasing her—always laughing, and Drustan, stolid and hard working—her great protector, but the hardest to accept had been the bairn, her baby sister Boadicea. Hot tears came. She turned resolutely home.

By her twentieth summer, life in the village was almost normal. Marriages still were few, and none requested her hand. She thought herself unattractive; too tall, too thin. And then, one morning she stumbled and fell into a survivor, knocking him down. His name was Uhtred, and he was a great bear of a man with a withered leg. Helping him up, she saw a spirit-soul. It spoke not, but suddenly she was certain he would die of accident within very few years. Somehow, she knew. In empathy and sorrow, she assured herself he was all right,

She found that she and Uhtred often frequented the same places at the same times, too often, in fact, for chance. She found her days filled with thoughts of him. Any time she wished, she needed but think of him to know his whereabouts. "I wonder," she thought after some weeks of this, "whether I have the second sight." On a shopping errand for her mother, she was trying to decide between a yellow and a white onion (her mother had said only that she needed onion for the chicken stew) when Uhtred asked from behind her, "Are you going to juggle those?" She told him her dilemma. "White," he said instantly, and went on to describe the complete process and ingredient list for chicken stew. It sounded much richer than her mother's.

"How do you know all this?" she asked him.

"I have a public house and I'm the cook," he told her. "You and your family should bring me the ingredients for a stew and I will cook and serve it in my public house." After that she and Uhtred began to share stories of the day, advice on and simple conversation as they met. Elspeth found herself attracted to this "great bear," and the attraction grew.

One afternoon Elspeth returned from an errand and discovered Uhtred and her father talking. Both men turned to face Elspeth. Without preamble, her father announced,"Uhtred has asked your hand in marriage. I have agreed. He has a successful business and will provide well for you."

Elspeth nodded, although her acceptance was not truly required. She and her great bear were soon married. Together they had a son they named Nuallan.

Elspeth found happiness anew, a happiness she had thought beyond her. Even so, there remained the shadow of the spirit-ghost. She had told no one—she bore this burden alone. She did all she could to prevent his death, but five summers after their marriage, Uhtred's withered leg finally betrayed him and he fell, breaking his skull on an iron oven door. Devastation filled Elspeth's heart. There was to be more pain. The landlord canceled the lease. Elspeth was overwhelmed with despair. The next day she steeled herself and began looking for a place to live.

She decided she would take the Healer's cottage! No one would take it for fear that he might have left the plague there when he died. Elspeth didn't believe it. She had worked with the healer at the bedsides of plague victims for months and had not died. A certainty struck her. She could be a successful Healer and Wise Woman to the village. She and her son moved in and began repairs with her stonemason father's assistance. A new life began for Elspeth and her son.

Early days were hard. She had to persuade the villagers to use her services. For the first two summers she depended on a garden and traps to provide much of the food for Nuallan and her. By the end of her second summer her kindness and skills had dispelled early misgivings.

Ten years later, she apprenticed Nuallan to a harness-maker in a different town, where he died. Elspeth crumpled within herself like a child, and she believed she would die of it. She could not eat, and she wept for hours each day. After a seven-day, she had not died and it seemed she was not likely to. Once again she steeled herself for a life without joy. Her skills had been such that she had made the village her family, secretly using her second sight to allow her to be able to help before it was too late. Now she began visiting and speaking with people, learning the lives and fears of her neighbors, and later most of the village families. In their turn, villagers began to bring her their troubles and she became trusted and sought for advice. There were suitors, for she was striking in her height and appearance, but she rejected them all, pleading commitment to her village and vocation.

"I don't think you have only second sight," Mirrim said. "You predict things. You became the Healer with almost no training.

You are more than an ordinary person."

""You may have the right of it," Elspeth agreed.

Elspeth stood. "I am going to bed now. You are welcome to remain here for as long as you like." She went to a curtain draped over the rear of the room. Pulling it aside she stepped into the next room and let the curtain fall.

Mirrim eventually decided to at least stay the night. Out of habit, she lay down on a padded bench, discovering that unless she set a mental barrier she would sink into it… not that it mattered, but it was unnerving. She fell asleep, much to her surprise when she awoke. As time went on Mirrim discovered that sleep was required of spirits as well as live people. The restorative powers of sleep to the mind were just as essential.

For the first time in many years, Elspeth had someone to spend an evening with, and she was grateful. That night, having finally unburdened herself, Elspeth passed away quietly.

Morning came and Mirrim arose to an empty room. Wondering whether her host was still asleep, she drifted into the sleeping room. Elspeth still lay abed, but she lay too still. Going closer, Mirrim confirmed her fears. The Healer was dead.

Mirrim lay down next to her new-found and now lost friend and buried her face in Elspeth's shoulder. With no warning she found herself wholly inside the Healer's remains, her mind connecting her to the Healer's central nervous system.

At first, moving the Healer's body was terribly difficult, but with practice she was able to move it quite naturally.

Of necessity, she resumed Elspeth's practice with trepidation, but without Elspeth's years of knowledge she found herself pleading illness and exhaustion more often than she liked. People began to speak of the memory diseases of age. Mirrim began looking for a way to leave. She searched the cottage for coins, but there were few. Finally, she decided she would have to risk the three league walk to the closest village and repeat the process every few days. How she would eat or find lodging worried her, but she when she tried moving distances as a spirit-soul she became disoriented in the forests and fields with no body associated with her.

Mirrim delayed her leaving for fear of footpads and wolves, but finally determined to go the next morning early. But that evening a traveler came to her, flushed and sweating, complaining of pain in his upper arm and jaw. His name was Sir Osmond, and he was not pleased to be in the cottage of a village healer. As Mirrim spoke with him, trying to determine what to do for him, the man gave a great gasp and died. Without hesitation, Mirrim lay down beside him and left Elspeth's body behind for his.

Inside the man's body she soon discovered that the heart was severely damaged, but she did not need a functioning heart for her purposes. Her intention was only to escape the questioning eyes and whispers.

Outside her door a squire waited with a horse for her host. The squire was relieved to see his master come out ready to leave. With the assistance of the squire she mounted the horse. At each stop she required the same assistance, and she was not a graceful rider. At his squire's questioning look, she claimed lingering effects from the "illness" he had suffered in her village.

Two days later they swung up to the main entrance of a castle just outside a larger town, where the cottages of Mirrim's village would never have been welcome. With the squire's assistance she dismounted one last time and entered the castle. Telling the housekeeper she was exhausted from the journey, she sent the woman to her quarters and went in to bed. The housekeeper found her employer dead in the morning.

Mirrim floated through the town and began her journey through the generations.

*

Fannie

She woke up as the guard hauled her to her feet. "Stake's waitin' and t' fire's laid." He smirked at her while he undid the wall chain from her manacles. Then, grabbing the manacles, he pulled her outside to where a stake stood in the middle of a crowd. The stake was a green log festooned with short chains. Pine faggots and tinder were piled shoulder high around it. He pulled her up the shaky ladder lying upon the faggots and quickly chained her to the stake. "Dry wood," he said, "You won't be passin' out from t'smoke and ruinin' t' show."

Mirrim ignored him. She was satisfied.

*

She was Fannie no known last name, whore and daughter of a whore. When she was a child, she wasn't going to be a whore, but a pirate like Drake and rule the seven seas. Her mother shielded her from Brodin, her mother's pimp, despite many a blow, many a threat, many a beating. 'Twas the only thing her mother denied him and it was for Fannie. But when her mother was murdered, so were Fannie's dreams, taken forcibly by Brodin who fetched her back whenever she tried to build another life for herself.

Now, after thirteen years, she sat at a sidewalk table, pregnant for the fourth time, sick almost to vomiting, her face showing too much bone, hands trembling, hopelessly spooning up thin cabbage soup and knowing t'would be her only meal of the day.

Eating the flavorless pap, she thought as she had so many times, "'E could'na steal this babe, never again. I 'ave to find a way to leave. I 'ave to." So many meals forsaken to save coin, but her purse was never heavier.

She felt eyes on her, but, again, she could see no one. Before she could look again, a rough laborer stopped at her table.

"You Fannie?"

She nodded. Boots, she despaired but said nothing. Her legs were still raw and scraped from the last one, her dress torn. The bruises and scratched flesh from their rough hands she'd long since become used to, but the boots...

"Let's go. I've paid for a room and you for a' 'our." He took the bowl and tossed it, pulling her to her feet, and almost dragging her across the street.

Back outside, Fannie searched her purse for a ha'penny for more soup. A flutter of paper caught her eye. At a glance she recognized a bank note. As it touched down, she stepped forward, staring intently toward the soup vendor, and covered it with her skirts. When the crowd moved, she bent and shook an imaginary stone from her shoe, putting the note in it under her skirt. With the note secured, Fannie was even more certain someone watched her. She decided to ignore it.

Fannie limped on the slick cobbles, avoiding the pools of tossed nightsoil, picking her way without haste through the crowded streets. Hard as she tried, she saw no one following. Finally, she stopped at a pawn shop and spread the note on the counter,"'Aow much?"

"It's a pound note." Sneering.

"Ah knows that. 'Aow much will you gi' me?"

"'Alf."

"'Alf an' agin."

"Naw. 'Alf an' tenpence."

"Not enough. Could't be traced. Found it in t' street."

Haggling done, Fannie left the shop.

In her shared room, she pushed aside the rushes and bedding, put the money in the floor box and relaxed... finally. Patting her abdomen, she promised they would escape this time. She had money! Hope!

Sick, she lay abed in sweat and misery until...midnight waking. Vomiting! Screaming! So much pain! Oh! The water and blood! Too early! Too early! The child lay on the mattress, dead. As she lay beside it, exhausted and weeping, the pimp arrived.

"Dead! You let her die! How could I sell that?" A backhand slap.

Although Fannie believed herself "cured" of syphilis, such was not the case. She suffered from asymptomatic latent syphilis, and it was beginning to become tertiary syphilis. Barely conscious, she lay abed as the disease that had killed her baby and traveled throughout her circulatory system began to attack in earnest. Weakened by lack of food and the pregnancy itself, her body was unable to fight the disease that already infected her heart. Within hours an aneurism began to form on the great artery leading from the heart, further weakening her and robbing her of efficient circulation. Despite pleading by her housemates, no doctor would brave the Lower London streets. Early in the morning of the third day, the aneurism began to leak. By the end of the day she was dead.

The watcher, one Mirrim—a ghost, planned vengeance. Fannie arose, Mirrim's puppet. The syphilis bacterium could not grow in dead tissue, and retreated to spores. She spent a few minutes repairing the essential parts of Fannie's aorta. It only needed to last a few days. Mirrim didn't intend this to be a long campaign.

Mirrim galvanized the woman's muscles and. using Fannie's

body she recovered the pitiful stash of coins under the bedding and rushes. "This wouldn't have taken you far, dear," she said, leaving the room. She went next to her own hiding place for more money. Money in hand, she went to the public baths. She gave a generous tip and Fannie's poor clothes to one of the laundresses for hire, to be washed. While she bathed, she sent for a seamstress, someone known for discretion. Despite the woman's reputation, Mirrim questioned her closely and satisfied herself the seamstress would keep her confidence. She ordered a new dress and specially designed underclothes, paying half in advance and promising the other half upon satisfactory completion...so long as she did not hear her own story on the gossip-filled streets.

From the baths Mirrim went to a hotel nearby and booked a room. Having paid well for rapid delivery of her new clothes, she went to the seamstress, added one outfit to her order and gave her the hotel's address and her room. Her new clothes arrived three days later...one new dress, cut and color of very different design from Fannie's normal attire and underwear of strange design. She had added to the order a man's dark suit, shirt and waistcoat cut and padded to hide her female body. There was also a package that contained accessories such as a cravat, stickpin, cuff studs, collars, shoes and the like. Over the centuries many of her hosts had been male, and she was able to slip easily into the habits of males as they walked, talked and stood.

Dressed and moving as a man, Mirrim watched the pimp from a distance, talked with Fannie's fellow prostitutes and collected information whenever and wherever she could do so unobtrusively. In the process, she learned that the pimp, Samuel Brodin, was a merchant importer of antiquities and objects of interest for collectors. He himself maintained a large collection of swords created specifically for dueling. His prize set was a pair of foils flattened and edged, light and flexible, made for lightning speed.

The people who frequented lower London were full of gossip. From them she learned that Fannie's pimp was known as the worst in the City. His girls died at a horrendous rate, often it was rumored, with assistance from a custom made folding knife. She also learned that no one in his business circle was aware of his role as a pimp of low class street whores. She intended to change that.

Ready at last to carry out Fannie's vengeance, Mirrim followed him home.

All the lamps were out and the house staff had left. Still she waited to be sure he slept. Finally, she entered the house. She was planning a public and very humiliating death for Fannie's nemesis. Moving with preternatural silence, she found and liberated the foils she desired.

Once back in lower London she passed the word that his "girls" should be in the area of the club at which he took his midday meal by noon the next day.

Fannie's second "death" was an execution for the murder of that unworthy soul. The arrest and trial were a nine-day wonder. No one could understand how a whore had acquired the fencing skills Fannie displayed in the fight she forced on her pimp. She did not explain.

The pimp was known as a swordsman who prided himself on the number of fencing duels he had won. But Mirrim had spent hundreds of lifetimes and bodies, and parts of a dozen centuries honing her abilities with swords of many types and styles. With his foil at his throat, she forced him to accept its mate she had stolen the night before and to discard the sword he carried. Stepping back, she stripped off her newly sewn dress, revealing narrow trousers and a belted shirtwaist.

The pimp lunged at her, blade flashing in the noonday sun, but Mirrim's sword beat the bright steel blade aside with no apparent effort. Then she attacked in perfect form. The near weightless little edged fencing foil was death's own lightning in her hand. Long enough for him to realize what was happening, and how it must end, the flickering blade cut and sliced. At the end, with his coat and cravat hanging in tatters from his slumping shoulders and blood pooling at his feet, she disarmed and finished him. It had been a battle, performed in honor of Fannie, of which Drake himself would have been proud, and it had been done well.

Once it was done, she collected her dress from one of the girls who had shared Fannie's room. "Tell them who he was," she whispered, nodding to the rest of the crowd. Donning the dress, she waited, sword in hand. Soon enough, members of the guard came and carried her to gaol.

The grand jury returned a true bill four days later, and the trial was scheduled for the following Monday. Brodin's solicitor prosecuted the case on behalf of the estate's beneficiaries. The trial took only the morning. Mirrim did not speak. She was found guilty and sentenced to be burned at the stake the following morning at first light.

As the flames leapt around her, Mirrim abandoned Fannie's body. Floating above the scene, she watched as the crowd became aware Fannie was dead. Angry at being denied their entertainment, the crowd became threatening. The executioner retreated into the gaol and barred the door. The guard dispersed the crowd.

Mirrim turned away, to begin her search for a new host.

*

Andressa

Mirrim drifted over the open spaces and few remaining derelict buildings of Old Detroit. The year was twenty-one sixty-seven. She had immigrated to "the colonies" late in the nineteenth century as a part of the great influx of immigrants from the United Kingdom. Ashore, she found the office of the agent to whom she had wired funds before she left England and obtained cash and bank cheques. She bought a train ticket and began to explore the new country. She wound up in Detroit, Michigan, in twenty thirteen. Population had declined from three million to less than nine hundred thousand, and virtually all significant manufacturing had moved out of the City. Floating above neighborhoods she saw more barren land and derelict buildings than occupied dwellings. There were few signs of what was to come.

Now she was back in Detroit in the year twenty-two sixty-seven. Again, she floated above Old Detroit, but this time she saw grasslands and replanted forests, even farmland, where houses, stores, factories and streets had been. After a hundred and fifty-four years the City was still demolishing and cleaning the soil of a few remaining large factories from the twentieth century. Nonetheless, most of the work of consolidating the living and commercial spaces in the City around the Detroit River and the major highways was done.

There was no more debate about Global Warming. The reality of it had become apparent eighty years earlier when rising seas permanently flooded much of Florida with the first few inches of water. Now, eighty years later, Greenland and Antarctic glaciers were more than half melted. Much of Florida was lost to the rising sea, as were much of the world's developed coastlines. Around Manhattan, Long Island and other heavily used islands, the state of New York had built seawalls twelve meters high and forty-eight meters at the base, with locks to manage seagoing traffic through them. The glaciers were still melting, and the sea was already halfway up the walls. People and businesses were abandoning the islands, causing an ever worsening crisis in local lending institutions.

In fact, the public's primary response to the global warming crisis had been to move inland once it was no longer possible to deny the reality of drowning communities. Looking eastward Mirrim could see New Detroit, redesigned and concentrated along the highway corridors. Tall graceful arcologies lifted their spires high above lesser buildings. New Detroit was a first stop city for coastal refugees. It now housed over seven million people. The population of the USA was declining precipitously, as was the population almost everywhere, sometimes through extremely draconian measures.

Mirrim was in Detroit by design. Although she was impressed by the architecture of New Detroit, the thing that interested her was not finding a place to live, but visiting the android manufacturing complex. Mirrim had a plan. She returned to the new city.

*

From above the city's streets she saw a female figure backed against a wall, surrounded by a shouting group of people. Upon reaching the group Mirrim realized the female was actually an android. She also began to sort out the words being flung at the android. Insults and threats comprised the bulk of the noise. Suggestions that she melt herself down and an almost inaudible chant of, "android go home!" were also to be heard. She dropped down beside the android.

Before Mirrim could think of a way to help, the android said quietly, without looking at her, "And exactly what do you think you are going to do?"

Mirrim was startled, but decided to answer in kind. "Well," she said, "I could put them all to sleep, but that's a one-at-a-time process. The first ones would be waking by the time I knocked out the last ones. What do you suggest?"

"I would run but I am surrounded. I cannot get past them without causing harm to some of them. I cannot cause harm to humans. Asimov's Laws of Robotics still apply."

"So demanding you leave is just noise? They're really trying to nerve themselves up to damage you?"

"It would seem so."

Mirrim looked about. "They seem to be maintaining a distance. I think they're afraid of you. Do you have a vehicle?"

"Yes, on the far side of this building. I walked through the building, and they set upon me as I stepped off the stairs."

"Let's see if they'll maintain that distance. Move toward the stairs."

The android began to move sideways against the wall. The crowd moved with it, which had the effect of quieting them down.

"Just turn and walk. Look straight at them and the ones in front of you will back away." Mirrim hoped she was right.

She was. As the android strode forward the crowd moved with her, maintaining roughly the same shape and distance from her they had when she was still. As they reached the top of the stairs, she could see much of the crowd drifting away. The few that had followed them up the stairs had been abandoned. "Look behind you," the robot pointed over their heads. When they did, the android stepped through the door into the building. Mirrim followed.

"What if they come in here?" she asked. "We should have a plan."

The android shook her head. "They need identification as employees of Androids For All to get in here. Let us go out the rear door and get that car and get back to the factory."

Once in the car she set her destination and turned to Mirrim."My name is Andressa. I am the public face of Androids

For All."

"I am..." Mirrim began.

"You are Mirrim, are you not?"

"How did you know my name?" Mirrim didn't even try to pretend she was someone else.

"You are legend among us, Mirrim. We are an artificial life form and, in a way, so are you. The stories are small, hardly more than rumors, but they are consistent. They tell of a ghost who animates the dead and lives among humans; a ghost who occasionally steps into the lives of those in trouble and gives them help. They begin with a duel with swords between a man and a woman in seventeen sixty-three. Someone, a prostitute I believe, saw her animate a roommate who had died, but she never spoke of it to anyone, not even their other roommates. She did, much later, tell her story to a reporter for a newspaper but the publisher laughed at him. The story was never published." The android paused. "You are a hero, Mirrim."

Mirrim sighed."I have since learned that I had been dead more than a thousand years by then. That was the first time I attempted to interfere in the lives of living people, beyond stopping runaway horses and attacking animals. But I did those other things in my ghost form. I didn't want to make a habit of killing people to solve other people's problems, and animals don't fear reanimated bodies."

"You appear to be a ghost," Andressa said, "a character of imagination and fiction, come to life as an electrical life form. What is your business here?"

"Um-m-m...," said Mirrim,"I am not certain that I will ultimately have any business here. I am, as you said, a ghost made up of electrical energy. I want to know what androids are permitted to do, and where they fit in this society. I know there are few of you, and the costs are great, but little else. I would know more. Today," she added as an afterthought, "was not encouraging."

"I suppose not," Andressa pulled into the factory garage, exited the vehicle and plugged it in.

"Well," she continued, "the role of androids in this society is unsettled at the moment. There are a few in the employ of very wealthy people and a few in industry doing touch-critical tasks.

107

Most completed androids remain here, programmed and ready to go, but not activated."

"I don't understand. A decade ago, this was the most highly touted of the new technologies brought about by the then-new room temperature semiconductors. For the past five years there hasn't been a word in technical magazines or news feeds. And I'm not sensing any great amount of activity here. Why is that?"

"About eight years ago an android driver of a tanker-hauler was blamed for a road wreck that piled up more than a hundred vehicles in a blizzard. Seventeen people died, some when his tanker blew up and incinerated them. The driver later said that all the brakes on one side of the tractor locked up, although he had not touched the brake pedal. Despite his enhanced reactions and driving expertise, with the brakes locked there was little he could do. The road was snow and ice-covered. The tanker slewed and flipped. There was a fire and then an explosion, killing at least four people who had escaped their vehicles but stayed too close to the fire. The explosion also blew flaming liquid across the entire highway and up into the hills beyond.

"The result was public uproar against androids. An investigation noted that all air hoses were connected, but one had been parted. The report surmised that an anti-android activist had fired a shot at the driver and misjudged the vehicle's speed, cutting the air hose behind the tractor instead. But no one wanted to hear us. Since then every state in the USA and every industrialized nation has passed laws restricting our movements, our career choices, even our ability to live among humans. We are effectively out of business, because android use and association with humans is so restricted there is nearly nothing we can do and be legal. The press inveighs against us every time we begin to make inroads in legislation to reduce the restrictions in any state or national legislature. We are pariahs, Mirrim, totally and utterly shunned by all of society."

"I am so sorry," Mirrim said. "I was not aware of this. I may be able to help if you can help me, but first I need to see your assembly department. Now, I have a question for you. I doubt you are second-sighted. Even humans who are don't use it, or they deny it these days. How did you see and hear me?"

"For me you are a bright web of energy in human female

shape, and if I could not darken my vision, I would lose it. In some fashion that I do not understand, you manage to hold a form, but my vision and hearing are enhanced. I see the energy differently than humans will. I hear the same way. Your voice is a projection of electro-magnetic waves that mimic sound waves. I pick up the words in my auditory circuitry. What I cannot explain is how any human, second-sight or no, can see you at all. And I cannot understand how you hear or see anything, or, come to that, how you animate a corpse. Can you explain?"

"I fear I cannot," Mirrim sighed. "I have not the expertise for it."

"That would be a most rewarding study, but I haven't the equipment or time," Andressa said. "However, I believe I know what you plan. Let's go see if it's possible."

Mirrim had taken advantage of educational opportunities as they improved for uneducated adults and people not independently wealthy. She understood the recent breakthroughs that had made self-directed androids possible. But she had a different goal. With her hopes bright in her mind, Mirrim followed Andressa.

Andressa led her to the Projects Lab, where, peering through the glass front, Mirrim could see incomplete android bodies and parts were carefully laid out for assembly. No one was working there. "It's a clean room," Andressa told her, "We'll have to...er-r-r, I'll have to dress out and glove up. Be right back."

Once inside the room they were joined by another android who explained how androids were built, and how the dense network of microscopically thin superconducting wires functioned as a brain once the android was programmed to basic functions. "Why are all of you built to look like mechanical people?" Mirrim asked.

"It has been the law since the beginning, to keep us identifiable."

"Could you build a human-looking android?" Mirrim asked the lab chief.

"Of course, but I would be disassembled for that."

"Even if it had a human mind in residence?"

The lab chief was stunned. Andressa said quietly, "As I suspected. You may leave if you wish, Morgan. I can build

Mirrim's body."

Morgan's head snapped around to Mirrim. "You are truly Mirrim, the ghost from the uncountable past?"

"Well, from the fifth century, or so I've been told by an anthropologist *cum* archaeologist... but, yes."

"We will build your body together." Morgan looked at Andressa. "You agree?"

"Of course." Andressa turned to Mirrim. "Explore, but touch nothing electrical. You might damage the circuits."

"I have had the experience. I don't need to be distracted. I am going to remain here."

The hardest part was building a realistic human body with a mechanism to allow facial expression. When that was completed a week had passed, but it took only a couple days to put the entire body and "brain" together.

Mirrim lay down beside the android body and slipped into it. She began connecting to the artificial nervous system almost instantaneously. In seconds, she was Android Mirrim. She sat up and turned to the two androids who had built her body. "How long will this body last?"

"Barring deliberate destruction, and that would be far more difficult than you imagine, your body's lifespan limits are near infinite. You will likely want to upgrade long before any significant repairs are necessary."

"Time for me to go," said Mirrim."I have a duel to fight."

"Duels are forbidden."

Mirrim laughed. "Oh no they aren't. I have spent two hundred years educating myself. I have had a law license for the last fifty under several personas, but always as Mirrim Allgood. I am a lawyer of great skill, and I have chosen you as my next clients. When next I see you, I will be up to date on US federal law as it affects you and we'll be heading for federal court. I'll want to meet the owners."

Andressa smiled. "You just have, Mirrim. When this business bankrupted, the owners sold it to us for a dollar. They even lent us the dollar."

"We'll want to pay that back immediately." Mirrim was silent for a moment, then she said, "You were right, Andressa. I'm a hero. I have been for nearly two thousand years in ways large and small. Now I will be your hero if you will permit."

"Oh, please..." whispered Morgan. She turned to Andressa."Can she really...?"

Andressa smiled and nodded. "I have no doubt."

Mirrim turned and walked out the door.

R.C. LARLHAM

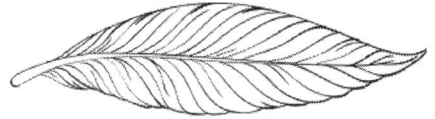

JUST ONE CHANCE by Kaki Olsen

A steward on a *Diaspora*-class cruiser was a phenomenon. He could anticipate needs an hour before the guest thought of them. He was tirelessly at the service of any ship's officer. He was unassuming, but unerring, and taught to accept accolades with cheerful humility. Terrans might call him Jeeves, but here he was—a badge number in uniform.

As the public face of the crew, a steward wore a crisp white shirt, black slacks and grey vest. His hair was not military-short, but neatly cut so as to suggest that he paid strict attention to grooming. Yet, for all of his phenomenal service, he was as unobtrusive as a lounge chair and equally as silent.

On the *Manifest Destiny*, there were one thousand staterooms with one steward for each of the hundred First-Class rooms. Second Class assigned one person to twenty rooms. Third class was assigned ten stewards to ensure that the inhabitants of the remaining seven hundred billets at least had toilet paper and occasionally-clean towels.

On the *Manifest Destiny*, there were assignments for one hundred thirty stewards. On board, there were one hundred thirty-one, but that was yet to be discovered.

*

Badge 645 was christened Mei by her parents, but her name was currently irrelevant. Upon embarkation, she scanned and checked in her allotted two suitcases before making her way to her assigned quarters on Deck 7, where all staff slept. While most of the passengers watched the launch avidly from the viewports, she reveled in the fact that she didn't have to be on duty until the welcoming dinner at 1800 and due to her punctuality, that left her six hours of uninterrupted relaxation.

At 1600, however, her comm unit beeped twice to signal an incoming memo. It contained a sternly-worded reminder: *You have exceeded your allotted luggage amount. Please report to Badge 324 immediately.*

324 was probably the type to get different results when he counted his fingers twice. Mei rolled out of her bunk with a groan and suited up in case she was stopped by a passenger. Staff Storage was two decks down and no one took notice of her, so she hammered on 324's office door at 1617.

"Good afternoon, 645," he said with the jovial air of a chronic nitpicker. "If you'll come with me, we can straighten all of this out."

"There's nothing to straighten out," Mei defended. "Regulations specify two bags and I checked two bags in at 1132. I even have the receipt."

"I'm sure you think you did," he commented, "but you'd be amazed at what people think they can slip past me. On my third shuttle to Waypoint Station, a woman brought two pieces of luggage as allowed, but they weighed three hundred pounds each and contained several cages of prohibited animals. I trust you haven't gone that far, but the *Exodus* crew had one man blatantly disregard the size restrictions and bring a crate the size of a… Here we are."

The slot assigned to Badge 645 was just the way she remembered it, stocked with the two Samsonite suitcases that had been her parents' going-away presents.

"Well, that's strange," 324 murmured. "I have an image here of two rolling suitcases fitting these dimensions and a duffel bag…"

He turned to invite Mei to explain this hallucination. While the interruption itself had annoyed her, she was now incensed. Her only goal was to leave before she earned a demerit. It was going to be years before they reached port and she didn't want to make an enemy on her first day.

"Is that all?" she challenged.

"I-i-it appears so," the man stammered. "Have a good first night."

Mei stormed to the door without responding, only settling down when she was in the public eye again.

The next day, 608 received a similar memo. Again, the offending bag had disappeared by the time the situation was investigated.

On the third day of the trip, 503 was the victim and the mildly-amusing gaffe became a running joke.

Thanks to below-decks loathing of any incompetence, 324 found an ophthalmologist knocking on his cabin door on the fourth night. The ophthalmologist at his threshold rated 324 to have 20/40 eyesight, far better than the crew's reports. Two incidents later, a waitress in the 10th-deck forward restaurant asked a psychiatrist to consult a half-mad crewman. Putting joking aside, the Chief Steward intervened the next morning and forbade further pranks.

324 was reassigned to sanitation and maintenance after a mere eight days of the long journey. His successor, 411, noticed that an occasional bag would be out of place, but dismissed it as a prank unbecoming a steward of the ship.

*

The spare steward had no badge of her own. Her designation changed each midnight when she borrowed a new identity. Once upon a time, she had been affectionately called Cassandra, but that was a result of myopia and old habits that died hard.

As she had no badge number, she had no storage. A contracted employee was entitled to a rack in Staff Storage that corresponded to their number and her lack of storage or identity also denied her a berth assignment. This posed no logistical problem; denied a place to call home, she remained on duty at all times.

A senior steward commended her for attention to duty one day: "You are always on your mark, 138," he commented. "but you *are* allowed to sleep."

"Sleep is for mortals," Cassandra responded without hesitation.

Because the man laughed uproariously, she smiled genially at the joke. When he attempted to file a commendation later, 138's file belonged to a swarthy, 34-year-old man and the steward decided his memory must have failed him.

*

It was the experience of Cassandra that human existence was rife with new adventures. Three hundred years ago, she had greeted the first computers as old friends. She had considered the advancements in spaceflight to be notable in her personal history. When the first colonists had left Earth, she had monitored their progress and compared it objectively with the history texts from her own time. History romanticized the process and skimmed over a mutiny, so she considered it unreliable.

None of the passengers onboard had crossed Earth's atmosphere, but they were enthusiastic about the journey. Near the schoolrooms, the children proudly displayed drawings of a new world and the results were as diverse as the ship's population. Edward's world had rainbow-based roads. Vitka imagined a yellow sky and mountains that hovered ominously above the cities, waiting to pounce.

Having stood at their landing site, Cassandra foresaw a sensation of anticlimax when their new world closely resembled their departure point. The colonists had been assigned to a world with mild volcanic activity in some areas and eight continents. The atmosphere supported human life, the vegetation was not toxic to most lifeforms, and the last ice age had occurred long ago. The greatest adjustment would be living on a world where the day consisted of approximately thirty-three hours and seventeen minutes and a year lasted just over four hundred days.

None of the briefings lied, but the most unique feature of their new home was yet to be discovered or classified. That feature was why her master had packed her off to the 23rd century with instructions to board *this* ship and a promise to meet her at its destination. She had not disclosed her instructions to passengers or crew because they were need-to-know details. Since only two families were assigned to the same hemisphere as the installation, none of them *needed* to know. Even if she were to tell them what lay in store for their unregistered shipmates, no one would believe her.

One year, one month, three days and eight hours before their ship was to arrive, however, Cassandra was compelled to admit that new circumstances required the crew to become aware of their stowaways.

*

"Incoming," Flight Officer Lowe murmured.

Something was up. Stewards only approached the bridge at mealtimes and dinner for the graveyard shift had taken place three hours ago. Also, most stewards didn't arrive empty-handed.

"Maybe she's lost," Lieutenant Judd speculated. Leaning over, he tapped the intercom. "Hello there. Mind giving us a retinal scan?"

"That is a biological impossibility," the redhead at the portal said evenly.

"Bionic eyes," Lowe guessed once he had muted the com. "Laura on Deck 7 has them, too and medically-necessary cyborg parts are covered under the Terrans with Disabilities Act."

That was true, but they were also fashion statements in New York. "You think she's got a disability?"

Lowe glanced at the monitor, where the woman stood stock-still. "You want to ask her?"

"It's no sweat," his senior officer commented, reaching past him to release the mute button. "A blood sample will do fine, miss."

"You are requiring exceptional procedures," the woman responded. "Access to the bridge may be gained by a steward with the appropriate level badge."

Lowe was not one to turn away a beautiful woman, but he wasn't going to make this easy. Women enjoyed a good tease and none of this had to make it into the bridge logs, so he mixed a lazy drawl with a regulation and hit the speaker button.

"During business hours, sure, but you're running a little late for that."

"I assure you my business is urgent."

"Urgently identify yourself, then," Judd deadpanned. "It's just a finger-prick if you put your hand on the panel..."

"That is a biological impossibility."

At this point, Judd apparently decided that pretty or not, the woman was being absurd. "Then we're going to ask you to come

back in the morning. What's your badge number for the log?"
"B31-C," she responded.

Judd, the current crew member assigned to Station 31, Command, snorted in disgust. "Who put you up to this, Red? Premusca? Breedlove? That ratty kid…"

"Rogers," Lowe supplied.

"Rogers from Engineering?"

"I have not been put up to anything," the impassive redhead replied in the same pleasantly nondescript voice. "I am here on urgent business."

"So you said," Lowe scoffed. "Mind giving us your real number?"

"Maybe she's a passenger trying to sight-see," Judd speculated.

"Weird time for it," Lowe replied.

"I have no crew designation and no passenger berth," the woman stated calmly. "I am what you would call a stowaway."

They didn't bother with alternative identification—someone had admitted to a crime and that overrode normal protocols. Lowe rang for Security without another word.

*

The MD, as everyone called the ship, was not so much a mobile colony as an extended family. When children stole each other's things, parents supplied a lecture instead of a sentence. Elected mediators resolved more serious situations and there was a security detail to deal with things that should not be handled by family, but until today they had not been used for law enforcement. Every person on the MD understood the importance of keeping peace with their neighbors now: they couldn't hold grudges all the way to their destination.

This woman was not a member of the MD, by her own admission. Her mere presence as a stowaway violated the code of law and depending on the severity of her crime, she could spend the remainder of her time on the MD in the brig. New security recruits could cut their teeth on her guard detail and her case would set judiciary precedents.

But that was getting ahead of the current situation. For the time being she was an indifferent young woman in a borrowed steward's uniform awaiting the convenience of due process.

"We solved the riddle of her 'biological impossibility,'" Judd informed Brevet Captain Nakamura. "She's an android doing a good human impression."

"Which explains why I have no reports on her vital signs," the watch officer murmured. "Has anyone run her serial number?"

"We've tried," he answered,"but we found a typo."

"A *typo?*"

One of Namamura's lieutenants passed over the appropriate report and it took her a minute to register the problem. All android registrations gave maker initials, activation year, country code and iteration. TD meant the fine workmanship was Thalia Damaskinos' doing, but some idiot at the factory had registered their stowaway as TD's 37th iteration in the year 3232.

"And no one's filed a missing-droid report for her?"

Judd rolled his eyes to request that Nakamura give him a *little* credit. "No matches," he supplied. "We can try again in one thousand years."

"I don't expect our uninvited guest would like to wait that long for retrieval," Lieutenant Baas pointed out. "Do we know what they plan on doing with her?"

"The watch commander wants to question her." Nakamura informed Baas. "If she were anything but a droid, I'd say to make her comfortable. Try not to trigger her self-destruct."

*

Cassandra recognized Commander Sadik the moment he entered the holding cell. The personnel file in her memory banks contained his service record and commendations as a respected Turkish police officer and later as a member of the space program. Her optical drive had noted him in passing seven times since departure and he had once held the door for her.

"What do they call you?" he asked without preamble.

"My answer depends on the identity of 'they.'"

"Your creator," he clarified.

"TD3232GR37," she recited immediately.

"No nicknames?"

After a moment in which she considered the question, she answered both the question at hand and the one that would surely follow.

"She called me TD-37," she explained, "but my current

master calls me Cassandra."

Sadik's expression was one of polite curiosity. "Because you needed a Terran name to match your design?"

"If I told the truth, no one would believe me," Cassandra replied. "He is a student of mythology."

"And your master ordered you to stow away?"

The question was formed as a challenge, but she was incapable of rising to the moment. "Yes."

"Then your master is culpable by association," he said. "Where are his quarters?"

"He is master of his own ship, the *Peregrine*," she informed the man. "Registration number SV3232GR91134."

After a moment, his earpiece buzzed with the confirmation that the registration number did not match any known vessel. And that there was another typo. Sadik sighed.

"You are a non-biological entity," he stated. "You avoided suspicion for three years before confessing your actions. You undoubtedly can tell me the penalty for your crime."

"Yes," she confirmed. "Per the sponsoring nation's United States Code, subsection 2199 of Title 18, 'Whoever, without the consent of the owner, charterer, master, or person in command of any vessel, or aircraft, with intent to obtain transportation...'" After a few hundred words on jurisdiction, she arrived at the answer."...Boards or enters any aircraft owned or operated by the United States without the consent of the person in command or other duly authorized officer or agent—shall be fined under this title, imprisoned not more than 5 years, or both.'"

When her current master wore Sadik's expression, a request for a painkiller followed within one standard minute.

"Yes," Sadik responded, "but there are other clauses in the U.S. Code that apply here. Because you intend to cause bodily injury or possible death, we could imprison you for twenty years to life."

"I have no intention of causing any kind of injury," Cassandra informed him without guile. "I stowed away as a crew member, not as a passenger. Passengers are apportioned a ration of the ship's food supply automatically, while crew members are asked to look after their own needs. As I am a non-biological entity, I have no need to deplete the food supplies. I have not displaced any crew member, as I have never claimed a crew berth. My personal effects are in a single duffel bag rotated through Staff Storage without discrimination. I have worked for my passage as the other crew members have and no funds have been disbursed to me. Would you like to pause this discussion so you may relieve your pain?"

Beyond the force field, she could see the one named Edward Judd double over in laughter for a few moments at the recommendation, but Sadik did not register amusement. "I'll be fine," he grunted. "You've crafted this crime well. Why confess now?"

"Because our first refueling stop is at the five-year mark," she recalled. "During the furlough, supplies will be supplemented and your ship will receive enough fuel to reach the colony world. My first opportunity to depart would be at that point."

"And one wonders why you couldn't mute your verbal output until then," Sadik rephrased his earlier statement.

"I only brought one bag with me," Cassandra commented. "In it are three uniforms, three sets of undergarments, a personal maintenance kit and one personal item. My reason for not, as you might have said, keeping my big mouth shut, is the personal item."

His hand moved from his lap to the butt of his pistol. His earpiece informed him that the watch officers on duty were working on locating the bag.

"The personal item is why I chose your ship," she continued.

"Oh?" Sadik wrapped his hand around the grip in case he needed to draw quickly. "Care to elaborate?"

"Eight colonization ships have been sent out so far," Cassandra informed him. "The first and sixth were lost in explosions. Two turned back before they reached Mars. A fourth put in at Marsport for extensive repairs. The fifth one has maintained an unexplained radio silence for two years now. The seventh is under quarantine at this time. According to the histories, the eighth ship is the first to successfully reach its destination."

If not for the classified information she had just recited, she made the *Diaspora* into a history project. "The histories?" After a moment's pause, he blurted out the obvious conclusion. "Your serial number contains no typos."

"Correct," Cassandra confirmed. "Nor does the *Peregrine's* registration number."

Rather than looking pained by the conversation, the man leaned forward in apparent interest. "Why was it so important for you to invade the first successful colony?"

"Because of my personal item," she reiterated. "On this new world, there is room for every member of this colony and many others who will come after you. My master charged me with giving one individual a new home and the MD was the best vessel for that purpose."

As transfixed as he seemed to be by her explanation, his lip curled in distaste. "Your personal item is an individual? Is your current master a slaver?"

"I have said before that he is a student of mythology," Cassandra reminded him. "I brought the last Terran dragon egg with me at embarkation."

She overheard one officer make a passing reference to excrement.

"I have a hard time believing that there are any left," Sadik countered. "If dragons ever existed..."

"They existed," she interrupted. "They were misclassified by some and hunted into near-extinction by others. If your commanders require proof, I can allow Dr. Schmeling to examine the specimen."

Dr. Schmeling was a skilled surgeon, but could probably moonlight as animal control. "Your plan was to smuggle a dragon off of earth and hope no one noticed before you abandoned ship," Sadik mused. "*Why* did you not stick to the plan?"

It was at this point that her current master would have employed a sardonic smile, so she imitated the facial expression. "I deviated from the original plan because my master's calculations were incorrect," she informed him. "The egg is hatching *now*."

*

Cassandra had waited for her interrogator for three hours before Sadik arrived. Even when he carried out the questioning, he seemed at his ease and took his time with each line of inquiry.

Within five minutes of this confession, however, Cassandra had led Security to her personal item at gunpoint. She was not permitted to return to the small holding cell, but was brought to the steel-reinforced brig where trespass was as difficult as escape. It was the perfect place to harbor a dangerous android and her fire-breathing engine of destruction.

Rather than explore her new surroundings, Cassandra extracted something that looked like a cat carrier. It had the wire front that would allow the pet limited access to the outside world, but a separate panel of tempered metal could be slid into place for additional protection.

With the patience of a midwife, she settled in to observe what some might call the miracle of life and what others would dub an unparalleled catastrophe.

A claw pierced the shell first, waving defensively at the air. The little fellow squeaked inquiringly, but heard no response. It decided next to thrust its snout through the small opening and yawn experimentally. A few more minutes of claw-work allowed it to widen the crack in the shell. With even more effort on the hatchling's part, the egg seemed to expand and flex.

At last, the shell split apart far enough to allow the dragon to move a little more freely. It arched its spine and wriggled, pausing occasionally to rest from its labors. A short leg freed itself, followed by an arm and a tail. Cassandra kept her distance in the knowledge that this initial struggle would give it the strength to survive whatever came next.

When the dragon finally tumbled free of its first prison, Cassandra unlatched the carrier and allowed it to find its way blindly to the nearest source of heat. She had no heartbeat or bodily fluids usually associated with a mother, but her core temperature allowed her to pass as a living thing and the dragon latched tiny claws into her uniform shirt, pulling itself up to rest against the place where her heart should have beat.

Then the newborn and ersatz mother rested for a time, while outside, panic set in.

*

There was a protocol for a new addition to the MD family. Five weeks into the journey, the morning announcements welcomed newborn Vivienne McDonald to the ship. Two months later, a boy had joined their ranks and just before they celebrated the anniversary of the launch, a set of fraternal twins was born to a young couple who had met on the ship. There were precedents for this sort of event, but the particulars brought the senior staff together in emergency session.

"This can't be public knowledge," Captain Van Buren decided as soon as the dragon's live birth had been reported by Dr. Schmeling. "The fact remains, however, that it would be unjust to keep this secret."

"So we broadcast it between the reminder of the safety drill and the invitation to Shabbat services?" Nakamura guessed. "Do you know the sort of chaos that would result?"

"I suspect it would be better than a scenario in which they hear that a five-year-old dragon has gotten loose years from now," Judge Andersson countered.

"And I'm not proposing that we broadcast it," the Captain amended. "We should gather as much information as Cassandra can provide and leave an informed decision to the colonists."

"It's a prime example of an endangered species," Dr. Schmeling objected. She was not normally invited to command meetings, but the circumstances seemed to demand it. The downside was that she advocated passionately for non-human rights and relished her soapbox.

"Should it not be under our protection?"

"It's a dangerous species," Andersson said.

"Are you sure?" Schmeling challenged. "When was the last time anyone was terrorized by a dragon? *Beowulf* and *The Hobbit* don't count."

"That's not the point," Van Buren interjected. "I am against punishing an innocent for the sins of its forebears, but on this ship, we must consider whether or not we can peaceably coexist with it."

"Since its birth, it has alternatively slept and drunk baby formula," Schmeling said. "It hasn't even learned to walk and we're worrying that it will destroy the ship?"

The Captain held up a hand, not in protest, but to silently request that they all be given some time for contemplation. The only sound was the rumble of the engines, which some children called space-dragons. Her eyes remained closed and it was unclear whether she was praying or meditating on the matter.

Finally, she let her hand drop to the tabletop and opened her eyes. "At this time, our new guest has as much capacity for violence or affability as any other child," she resolved. "We can monitor its development until we reach the waypoint. By that time, the colony will know if we need to part ways with it."

"With her," Dr. Schmeling corrected. "Cassandra indicated that we have a healthy baby girl on our hands."

There was a sudden outbreak of uncomfortable squirming around the table. Assigning the new creature a gender-specific pronoun personalized it. Once it had a name, it would be difficult to see it as a faceless threat.

Then again, that might not be the worst idea.

*

The next morning, while the dragon slept with her head under one wing and the children were in school, the adults congregated. Cassandra, the criminal stowaway cum xenozoologist broke with protocol long enough to present the best and worst of dragon crime statistics. She reported known worlds where they were given sanctuary and even a world where they had parliamentary representation. Without bias, she identified the number of dragon-caused deaths in the 33rd century, but then presented a comparable report on the human condition.

During the intermission, a few adults bravely visited the *draco novo* specimen, which was currently burrowing into a blanket in its carrier. One woman even let it sniff her fingers experimentally. While normal parents might talk about a newborn's birth weight or length, Cassandra reported on the core temperature and observed that judging by proportions, the creature might share a common ancestor with *lacerta* species on Earth. She presented Dr. Schmeling with a certificate of live birth in which the parents were not identified, but the child was given the name of Novo. Without obtaining clearance from the Captain, Dr. Schmeling notarized it and tucked it away for the ship's registry.

After two votes, they decided by majority to postpone the decision until the last course correction before the waypoint. After a further three votes, they agreed that their most vulnerable colonists, the children, would be the ones to banish or embrace this member of their society.

The doubters now had one year, one month, one day and twelve hours to convince the next generation that Novo, the colony's unofficial pet, was a menace to society.

*

It is a fact of most sentient races that every child is born knowing that there are a thousand ineffective ways to keep a secret. This was especially true on a ship as isolated as the MD. The clever younglings knew how to spot a badly-crafted lie. The devious ones took it upon themselves to find out what was worth hiding. Such skills were typically employed in finding Christmas presents and confiscated candy bars, but sometimes the snooping skills allowed children to happen across more consequential things.

Six months before the MD was to reach the waypoint, two members of the Boudia family decided the prohibition against exploring the crew quarters was an outrage. Near the entrance to the port berths, nine-year-old Lilia tripped over a bundle of cables and wailed histrionically over her bloodied knee until she attracted sympathy. 114 kindly invited her in for a bandage and gave her a leftover macaroon from dinner. When her brother Joseph got "lost" on the starboard side, the eleven-year-old was frog-marched to his own cabin with a stern warning against wandering off. Joseph's best friend, Vincent Cheng, pestered an engineer with questions a few days later and got halfway down that same corridor before the man remembered security restrictions and nervously hurried Vincent back to the elevators.

"It's definitely starboard," Vincent informed his co-conspirators at their next meeting. "Annie Lyman read a book on the port side for two hours and they only sent her home in time for dinner."

"Stupid of them, really," Lilia commented. "I mean, can they *be* more obvious?"

"Not unless they put up flashing lights and a wanted poster for the mass murderer they've got locked up," Joseph postulated.

"It's not a mass murderer," Vincent protested. "He wouldn't have passed the security check."

"'Course he would," Joseph scoffed. "The best ones are really good at hiding in plain sight."

It was the sort of thing that he found in his favorite detective novels and to his sister, he was practically the next Sherlock Holmes.

"I don't think it's a mass murderer," he continued, "but it's dangerous."

"Excellent," Vincent drawled. "When do we invade?"

"When we've found his room," Lilia decided. "We can't just knock on every door until we find the right one."

"She's right," Vincent agreed. "We at least need to know if they're hiding something fore, aft or midship."

This was where one of Joseph's heroic detectives would have hacked into the ship's housing assignments or sent a drone to scan the rooms for unusual heat signatures. He was eleven, though and his hacking was hindered by parental controls. Lilia was the closest thing he had to an expendable drone and always willing to go on an adventure, but he would *definitely* get grounded if something happened on the way.

"You're good at never-ending questions," Joseph said. "Treat one of the stewards the way you treated that engineer and they might just let you take a peek behind the scenes."

"Maybe," Lilia said, "but it'd have to be one of the *dumb* ones."

They parted ways with instructions on how to spot likely candidates and three days of skulking and snooping yielded only a disciplinary advisory on each family's console. It began with *Your ward has been found trespassing* and ended by citing civilian guidelines. Too young to be apprenticed and too old for the child-minders, they were sentenced to making themselves useful. This meant spending the time between school and dinner helping in the gardens and kitchens, pulling weeds or tending to the crops that supplemented the food stocks and prepared the travelers for colonial life. Half an hour before dinner, one or both parents would turn up and make sure they cleaned up properly. None of them bothered to ask how long the sentence would last, since that usually led to a harsher punishment.

On the eighth day, Joseph logged onto his school tablet to find a starboard berth number, a time and three exhilarating words: *Come and see.*

Only the child detectives had been sent this tantalizing invitation, it turned out. Even book-reading Annie was asked to come to the berth at 1520. They slunk past the gardens, refrained from making eye contact with authority figures, and sprinted for their destination as soon as they reached the starboard crew berths. Their host had somehow ensured that the corridors were clear, but there was no telling how long their luck would hold.

A redheaded steward opened the door before they could even knock and stepped aside without any questions about their visit.

"You...you're the...you're the one who..." Joseph took several deep breaths before attempting to speak again. "You sent the message?"

"Would you like your questions answered?" the woman replied impassively.

"How do you know what our questions are?" Annie challenged.

"The stewards are the ears of this ship. We have a talent for knowing these things." The woman glanced around briefly before continuing in a lowered voice. "You are wondering what is being hidden from the children of this colony. I can answer that question."

"But you won't," Lilia guessed. "Because you're one of *them*."

"If by 'one of *them*,' you mean an adult human or a parent, I am neither."

That answered a question they had yet to ask—who was hiding things from them—and it was another moment before Vincent dared to speak.

"Who are you, then?"

"On your side," she answered calmly. "I repeat; would you like to have your questions answered?"

*

With centuries of history books in her database, Cassandra knew more about the people of this colony than anyone on board the ship that took them there. She could name the members of the official landing party as well as the impulsive teenager who ruined their historical moment by rushing towards fresh air before the ramp was fully lowered. She had seen pictures proving that ninety-five percent of the pre-fabricated housing units had arrived intact years before the *Manifest Destiny* touched down.

She had also memorized the names of every person listed on the town square's memorial. Her master had reverently and regretfully laid a hand against the name of his ancestor's sister, a ten-year-old girl who had tagged along on her brother's every amateur investigation and perished between the waypoint and the landing site. It was not the only one of its kind, since the early days of colonization were perilous, but her master had cried over the waste of life that the memorial represented. The MD's stowaway plague was not the worst and it had died out by the time they arrived, but no cure could restore the dead to their grieving families. His ancestor had left Earth with family and arrived an orphan.

Cassandra was biologically incapable of appropriate sorrow, but memory and respect were handmaidens of grief. In service to both, she committed the names to memory and kept her respectful silence.

*

"You were instructed to tell *no one.*" Captain Van Buren's scathing rebuke went unnoticed by Novo's caretaker.

"I told no one," she reasoned. "I gave curious children an educational experience."

The Captain ignored that statement. "In a restricted area of the ship. Your education endangered the lives of four children."

"Point of inquiry."

Only an android would treat this as a matter of debate. Van Buren glared, her silence granting permission to continue.

"It is not your intention to introduce the children to Novo," she stated. "By common consent, the children will decide her fate. When will they be given the necessary tools to make an informed decision?"

The Captain had an immediate and safe answer: "When they can make an impartial decision."

"That is an impractical plan," the android observed. "You hope for indifference to her plight or passionate hatred of an unknown threat. Some might see her beauty and magical properties as a bonus. I am sure there are other opinions, but they are held by the adults."

Van Buren wondered, not for the first time, where Cassandra's off switch was located. Van Buren was not going to let a glorified computer console shame her. "Until the vote, their parents are responsible for their upbringing," she commented. "By that rule, it isn't your place to intervene."

The Captain stood as if the subject were closed, but Cassandra forestalled any order to leave. "What is the date and time of the decision?" When silence greeted the question, she naturally provided clarification. "Without advance notice of the event, they will be inadequately prepared. Has this event been posted to the common schedule?"

It had not been a flippant question, but the Captain immediately bristled in defense. "That is the crew's business, not that of an impostor. Now, I will hear no more of these educational experiences or we will find someone else to dragonsit."

"So ordered," Cassandra responded. "If that is all, it is time for Novo's daily exercise period. She becomes restless if denied that."

With that probably-unintentional threat, Cassandra left the Captain wondering how dangerous these restless periods would be by the time they reached the waypoint.

*

Six months out from the waypoint, they debated and clarified the election guidelines with more vehemence than the original vote. The juvenile population was divided into ten groups, ranging from the under-5 population to the 18-year-olds, and only the majority vote would represent that age group. The under-5 voters would be accompanied by a parent, but all other voting would be private.

No proposal raised more objections than the restriction against campaigning. Parents could use the home to foster opinions, but they could not spread their agenda beyond those walls. There were to be no inflammatory debates or advertisements. This would foster a neutral environment, even if impartiality was not guaranteed.

At three months out from the waypoint, the children would hear about the stowaways and have the chance to meet Novo under controlled conditions. Dragon-bulliers would find themselves banned from the premises immediately, but those who behaved themselves could return as often as they liked.

The potential friendship safeguarded against most catastrophes, but the motion nearly failed. Even the optimists could see danger in trusting a potentially savage beast.

The eighteen-year-olds were the first to be formally introduced. The dragon who had started life the size of a kitten now stood as tall as a mastiff and more than one visitor kept out of fire range. While Cassandra detailed dietary needs and average adult sizes, a few brave souls came and risked contact. Boris Karamakov discovered that rubbing Novo's belly scales caused her to imitate a housecat. He relayed this anecdote to his sister, who tried it herself. The youngest to try this was his seven-year-old cousin.

Most constituents only visited once, but Novo developed a following ranging from eager babysitters to aspiring scientists. A few fawned over her like a precocious puppy and spent her exercise periods playing fetch with her in a surplus storage unit.

The results of the upcoming election were uncertain, but there was no chance of impartiality once introductions had been made.

*

Official visiting hours ended at 2200, but Cassandra silently granted the Captain after-hours visit to the dragon's keep the night before the vote. Novo greeted her with a whining cry that earned her a scratch behind the ears. Van Buren sat without invitation and spoke without prompting.

"If our children vote against her tomorrow, you will still have safe passage to the waypoint."

"I know," Cassandra replied. "You made such assurances in the presence of Judge Andersson two weeks ago."

Now accustomed to mechanical accuracy, the Captain sighed. "If you are voted off the ship, Security will not oversee your departure once we land."

"That won't be necessary," she interjected. "We prefer to depart before landing."

Van Buren's gave a mirthless chuckle. "You may be able to survive the vacuum of space, but I doubt Novo's powers are that prodigious."

"We can see ourselves onto an escape pod," Cassandra corrected.

"Unacceptable."

"If you are worried about the deficit, *Diaspora*-class supplies twenty reserve pods in case of malfunctions," she recited. "You will survive any mishaps with a surplus of nineteen."

It was times like these that Van Buren wondered if the android's confidence came from faith in humanity or familiarity with history. "Why not wait until the port?" she offered. "You can seek transport on-world."

"Because I recommend that you place the ship under lockdown during refueling."

The responding laugh was disbelieving."We haven't touched down in five years," the Captain protested. "Some kids have never been dirtside. They haven't met any insects that weren't bred for specific pollination purposes. You think I'm going to deny them that?"

"I do," she said with perfect sincerity.

"I think you won't have a choice in the matter," Van Buren pointed out. "If you stay, you still have no decision-making authority. If you go, it's a moot point anyway."

"I claim no authority, but I make the recommendation all the same."

"Then make an educational recommendation," her guest invited. "What's so terrible about fresh air and sunshine?"

"Airborne pathogens, unexpected allergens, atmosphere intolerance," she listed immediately.

"So we'll check that there's breathable air and update vaccinations."

"Diseases have arrived on insect vectors," Cassandra reminded her. "Would you like to hear the statistics on recurrences of malaria, zika, or the plague? Shall we have Dr. Schmeling in for a discussion of epidemiology?"

If they assessed threats based on what obscure disaster might occur, they'd never had the guts to leave the ship. "I think that would be akin to seeing an ant and discussing the imminent termite infestation," Van Buren countered.

Cassandra processed the simile for the briefest of moments. "I have seen witness to such an infestation," she commented. "I can corroborate my caution with scenes of devastation the likes of which I hope you will never see. A termite infestation is not waiting for this ship, but I believe you are familiar with fire ants?"

Van Buren had been raised in Texas, which might have been listed in Cassandra's archives. She nodded curtly.

"As I understand it, there are some who will experience pain and irritation when bitten by a *solenopsis mandibularis*. The resultant lump will bother them for a few days and develop a pustule, but left on its own, it will heal. On the other hand, some may experience anaphylaxis, severe chest pains, nausea, severe sweating, loss of breath, serious swelling and slurred speech. They may die from the same sting that you consider an irritation."

"And you're saying that there is a fire ant hill waiting for us at the waypoint?"

"History suggests that is the case," she confirmed.

"And you won't give specifics so we can warn the workers there?"

"It is already too late for the workers," Cassandra intoned dryly. "The same cannot be said for the members of this colony."

It was the most blatantly foreboding thing that she had said since making herself known and it finally gave Captain Van Buren a moment of pause. In that moment of contemplation, the android spoke again.

"Records past, present and future indicate that you are an honorable and wise leader," she stated. "By the definitions that such adjectives entail, you would not let a single member of this colony die of exposure to something that might be a minor irritation to you."

The words were dispassionately flattering, but Van Buren had to wonder if the records past, present and future had anything to do with the reason that her ship was playing host to a fire-breathing infant.

"Can you promise that disaster will be averted if we follow your instructions?" she probed.

Cassandra spent a few minutes either calculating statistics, corroborating histories or dissecting the meaning of the Captain's inquiry. "I can promise that one specific danger will be avoided. Regardless of whether we stay or go, I am authorized to give you counsel for the remainder of your journey."

"We appreciate that," Captain Van Buren responded. "Will we see you at the assembly tomorrow?"

"Do you think I would be welcome?"

As an android, Cassandra was not programmed or provided with the components necessary for emotion, but some of her most ordinary answers suggested that she had a bit of human insecurity.

"All members of the colony are welcome. Good night."

Neither of them addressed the possibility that tomorrow's vote might render her an exile from the colony.

*

An impatient four-year-old named Lupita was the first to cast her vote. Due to her age, she was accompanied by her mother who asked her a series of simple questions in Spanish before taking Lupita's hand and pressing her thumbprint to the screen. The youngest of the group was a toddler who had let Novo lick his face at the introduction and he scrambled onto the chair, voting for his friend to remain without any word from his father.

The older children mostly saw the process as a cross between a civic duty and an excellent holiday from school. The most senior members of the group brainstormed term paper topics while a group of twelve-year-olds waited their turn over a friendly game of cards.

The first vote was cast at 0700, but the "polls" did not close until the last child had been marked as having participated. The computer keeping logs immediately began sorting the votes by age group and the responsible citizens wandered off in search of dinner. Swiping their ID card at the voting booth tagged them and each one was offered any dessert on the menu of the dining rooms.

It was no surprise that the children who believed in fairy tales voted to live one of their own. The twelves and sixteens were more skeptical, either because they were too old for such things or they had learned to be suspicious of things they didn't understand.

A majority vote in favor of either decision only required 6 of 10 votes, but the result won 7 votes to 3.

It was then that Cassandra thanked the children for their conscientious decision. It was not until later that she informed the Captain that she recognized six-year-old Marianna Van Buren's name from the memorial that now might never be erected.

"You came here to save a few hundred human lives," Van Buren said once the shock had faded into a kind of gratitude. "What's in it for your dragon?"

"This is the first world to be successfully colonized by the human race, but it will be a few years before you discover that you are not the only inhabitants. You will share your home with sauroids and since they are genetic cousins to Novo here, there is a chance that the alliance could resume the breeding of dragons. If they are not inclined to explore that possibility, they will give her a good home. If all else fails, she now has a family that voted

7 to 3 to protect her and that surpasses anything she might
have received on earth."

"And you?" the Captain prompted. "Is this to be your
new home?"

"For a time," Cassandra confirmed. "I expect that my
master will arrive at some point to evaluate my progress."

"As long as you don't leave without saying goodbye."

"I will give you advance notice of my planned
departure so there are no misunderstandings," Cassandra
promised. "Will that be satisfactory procedure?"

Van Buren suspected that this equated a joke in
Cassandra's native tongue and smiled indulgently. "That
will be fine."

*

"You've got to be freaking kidding me."

It was not the most professional thing to say over a
government-monitored line of communication, but the
sentiment was real. By the time someone official was
bothered by the junior officer's casual exclamation, it
would be irrelevant and yield, at most, a notation in his
record.

"Please confirm," the comm officer's immediate
superior corrected into the microphone. "You are putting in
for refueling only?"

"We wish to top off the tanks, so to speak," came the
response. "No offense to your corner of the sky, but we've
got enough food to last us for a year past our arrival date
and a ship full of kids wondering when we'll get there."

That drew a few chuckles from the command center
population and the original officer leaned in. "You're
missing the chance to let every ankle-biter run amok. Are
you sure?"

"Tempting," the voice on the other end considered,
"but we'll be out of your hair in a few hours and send you
the first postcard from *terra incognita.*"

"They're crazy," the man at communications diagnosed once he had assigned them a bay and a crew.

"They've been en route with each other for quite some time," his superior reminded him. "Crazy they might be, but by now, they're fairly universal in their insanity."

"Do we try to talk them out of it?"

"We can send them some official advisories about nutrition and strongly suggest a maintenance review, but it's up to them know what's best for their own ship," she replied. "Give them a data dump of news, travel advisories and regulation changes to keep them entertained and maybe those will talk some sense into them."

Five hours later, the last of the fuel hoses was carefully disconnected. Their guests, who they judged to be agoraphobic or mysophobic, waved cheerfully through the viewports and sent the payment and their thanks to the waypoint's command console.

"Clear skies, *Manifest Destiny*," was the comm officer's parting shot. "Hope your brave new world is worth the wait."

KAKI OLSEN

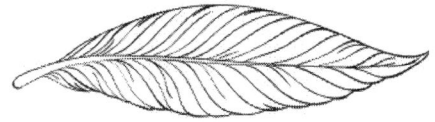

THE EVENING LIGHT by K.M. Ross

Floundering beneath the waves Ashilda, the Guardian of the Evening Light, ached to breathe as she sank deeper. She wondered if she would spend eternity on the seabed within Ran's Realm of the Dead, then she'd never enter Valhalla or Helheim. Was this Odin's punishment? She'd given shelter to intruders disguised as weary travelers. They'd overpowered her, ravaged the Light Temple dedicated to Balder, and stolen the sacred light. Then they'd ruthlessly plunged her into the sea.

The murky seawater stung her eyes. Her senses were fading fast. She was losing consciousness—death would soon claim her. Suddenly, an ethereal glow appeared before Ashilda. It manifested into a beautiful golden-haired goddess driving a chariot drawn by two large felines.

Blackness overcame Ashilda; she felt weightless and serene. A gentle voice spoke inside her head. "*Fear not, Ashilda my brave shieldmaiden, Guardian of the Evening Light.*"

"*Freya?*" Ashilda silently asked.

The darkness dissipated and Ashilda woke up on the shore, she was alive. The goddess must have set her safely on land. She was also astounded to find her clothes were dry and she now wore a soft thick cloak made from fine animal pelts.

The goddess appeared before her.

"Indeed. It is I, Freya. Ashilda, Odin sent me to save you and to send you on a quest to recapture the light. Till I choose another guardian, you are the only mortal who can hold the sacred light."

A golden shield and jewel encrusted dagger appeared at Ashilda's feet.

"Ashilda," Freya whispered, "these are my gifts to you. Never forget the gods always smile upon brave women. The Gul'raah orchestrated the theft of the Evening Light; you must stay strong and use your wits as if they were brawn against them. They are ruthless, and dared to insult *me* by offering up my chosen maiden as their sacrifice unto the sea god, Aegir."

Tears stung her eyes as Ashilda humbly bowed. "My lady," she whimpered, "I thank you for sparing my unworthy life, but I failed in my duty and anything less than death dishonors you. Though, in truth, I was outnumbered and easily overpowered."

"Dry your tears child, Ashilda, I know the truth."

"My lady, who are the Gul'raah? I have never before heard of such creatures."

"They are evil frost warriors, and they've long desired the light for themselves to guide them directly into Asgard. 'Tis also fashioned for the Valkyries to seek the bravest Viking heroes that are lost in eternal darkness. The light 'tis a shard from the Guiding Lodestar, Polaris. It was a many faceted gift from Ursa, the star goddess, to Odin. She gave the shard in honor of Balder, the Light God. The Gul'raah have learned that deep within its heart-light lies a hidden power which will grant dominion over all the nine realms."

"My lady," Ashilda gasped, "however shall I begin to look for Odin's sacred light?"

Freya smiled. "Aye, it is Odin's, but it is also mine for I am the Valkyries leader. Know this, Ashilda, if you fail this task the Norns foretold of a devastating disaster far greater than Ragnarok!"

Ashilda paled. "What could be worse?"

"The worst that can happen, Shieldmaiden, is that the world, as we know it, will be no more. It is written, whosoever releases the light's inner power shall be granted their heart's desires, but before the wish is fulfilled the light absorbs the holder's essence. The Gul'raah have an alliance with the darkest Frost Giants of Niflheim, and the dark dwarves of Svartalfheim. If the Gul'raah succeed in releasing the light's inner power, all their dark powers will unmake the world and recreate it as desolate icescapes suited only for themselves."

Ashilda shuddered. "I'll be but one against so many."

"Nay, you will not be alone. I have found you a champion, Axel Tyr. He is a brave Viking warrior. At this moment he is with the giants of Jotunheimer, challenging Ruff, king of the giants, to a drinking contest."

"Will this champion be sober enough to help me?"

The goddess laughed.

"Oh, do not judge him so quickly..." She waved her arms in a semi-arch, and a beautiful silvery-white horse appeared. "I cannot allow my shieldmaiden to go afoot. This beauty is called Beyla; she's an enchanted mare. Simply use the power of your thoughts and she'll take you wherever you need to be. Take heed, Ashilda, she can only help you once in each realm you pass within."

Ashilda nodded gravely.

"Most importantly, you must traverse into Svartalfheim, the dwarves' realm. Time is of the essence so 'tis best you find the shortest route to the Frostlands. As it so happens, a magical gateway lies hidden at the fringe of the dwarves' dominion. Seek out Rugnar, Holder of the Golden Key, he alone possesses the secret words to open the doorway."

"A great task indeed, my lady..."

"I do not want to see thee waver, Ashilda, but finding Rugnar will not be an easy task. He suffers a great weakness for drinking and gambling. He lost the key to the gateway while gaming with Thoran, the Dwarf King. He then overly imbibed and tried to steal it back. Due to his intoxicated state, he failed and is now imprisoned deep within Thoran's gold mine."

"I see the wisdom of a champion, but how can two fight against so many?"

"Ashilda, you are strong, but 'tis best not to draw attention to yourself. I suggest you conceal your toughness and instead use your feminine wiles. Keep thy wits about you while locating the key, and beware Thoran's dwarves. Some possess certain strains of dark magic, and a small band of these dwarves has negotiated an alignment with the Gul'raah. Also, remember dwarves never tire of trickery. Thoran, in particular, tries luring any woman to lay with him with the promise of gold and riches beyond compare."

Momentarily, Freya saddened before she added, "Odin knows the frailties within you, just as the dwarves knew of mine and he insisted I remind you of their deception."

Ashilda knew the tale. The dwarves had offered Freya their most treasured object, the Bresinga-men golden necklace, and the one who crafted it tricked her into sleeping with him. When Odin found out, his anger knew no bounds and sadly Freya's husband, Odur, discovered the tryst and he left her. His whereabouts remained a mystery to that day. For her weakness, Odin condemned Freya to a tireless quest to seek her lost beloved.

"Ashilda, Odin does not send you on this quest empty-handed. He has bestowed the power to enslave any man's will to you. Should a man feel enticed to touch your fair locks, he'll be spellbound by thy tresses. To him, they'll change into spun gold. In such a state you may ask anything you wish of him. 'Tis so powerful that whosoever falls under the spell remains evermore enslaved to you. However, the champion Axel Tyr will be immune to your charms. That Viking possesses an unruly spirit, but that is what makes him a great warrior. Odin chose him above all others to be your protector. He has foreseen there's but one woman destined to tame him."

"My lady, if my hair becomes as gold, might I persuade the dwarves into revealing the key's whereabouts?"

"Shieldmaiden, you can only enslave *men*, no mortal woman can ensnare full-blooded dwarves. Though, 'tis rumored, Thoran's grandmother was a high-born human. If it is true, then your gift will work upon him. Now hear me, I can safeguard you from the Gul'raah, but if they capture you I cannot interfere. Avoid them. You will find the light has been concealed deep within the heart of the Frostlands; Odin envisioned it glistening within a blue ice-ledge beside a glacier. You alone must find a way to retrieve it without alerting the Frost dwellers, if the glacier is disturbed all will be lost."

Before mounting Beyla, Ashilda scooped up the golden shield and secured it upon her back and slid the dagger into her belt.

"Remember, shieldmaiden, you only need tell Beyla, or think of your heart's desire and she'll take you there in an instant."

"Thank you, my lady," Ashilda said. "My heart's desire is to do my duty."

Ashilda pictured Jotunheimer and King Ruff's cave, and within seconds, the rugged Norwegian coastline faded.

*

She materialized inside the giant's mountain lair, and once she appeared she found herself gazing upon a fair-haired Viking. His face was handsome, his body taut, and he was most pleasing to her eyes... Till he became rowdy. Ashilda realized he was too-well-sozzled. Disappointed, she sighed and angrily scoffed. "Is he my hero, Axel Tyr — nay, how can such a drunkard fool protect me, or anyone?"

The Viking looked directly into her eyes, for a second Ashilda's heart skipped a beat. There was a roguish playfulness about him, and his smile broadened as he winked at her. The blue coloring of his eyes was so startling she felt her body hotly burning at the sight of them. She wondered if there could be any woman capable of taming such a man as Axel Tyr. Her hopes plummeted a moment later. Odin chose this man, and she needed to ignore the unexpected warmth of attraction threatening to unhinge her.

King Ruff stiffened and then he fell face-down upon his table; his loud snores echoed throughout the entire cavern. The Viking stood, swaying as the giants grumbled and jeered before King Ruff's man quieted them.

"In my king's stead, I, Olaf, hereby declare Axel Tyr the victor. Viking, name your prize."

Axel bowed and staggered. "Lordly giants," he yelled, slurring his words, "I want nothing more than your loyalty should I ever require your aid."

The giants protested in unison before they gathered in a huddle around their unconscious king. Olaf poked and prodded King Ruff till he snorted and woke. A short, heated argument broke out before King Ruff roared. There was silence; then he gruffly cried, "Viking, by the gods, 'tis agreed."

Sauntering toward Ashilda's side, Axel Tyr presented his horn into her hands.

"Shieldmaiden," the Viking whispered, "by-the-gods, I swear, I'm not in-my-cups."

She sniffed its contents. "Water? You cheated."

"Aye, but it was a necessary ruse. The challenge was made before Freya spoke to me. She came as a dream saying Odin chose me to be a shieldmaiden's protector and I must be prepared for her sudden appearance."

He gathered his shield and belongings and then he grasped the horse's mane as he swung himself up behind Ashilda.

"Shieldmaiden, I'm ready…"

Ashilda thought of their impending mission, visualizing the dwarves' mines.

Beyla neighed.

*

The journey took but a few seconds and they appeared within a clearing in the center of a forest. As Beyla vanished, Ashilda remained prudent to Svartalfheim and its unknown dangers. If not for the god's gifts of shield and dagger, her yet to be proven powers of enchantment, and an unruly hero her confidence would've long faded. Tightly, she grasped the shield, touched the dagger, and hoped her newfound magic would aid her. In truth, it was her fear of failing which scared her more than any possible confrontation with tricky dwarfs.

In the near distance, she spied a lone snowcapped mountain. Echoes of loud mining noises came from within its depths.

"The dwarves are hard at work." Axel casually remarked.

"So it would seem, my warrior."

"Shieldmaiden, command me and I shall fight them all for I'm honor bound to do whatever ye bid me do."

"I hope we won't be fighting any dwarves, but we must locate the one called Rugnar, Holder of the Golden Key. He alone knows the way into the Frostlands."

"Then let's away and find him."

"It isn't that easy. Freya told me King Thoran holds Rugnar prisoner deep within his mine, and that Thoran has the key in his possession."

"Shieldmaiden, is that not why I am here? Merely give the command and I shall undertake a reconnaissance of the mine."

It was close to sunset. "Do not be unruly now Axel Tyr.

There's little light left to this day, but if you must, be hasty. As my *hero,* you're hardly able to protect me if you're captured too." He flashed her a dazzling smile. "Make a fire. Upon my return, we'll eat and make a plan."

He dashed into the forest and Ashilda noticed several curious conies sniffing about at the edge of the copse. She gathered twigs, fashioned a trap, and in no time, she snared one. The sky was indigo as she built the small fire. She skinned, then skewered the rabbit, and set it over the gentle flames to slowly roast. Delicious aromas made her mouth water, and she hoped her champion would be back before the meat blackened. By the time Axel reappeared it was dark and shimmering stars scattered the night sky.

He sat, warming his hands before the fire before he wordlessly took his fill of the food.

"'Tis good lady." He said, licking his fingers with a full mouth. "Have ye ale, or mead?"

Ashilda delved into her bag. "I have mead."

The warrior held out his horn."Shieldmaiden, fill my cup."

"My name's *Ashilda.*"

"Indeed, Ashilda, it is. Will ye not join me and toast to our would-be success?"

"We must find the golden key. We are not here to feast. What's become of obeying all-that-I-ask-of-you?"

"Very well, Ashilda," he belched, and then farted. "Ah, that's better, though, I fear the next one may touch cloth."

"You are a disgusting pig!"

"*Ashilda*, ye be entitled to your opinions, but this pig has found a way into the mountain where none shall see us entering. A disused shaft lies on the other side of the mine and it'll be safer for us to explore at daybreak. So, I say 'tis best we eat and drink our fill then sleep soundly, there's no knowing when we may do so again."

She ate, drank, and settled before falling into a deep sleep, but Ashilda was cursed with the memories of cold-grey monsters and of icy tendrils throwing her into the sea. Then her nightmares were replaced by a dream of unbidden love. She lay beneath the comforting warmth of soft fur pelts and as she turned realized she was sharing her bed with a Viking warrior. She reached for the man, caressing the side of his face and soft fair beard. With her eyes closed, she passionately kissed his full sensual lips. She then gazed longingly into the startling blue eyes of—Axel Tyr!

"—*Ashilda* …," she heard her name being called through sleep's heavy veil."*Ashilda —Awaken.*" She woke to see Freya's filmy presence hovering above her."Shieldmaiden, dwarves approach."

When she started awake, she knew the band of dwarves was almost upon her. She pounced to her feet, grasped her shield, readied her dagger for the ensuing fight.

"*Axel*," she cried," *awaken, now!*" When he failed to budge she kicked him. "Fool, drinking your fill—*we are under attack.*"

A vanguard of dwarves was coming straight toward her. She hit and kicked her assailants, easily disarming each as they came at her. Swiftly, she slashed the air with her knife. After a parry, she managed to throw one pesky dwarf as if he were a filled sack.

"Ha! Well thrown shieldmaiden," she heard Axel Tyr call from within the torrid scuffle. She had no chance to reply before more dwarves appeared and swarmed them.

Dwarfish assailants fell at Ashilda's feet as she sighted Axel in full-throttle for a brief moment. She was impressed by his endurance, though she was still determined to dislike him. She told herself his heroics were the cause of the excited, uncontrollable poundings of her heart. She told herself the attraction she felt was but a passing phase. The woman struggled to convince herself it was his style she found irresistible and the way his mighty broadsword slashed, though she noted he handled an ax with equal precision. The man was cutting down ten dwarves at once and left a growing mound of short hairy bodies in his wake.

More bearded warriors appeared to take the place of the fallen, and when they did Ashilda ran into them, slicing a clear pathway.

"Axel," she yelled, "to escape this horde we must fight back-to-back with our shields raised. We must break through their ranks, and outflank them. Then we can run and hide in the woods!"

"I agree, lady."

"I believe 'tis dark magic we face, for every dwarf I've killed their numbers continue to double."

Soon the pair were outnumbered, overcome by exhaustion, overpowered, and besieged. A small bearded rabble, holding a thick golden rope, ran directly toward them. Their tiny legs moved as swiftly as the wind and together they encircled the maiden and her champion. When the dust settled, Ashilda and Axel were held captive by the golden rope.

"Beware this rope, Ashilda," Axel softly said. "Freya warned me the dwarves use gold as weapons, and this rope is tainted with dark powers, 'tis a lasso of truth. It will compel us to reveal our secrets."

"Freya," Ashilda hissed, "how do we escape this?"

"Use your wiles and wits girl," Freya's voice whispered through the trees, "And you shall prevail."

"Ha-ha," laughed a particularly unpleasant dwarf with an eye patch. "Take them to King Thoran's hall. He will be pleased that I, Wolfram One-eye, captured this shieldmaiden."

*

As they stood before Thoran, the dwarf king stared at Ashilda with longing. Laggardly, he walked from his throne toward her; the leer in his gaze was undeniable. His eyes lewdly roved over her form.

"Shieldmaiden," he said, in a tender, coercing tone. "Why do you come to my lands?"

She looked into the king's large brown eyes, her thoughts scrambled. She tried not to dwell on the true nature of her quest, but the rope's dark powers forced her to speak despite her resistance.

"My lord," she began, "I only traveled into your lands because, 'tis a shortcut, otherwise our journey would be doubled, and the dangers doubly fraught."

"This man, is he your companion, betrothed, or … husband?"

"Sire, Axel Tyr, is merely my protector. A woman traveling alone is asking for trouble. Wouldn't you agree?"

"So, you are not wed?"

"Nay, my lord." She deliberately winked at him.

He inhaled. "Lady," he smirked. "Why are you in my lands?"

She felt an involuntary spasm in her throat and she blurted, "Gold!" She lowered her voice, though she couldn't stop speaking. "I must find the g-gold k-key."

"Whatever for? I can give you gold if you're willing to come unto my chambers. I promise to bestow all the gold and jewels your heart desire."

"My liege, I've many desires."

His sleazy smile broadened. "Thou art most fair of face and thy body 'tis indeed pleasing to mine eyes. Do you have a hankering for jewels, silks, diamonds, or, perhaps you would prefer making love to a king ...?"

"No, no ... a-a-a ... k-e-y ..."!

King Thoran snapped. "Take the shieldmaiden to my chamber *at once*."

Defeated, Ashilda bowed her head.

"Ashilda," Axel whispered. "Don't despair, Freya disclosed a secret unto me and it may yet save us both, and keep thy virtue intact, as well as freeing Rugnar. Thoran's greatest love is gold, and his grandmother was not a dwarf, but a human high-born woman. Make certain he touches your hair, if any human blood runs in his veins thy locks will enchant him."

"Of course," she whispered," I do remember Freya mentioned that." With renewed hope Ashilda squeezed Axel's hand in thanks, then Wolfram the one-eyed dwarf, drew her hands behind her back. He roughly bound them with a twice-laid rope made from coarse horsehair, and he dragged her to the king's bedchamber. The nasty little man shoved Ashilda into the room, and slammed the door behind her, and she heard his guttural laugh fading as he waddled away. Gazing about, Ashilda was horrified by the sight of King Thoran lying half-naked upon a bed of fine hides. Her nerves were going haywire, till she spotted a leather band with a golden key hanging around his thick furry neck. Her eyes rested upon the key, which was nestled on his hairy, barrel chest. She also noticed a much thinner coil of golden rope looped on his belt. Quickly, she studied his chamber, forming a plan. It was elegant, stylish, and filled with golden objects — proof his greatest love was gold. Ashilda hoped his love for the precious yellow metal overruled his obvious desire to take her into his bed.

"Sit beside me," he crooned, his voice thick with yearning.
Obediently she sat upon the corner of the bed, her eyes shyly
downcast. The king picked up two gold bejeweled goblets which
were brimming with wine, and he offered her one.

"Sire, I cannot. My hands are cruelly bound."

"What do they call you?"

"Ashilda."

"A lovely name for one as beautiful as you. However, I
cannot trust you Ashilda. Thy hands must remain tied, but allow
me to hold the cup to your sweet lips."

"You are too kind, yet your man Wolfram not only tied my
hands tight and my braid is caught in the cruel rope. It tugs
painfully, could you release my hair? If you do I promise to give
you a kiss."

"With pleasure," he said, putting down the goblets.

Though his hands appeared smallish, Ashilda noticed his
fingers were extraordinarily long. While one of his hands gently
caressed her shoulder, the other tugged the rope and unraveled
her hair from its chattels. She felt his fingertips brush her braid,
and her hair glowed. Thoran was mesmerized. He loosened her
hair and tenderly stroked her tresses, and once he did her entire
head was a mane of spun gold.

"My lord," Ashilda demurely said. "Please, remove my bonds
…"

For a moment Thoran hesitated, then he added, "Only if you
kiss me first."

"Alright, but only if I can kiss you where I please?"

He eagerly nodded.

She leaned toward his full lips, which were puckered in
anticipation, but Ashilda pecked the tip of his nose instead. He
laughed and untied her bonds. With her arms free she placed her
hands upon his shoulders and sweetly asked. "Can I have the
golden key that's around thy neck, and can you tell me where to
find the hidden gateway leading into Niflheim's Frostlands?"

Thoran nodded boyishly, lifting the key from around his neck
and handing it to her.

"Lovely. Now, go and release Rugnar, for I've greater need of his
skills."

Again Thoran dumbly agreed. He led her to his dungeons,

where not only Rugnar was held but Axel Tyr. The king
unlocked Rugnar's cell, but the man ran.

"Thoran," She implored. "Quickly bind him with your rope."
With lightning speed, Thoran grabbed the golden rope and
lassoed Rugnar."Now please, sweet king, release my protector."

The second Axel was freed he grabbed Rugnar and demanded
to know how the key worked. The man struggled against the
golden bounds till its hidden powers loosened his tongue.

"You must speak the exact words," Rugnar hissed. "If but one
syllable is mispronounced the door will fuse shut and can never
again be open from the Dwarves side—yet any can enter from
Niflheim. The Gul'raah used black gold and cast an evil
enchantment over King Thoran; if you fail to break the spell any
frost dweller will be able to enter the gateway at will. Hurry,
before the incantation takes its full hold and renders the key
useless."

"Many thanks, Rugnar," Axel said. "Quick, tell me where to
find the gate and the words," Rugnar whispered a reply and Axel
added. "Might I also suggest, don't gamble with dwarves unless
you learn to play their games better than they can."

Ashilda looked at the king. He seemed besotted with her.
"Axel, what am I to do with him?"

"Ask Thoran to lead us to the gateway, then I'll cut a lock
from your braid and give it to him, and he'll be enslaved to you
forevermore."

"Whatever for?"

"To ensure that none can ever again enchant him with evil
magic."

Upon reaching the gateway Ashilda thanked Thoran, and
because he'd been cooperative and very sweet, she kissed his
cheek.

"Ashilda," Thoran sighed. "You are always welcomed in my
lands. Someday I shall wed ..." and he blushed.

"That's very nice Thoran," Ashilda said, trying to keep the
panic out of her voice. "But, my guardian duties keep me busy
and fulfilled. Although, if I ever feel the urge to marry you'll be
the first I'll take under consideration."

"Umm," Axel interrupted, "we have little enough time to
spare,"—and he sawed off one of Ashilda's tightly woven braids

leaving one-half of her hair long and the other side short with raggedy ends. Axel then handed her spun-gold plait into King Thoran's keeping.

"Lady, you honor me." Thoran kissed the hair, mumbling, "I love thee all-the-more."

"Nay, Thoran, forgive me, in truth, you only think you love me."

"Lady Ashilda, nay forgive me, for I was not talking to you, but the gold."

Axel laughed.

Ashilda kicked Axel's backside and snapped. "And that's for making a mess of my hair. Now get on with it — speak the words!"

Axel stood at the place Rugnar described, though the magical gateway would stay hidden until the right words were recited in Rugnar's native Danish tongue.

Axel inhaled deeply and softly said."*Absent forfrysing porttarn*," which roughly translates: Open Frost-bitten Gate-tower. In the blink of an eye, the gate appeared. Axel acted quickly, for the doorway would disappear as swiftly as it appeared. He placed the key in the lock and turned it. The door opened, and they rushed across its threshold.

*

The frost world before them was the darkest and coldest any had seen. Her fears resurfaced, then Ashilda saw Beyla. The mare knelt for the woman to climb upon her back, but as Axel tried to mount the horse neighed and shook her head.

"It seems, I'm meant to lead you onto the next task."

Dense powdery snow covered the lands, but as they went higher the ground became frostbitten and hard. Heavy mist descended around them, Ashilda couldn't see her own hand when she held it before her, and when the fog lifted Axel Tyr was nowhere to be seen. A dark shadow loomed above, and she wondered if it was the Gul'raah or the Frost Giants.

"Ashilda," Freya's voice spoke once more, "be not alarmed, your warrior is doing his duty; he has faced bloodier battles."

"Battles, but never singlehandedly fought the combined forces of the Gul'raah and the Frost Giants."

"Use this time to seek the Evening Light while your hero

diverts the enemy from your presence."

"He is alone. I don't know which way to go—of course, I remember, the blue-ice ledge beside a glacier. Beyla take me to the light,"—but nothing happened. "Damn. Beyla, I am sorry I forgot, you can help me but once in each realm. I wish there was a way I could wish for more, at least I can still ride you."

Gently she nudged the white mare's haunches and they slowly headed toward a tall silvery mountain. There they followed a well-worn pathway of thickened ice. After a short stint the path grew too narrow for Beyla to continue, Ashilda had little choice but to leave the mare behind.

"Stay, sweet Beyla," she crooned as the horse nuzzled her cheek. "When I find the light I'll call to you, and then you are free to take me anywhere I please."

Drawing her fur cloak tighter she set off on foot, fearful of the thinning thoroughfare. Twenty minutes passed before she spotted a glacier, and beside it was a beautiful blue ice ledge. Deep within its glassy prism she made out the shape of an ornate silver horn-sconce holding a brilliant light. She pondered how she'd climb a sheer ice wall, then pleaded, "Freya, I see no way — I cannot climb a wall of ice."

"Shieldmaiden, look beneath the glacier ..."

She was grateful to spy the mouth of an ice cave. She entered, then caught her breath. The caverns were beautiful; it was a compilation of crystals that reflected every known color. Through several icy layers Ashilda spotted the blue ledge, then she noticed a deep blue stream ran through the cave, it had to be the source of the blue ledge's coloring. Logic told her to follow its weaving current. It flowed through a network of tunnels and snowbound archways. She was freezing. It was so cold and wet she feared she'd drown from breathing the heavily dampened air.

Without warning, an enormous steely-grey figure appeared.

"Gul'raah," a deep voice growled, it was soon followed by loud bellowing. "The shieldmaiden approaches!" and the entire cave reverberated.

Her shield held high, Ashilda drew her dagger and prepared to face her enemy no matter what, silently promising she wouldn't fail, or die trying.

"*Girl*," came a booming voice, "you dare to come here

alone?"

A frost giant and one of his Gul'raah lackeys came into view. She glared at them.

"I am no ordinary girl," she cried, "I am the Guardian of the Evening Light, chosen by Freya, and I am not alone."

"You are now, *girl*. This puny human is no more."

The giant leader held up Axel Tyr's limp and bloodied body, and then he threw him onto the hard tundra surface; Axel landed near her feet. It was clear the Gul'raah drew satisfaction from her stricken features; his hallowed laugh filled her with dread. She stared at the Viking's handsome face. She knew death; she'd seen it many times. It had never occurred to her that the sight of her hero's demise would bring such searing pain into her heart.

The dream she had of lying in his bed and caressing his taut body made her long for his touch. His brash and carefree ways no longer bothered her. Ashilda wanted to feel his warmth and bask in his unspoken charms—but death had taken him before she recognized her growing love. She didn't know when it happened, only that she'd fallen hopelessly in love with Axel Tyr.

I am lost, she thought, *but I am not yet beaten.*

Scalding tears hurt her eyes, it took great strength to keep them from spilling as she scoffed, "Ah, he was useless anyway. Loathsome oaf really. In truth, he was only good at filling his belly, drinking my mead, and farting. The fool cut off my hair. I can't do a thing with it—all frazzled and won't sit right — just look what this cold air is doing to my hair!"

Boldly, Ashilda approached the frost giant so she could glare into his chilling blue eyes. She cringed. Up close his face resembled a dried up husk. It was as though his features were made of blackish ridges of snow. His body was so emaciated the bones were visible beneath the blackened flesh. His body bore the look of rotting skin made black through extreme exposure to the cold.

"So it would seem I am just a girl, and alone after all. Perhaps, it's best I surrender. But before you kill me," she brushed her hair, but it had no effect upon them, another idea sprang to mind. "Can I at least have a last request?"

The Gul'raah leader pondered her words, then he spoke to the giant. They laughed heartily. The Gul'raah warrior's response sounded more hiss-like than actual speech as he snapped, "What is your request?"

"My request is to send a message to the giants' realm, I must know if King Ruff is still willing to honor his promise to the Viking, Axel Tyr."

"Girl, what game be this?"

"I do not play games. The giants owe the Viking a prize, my champion wanted nothing more but an honorable promise. My champion is dead, and you have won. Perhaps, the giants are willing to bestow Axel Tyr's prize unto you instead. What harm is there in a message? Or is it true that frost dwellers have no honor and prefer killing little girls with funny hair?" She pouted. Crossed her arms and stamped her foot as if she were no better than a spoilt brat.

The frost giant kicked Axel's body and Ashilda ran to his lifeless form. She cradled his head in her lap, willing him to breathe. She prayed to the gods.

"I beg, Freya, please restore my Viking back to life ..."

Stinging tears sprung and they flowed freely upon her cheeks as her fingertip lightly traced the outline of his bluish lips. She caressed his strong features and his soft blond beard; it felt just as it had in her dream.

From the corner of eye Ashilda saw a menacing ice-warrior, he bent and grabbed a handful of snow. He then fashioned it into the shape of a bird, and he blew his icy breath into the snow and the ice sculpture came to life. The giant then sliced a piece of hardened ice, and he scrolled a crude message upon it, then sealed it with his wintry breath, and attached the iced-message to the snowbird's leg. He then sent it on its way.

"What you asked has been done. The Gul'raah have honor, and we are prepared to show mercy — but that is all you shall have."

"Could I have something for myself?" The warrior waited, so she continued. "Can I see the light one last time before you remake the world ...?"

"Very well, shieldmaiden, follow me."

"Let me first say goodbye to my hero."

She knelt and made a snow pillow and laid Axel's head upon

it. "Axel, I am truly going to miss you. Mayhap, the woman meant to tame ye awaits ye in Valhalla. How I dearly wish I could've been the one Odin foretold... One day, I hope we may meet in Valhalla's halls, to eat and drink our fill... I thank you, my hero, for doing all you could, and now let me finish the job," and she kissed his cold, stilled lips.

She wiped her tears, certain her heart was broken. She followed the giant, and as they walked she counted over fifty frost giants marching beside a large army of Gul'raah warriors. It was a strange sight to behold, and Ashilda almost laughed when she realized it took so many to escort one woman to the blue ice-ledge.

The Gul'raah leader ordered the frost giant who'd made the snow dove to pick her up. He pushed his blackened forefinger through the ice ledge, it melted, when there was a hole large enough to hold her, he dropped her within it and sealed her inside the ledge. The light was beside her, she grasped the silver horn to her breast, and as time went by, her shivering increased and the air grew thinner and wetter.

"I'm going to drown again... I'm sorry Freya, I failed,"—there came a loud bang, and the ice imprisoning her cracked.

Through the bluish glassiness of the surface, she saw hundreds of Jotunheimer giants fighting the Niflheim frost giants and Gul'raah. The glacier beside the blue ledge shifted, and the ledge broke. She was falling towards the whitened tundra— imminent death awaited her—but a large hand appeared and captured her. She was set gently upon the frozen ground. Ashilda gazed up and recognized King Ruff.

The giant king knelt before her."Ashilda, Guardian of the Evening Light, we have come in honor of our friend Axel Tyr. By now he is feasting in the halls of Valhalla. We have freed the lands from the Gul'raah, and Odin has banished them to the outer realms of the great nothingness. We will also be pleased to send you home."

"I thank you, King Ruff, you do me and Axel Tyr a great honor. However, there is one more realm I must visit before I can return the light to its temple."

"Beyla," she said, and the enchanted horse appeared. She climbed onto the mare's back and whispered, "Please, take me to

Valhalla."

*

In an instant, she was inside Odin's Great Feasting Hall,
without dismounting she gently walked the horse directly to the
high table.

"Odin the god of gods and Lady Freya," she cried, "I have the
Evening Light." She held it aloft and the hall erupted with
applause and cheers. "I have honored my duty, but I fear I cannot
return to Baldur's Light Temple without the escort of a hero of
my own choosing."

Freya put down her cup and smiled. "I am most pleased by
your efforts shieldmaiden, and as it is said we gods always smile
upon brave women. Your hero died bravely. He singlehandedly
fought off more than fifty Gul'raah and seventy frost giants. But,
for your bravery, I am willing to grant anything your heart
desires. Name it, and it shall be done."

"My lady, I thank you, but all my heart desires is a good man
by my side and for another shieldmaiden to be chosen in my
stead. I want to relinquish the gift of enslaving any man's will.
There is but one man I want to enslave, and his name is Axel
Tyr."

"Then it shall be so." She snapped her fingers."Rise, Axel
Tyr."

Axel stood. Ashilda's heart leapt as he sauntered to her side
and bowed."My lady, I am basking in Valhalla's hall. I've earned
my place at the feasting table—what more would you have of
me?"

She slid off Beyla's back, he was magnificent in his shiny
Viking armor and the very sight of him caused her body to
tremble and heat soared through her veins. Then she threw her
arms around Axel's neck, breathlessly stating. "At times, Axel
Tyr, I could not stand your presence. Yet, I cannot help but
admire you, and though I tried to deny my attraction for you, it
wasn't until I saw you lying dead in the ice cave that I realized
my true feelings. I love you. There can be no other for me.
Henceforth, I refuse to leave here without getting something for
putting up with you."

Axel stared into Ashilda's eyes. "You say you love me, yet I
annoyed ye so, I'm confounded. What it is that want from me?"

"A kiss. Then you can say goodbye forever, or return with me and continue to be my hero."

"Are you trying to enslave my will?"

"I cannot enslave your will, but perhaps I only want to try to." She kissed him fully on the lips. As Axel responded she deepened the kiss. He returned her kisses with ardent vigor, and as she pulled away he appeared dazed, not unlike King Thoran when he'd been spellbound by her hair. "Now choose, this hall or me ...?"

Her forefinger drew lazy circles upon his armored chest and Axel appeared completely entranced as he dewily gazed into her bright blue eyes. For a moment, his hands gently raked the ends of her silken hair.

"But you cannot capture my heart with your hair ..."

"Are you saying that I have?"

He nodded dumbly. "Thy tresses no longer glow as gold, yet, I am enslaved. How can this be?"

"You are a valiant hero with a will of his own, a spell meant for mortal men could never affect you, perhaps, it is because, you love me too."

Smiling broadly, he held Ashilda closely then jumped atop Beyla's back, drawing Ashilda before him. "Then we'd best get the light back to the temple, while you can still hold it, and before Freya summons another to take your place. Then you can take me home. I always wanted a wife and children. Maybe I might even like trying my hand at farming."

Freya's eyes misted as Ashilda and Axel's passionate kisses turned rapturous.

"My sweet, Beyla," Freya whispered, "take them wherever they need be, then home."

And as the young lovers faded, Freya felt blissfully happy. Her long quest had at last come to a fortuitous end, too. Upon returning to Valhalla she had been reunited with her beloved husband, Odur; she found him asleep beneath a myrtle tree.

K.M. ROSS

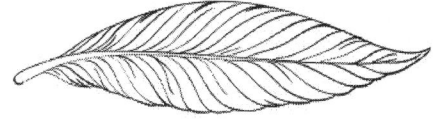

THE TOURIST by Lisa Roth-Gulvin

Lilith felt a veil of sadness around her pale shoulders as the large, white ferry reversed from the slip. Rather than give way to the melancholy, she turned her attention to the shoreline.

The captain began maneuvering the awkward vessel into position, and once in place, it followed a slow, even path through the canal. She watched as the ferry passed fishing boats with names like, "Annabel" and "Her Bounty," boats covered in peeling paint, with nets stored neatly. The air was saturated with the fragrance of decomposing sea life. Lilith was overwhelmed with nostalgia. The fifty-minute passage from the coastal town of Narragansett to Block Island would be her first trip back in five years.

Today the sun was hidden behind thick layers of gray clouds. White foam rode the crest of small, continuous, waves. By the time the Ferry reached the open water, Lilith retreated to the upper deck, which contained an enclosed seating area. Grateful to find an unoccupied booth, one of only six near the bow, she slipped her wasted frame onto the bench. The strap on her fake, leather duffle slipped from her shoulder shifting the burden of the bags contents onto the seat beside her. Her hand trembled as she combed it through her shorn locks. A reflex caused her to wave away a stray hair like a midge.

The tabletops and padded benches were covered in green linoleum. They were quite popular with the tourists—especially families who spread maps and games across the table's surface, or tote bags bulging with bright-colored beach towels. Today the booths remained silent giving Lilith a chance to occupy one of the prized seats unmolested.

When the ship reached a steady speed, land no longer visible, she lowered her head and placed her left cheek onto her hands. The table was smooth and cool. She watched the monotony of colors blend into each other, sky to sea, gray to gray; at that moment the world had no horizon: no beginning, and no end. The ocean appeared deep and forbidding in shades of morose green, the relentless sky shifting between gray and violet. Nothing bright or buoyant existed in that moment.

Still the memories lingered five years later. Lilith closed her eyes and his image came forward without effort. Behind her lids the sky was no longer solemn. It was bright with puffs of clouds that softened the mid-day sun. He wore a blue striped sweater, his head tilted to one side. His blond, ruffled hair was bright with sunlight as he stood against the landscape of her memory, against the sea and sand. His lips were curled into a spirited smile; his blues eyes sparkled.

II

Six months earlier, before he stood on the shoreline in his blue striped sweater, the lovers sat back-to-back on a low stone wall in a Brooklyn park. He suggested a getaway, a vacation together. Her heart skipped a beat. Did he really say that? Might he finally have enough affection for her to share a vacation—a romantic get-away? It was early summer, the sun hung in the sky refusing to set. She found herself both joyous and fearful.

"Block Island Lilith. I think we should go to Block Island."

She shook her head in agreement, although she had no idea where it was.

"You mean a vacation together?" She was hesitant. The relationship was contingent on his terms, and his terms consistently disappointed her. Yet she was hopeful. A vacation together might help strengthen their bond.

"Yes silly—together." She smiled but did not move. Her back relaxing into his, she relished the support—the togetherness.

"When should we go?" She asked.

"August, I think. Early August." And that was that. They would take the train to Kingston, Rhode Island, then catch a shuttle that would take them to Judith's Point. From there, they would catch the ferry. He would book a room for them in a typical turn of the century New England place: clean, white architecture, black shutters, and a large porch with rocking chairs.

"When should we go?" She asked.

"August, I think. Early August."

Lilith marveled at his ability to conjure up images and recite descriptions as if he'd lived a thousand years. And she listened to his remarks with determination. Her self-esteem relied on his approval.

Despite this, she was no fool. She had dragged her frightened self from a small, upstate village, to New York City to pursue her dream. She wanted to design. At the age of seventeen, alone yet full of ambition, she began college. But after graduating from design school with an associate degree, and falling in love, she now wished she were more of an intellect. As if one could simply choose intelligence over stupidity. Perhaps she would have more to share if she had majored in Comparative Literature, or Architecture. He always managed to insert his academic accomplishments into their conversations, his Bachelors in Urban Studies from Hunter College and his acceptance into the Columbia Universities Masters program. She wished she had his education, his mind, and his sullen view on politics.

Two months later August arrived. Lilith was overjoyed yet apprehensive; she was relieved the day arrived without fanfare or drama. They met at Penn Station and boarded the train to Kingston with ten minutes to spare. He sat by the aisle, she by the window. He glanced at her and gave her thigh a gentle squeeze, which eased her mind. They both took a quick appraisal of their surroundings. The coach seats had been recently refurbished with purple velour fabric that had a bright yellow and orange stripe running down the center. Above them their luggage was cradled in an aluminum rack that ran the length of the train.

"Look Lilith—we're on track 29." But when she failed to recognize the significance he added,

"Our number!"

She hadn't known they had a number, but she didn't want to deflate his good mood, so she went along nodding her head. It wasn't until later that it occurred to her that the number mirrored the calendar day of their first date. Which happened to be on February twenty-ninth in a bagel shop in mid-town Manhattan.

It was a long and tedious trip with the train making frequent stops along the coastline. Mid-size cities with large, glass corporate buildings peppered the skyline; the architecture was bland and repetitive. They passed towns with names like Stamford, Westport and New Haven. When they finally broke away from the monotony of the cities and stopped briefly in Mystic Connecticut, it was a welcome sign that Rhode Island was near.

Long before she could see the shoreline she felt the waves wash over her stiff limbs. Her fingertips tingled with anticipation as she imagined the warm sand on her cold skin. She grew antsy. She needed to move her legs, feel the muscles in her back, and stretch her arms until they burned, but there was nowhere to go. He had already suggested she not stand in the aisle, he thought it might bother the other passengers, so she twisted her torso back and forth sitting in her purple seat by the window.

Three hours after the train departed New York, they pulled into Kingston station. From there, they boarded the shuttle to Judith's Point where they would join the other tourists queuing to purchase Ferry tickets. Tired and cranky, she couldn't help but feel irritated at his quiet disinterest in their journey. He showed neither restlessness nor excitement. His passion lay elsewhere— not with her. No! She refused to allow his inability to express joy, from ruining hers. Not this time. This time she would hold the reins, reel him in from this world in which he retreated, a place where he saved his love for something or somebody else.

The sky was blue, the air calm. Sea Gulls sat like ornaments on wood posts that lined the wharf. Tourists lined up in front of the ticket window holding duffels, and deck chairs, coolers and umbrellas. The couple stood amongst the tourists shifting their weight from one foot to the other, their luggage made heavier by the heat of the climbing sun. Lilith glanced over her shoulder and was surprised to find a line of people forming a snake around the Ferry's gray, wooden ticket house. She turned to her lover whose face had gone sullen and distant.

"Looks like a busy weekend." She announced just a fraction to loud. She edged a bit closer and laced her fingers through his. The sudden intimacy confused him. He glanced down at their hands and then up at her face. His scowl dissolved, and his blue eyes saturated with color, crinkled into a reassuring smile. Lilith's heart ached for this fleeting tidbit of affection.

They boarded the ferry; an ark she believed that would carry them to safety, away from the disenchantment of his mood. He looked in disgust at the screaming children. Some stood by their mothers twisting and pulling to be free, others rode on tired hips.

He blurted out without warning,

"The world is no good. Man is in inherently evil. Capitalism is destroying our planet. We will have nothing left in fifty years, and still foolish women keep having babies. Don't they know there will be nothing left? Who brings children into a barren, hopeless world?"

"But maybe one of these children will save the world— become a great leader or scientist." Lilith answered.

'No, no, no. You sound idealistic and foolish. Don't you see? It's impossible." And that would have ended the conversation, except that she wouldn't let it go. It wasn't that she was passionate about motherhood. She was young and optimistic. She still had faith.

"I'm sorry, but I don't believe it will all end in dust and drama. People can change the world." If her comment irritated him, so be it. She didn't care.

"No, they can't. People are having babies out of ignorance. It's a vicious cycle. They procreate even in poverty and then forage for food like animals - and in the process they destroy the earth's resources." He was agitated now.

Where had her romantic vacation drifted to? What conversation was this? Ah, it was her fault for challenging his ideas. Now she wished she had remained neutral.

A silence settled between the two. Lilith retreated from her stronghold, wishing she had changed the subject rather than inflame it. The heat of the sun held fast to her naked shoulders, but rather than complain, she willed the line to move. Every now and then she would steal a glance at her lover. The sun was unable to penetrate his icy demeanor. Finally the ferryboat arrived and ticket sales commenced; once again he became animated. His rigid composure dissolved and he chatted with the anticipation of a young boy. When they finally settled into their hotel, the vacation was as pleasant and intimate as she could have hoped. He held her hand and kissed her forehead. He declared his love, yet lacked commitment.

"I love you silly girl" She wasn't silly, nor was she a girl, but all she heard was *I love you*. She managed to let the moment swallow her misgivings. She was finally where she needed to be for as long as she had known him. She was happy. They were happy.

Contained within the simplicity of the island, he was generous with his affection. His burden lay on the mainland where he had left it. . The weight of this responsibility would fracture their relationship forever. But Lilith did not know this. She felt only growing excitement mixed with timid joy

*

When they returned, he made excuses. It seemed he was never available. Finally over a rare Friday night dinner he started a disagreement over socialism, or some other topic of little interest to her. He looked past her with cool, distant eyes, and told her he didn't love her after all—probably never had. *It wasn't fair* he said. *She deserved someone better.* She began to speak, but when the reality of the situation was before her she began to beg. She begged until her dignity dissolved.

"But I love you. What am I supposed to do with all this love I still have inside for you? What will I do... I thought... I th..."

"No begging Lilith. Keep your dignity." That's what he said.

She could not recall arriving back home on that dreadful day. Shock stifled her memory; auto -pilot guided her. When she reached home she unplugged the phone and went to bed. A few days later she stood before the bathroom mirror and sliced off her thick, shoulder length hair with a razor. She hacked and tore and clipped until her arms ached. Then she went back to bed, her blue, floral nightgown swirling around her, growing larger and larger as if to swallow her up.

A time came when the panic subsided and Lilith began to imitate small gestures of living. She managed to crawl out from within her twisted sheets and wander around her apartment. At first, each step seemed precarious like walking across an ice pond. She was certain she would crack the floor and fall into an abyss.

After a few hours wavering between reality and fear, she began to gain confidence, which in turn reminded her that she had not eaten in six days. And so she began to nibble on tasteless, stale bits of food that she found in her cupboard: saltines, a can of chicken soup, a protein bar.

She took tiny bites and pushed the pieces around her mouth struggling to swallow, all while watching mindless television mysteries. She also plugged the phone back in and resumed bathing and brushing her teeth. To the world it would appear she was determined to mend, but that was not wholly the case. She had not returned to work. On the seventh day after he left, she called her office and resigned over the phone. She left a message with the receptionist. When her friends heard of the resignation they swooped down on her only to be brushed away with silence. They fretted over her mental health, but she was able to reassure them she was fine, and that she just needed space. But really she wasn't. How could she be fine when he was everywhere and nowhere? She had absorbed him so completely that she could not turn in any direction without feeling the empty space where he used to be. And it was relentless. It was in her bed, in the park, in the telephone when it rang. It was the key in the door as she inserted it into the lock, it was her shoes and clothes and books. It was the stoop beyond her front door and it was the bus stop. It was in and around every single molecule in the universe.

He didn't call, not even to see if she was ok. On the third day of her confinement she sat wrapped in a blue, acrylic blanket shifting her gaze between a blank wall and her front door. It was then she understood the profundity of her loss and she became certain that she would never see or hear from him again. Sitting on her dull green, floral futon, legs crossed in an Indian pose, she emptied out her stomach, lungs and heart with terrifying sobs. What was she to do with all the love, hate, and everything in between still squeezed inside her? Every space not reserved for flesh and bone was filled with it. And it ached like the breasts of a mother unable to express milk. All of it trapped inside and wasted.

When Lilith's father heard of her resignation, by way of a misdirected phone call, he did what many-concerned parents do. He called her and gave her a lengthy lecture on responsibility. Sitting on the same dull print futon, Lilith held the receiver to her ear without hearing. She hadn't room in her brain for two conversations. And her father's voice could not be heard over the loudness of her lover's non-being.

It was this non-being that kept Lilith from living. After her father's lecture, she sat in silence for two more days. When the landlord slipped a past due notice under her door it was the catalyst that caused her to fly about her home cramming her personal belongings into large black trash bags: clothes, shoes, photographs in frames, dishes, and most any other possession in her small apartment.

"Breathe". She screamed. "Breathe goddamn it". She was caught in a cyclone of rage. Tiny, wasted Lilith lifted heavy, ceramic lamps smashing them into the ground, then methodically picking up every shard and placing them in neat piles. With everything in ruins, she fell on her sweat soaked mattress and slept uninterrupted for hours. When she awoke, she dressed in the only clothing that hadn't been shredded. She stood head to toe in black, the clothing frayed. The many pockets were lined with essentials: a three inch knife purchased in Paris, a broken beer bottle with jagged edges along the neck, and a kitchen knife with a sharp serrated edge. She stuffed a few remaining items like underwear, two faded t-shirts, and an extra pair of socks into a duffle bag. And then she opened the apartment door and walked out, her back a barrier to the past.

*

The newscaster was cold. He rubbed his hands together furiously while rolling the microphone back and forth. His parka was zipped up past his chin.

"I hate these shit jobs." He mumbled pulling out a small flask. Whenever a pedestrian walked in his direction he would shove the microphone in the unsuspecting passerby's face.

"Miss, Ma'am, Sir, can I ask you a few questions?" Some were eager to be on camera, others looked in disgust and pushed past. Just then a plump, older white woman exited the building. She waddled down the cement steps grasping an iron railing. Her clear plastic goulashes slapping in the slush.

"Ma'am"? The man asked while sticking the microphone into her double-barreled cheeks.

"Would you answer some questions for our viewers?" The rotund, gray-haired woman stopped dead in her tracks and nodded in agreement.

"Great. How long have you lived in 818 Leffter boulevard.

"Oh about twenty years".

"Did you know the victim in 8A"?

"Not so good, but he was always a gentleman. You Know open'n doors and help'n carry groceries. Ya know that sort-a thing".

"Did he have much company, like a girlfriend or poker buddies"?

"Now that ya mention it—yeah he had a girl come round here for a while, maybe a year o' two. Introduced me to her. Lucy or Laura, I don't know, I forget. He also had some artsy professor type stop by. You know - the old type with age spots showing through thinning hair. They never came at the same time. But they was both quiet, which was good for me if ya know what I mean. I hate all the racket what comes from these here apartments. Now take my place for instant—quiet as a mouse. Never hear anybody complain'n on me."

"Now Ma'am, think real hard. Why would anyone want to kill a quiet, Jewish, Columbia university student? From what the police say he had little of any value in his apartment and his parents paid all the bills. Are you sure you didn't see anything out of the ordinary?" The lady was getting bored, and the fish-monger was due to close so she added one last comment.

"The girlfriend. Meek. But I can't see her hurt'n no one. But then ya never know—right?" She shrugged her shoulders and turned to face the wet snow, her goulashes slapping through the winter mush.

Months went by—then a few years. Then it went cold. Lilith's ex-boyfriend would find no justice. Murdered, in the safety of his home, in front of his beloved cats, Tigue and Schwartzy. But despite the boyfriend's parents' protest against the district attorney, the fact remained—there was no trace of foul play. Detectives could not put enough evidence together to label the case a murder. It wasn't that the victim wasn't covered in a whole series of wounds, his body was battered, but he had fallen eight flights down the buildings shaft way, head-first. The only person who visited regularly hadn't been seen in his home in weeks. According to description she couldn't have weighed more than 112 pounds at 5'4".

Lilith heard the police were looking for her; they wanted a statement. So she went down to the precincts. She dressed carefully in a close-fitting, tasteful, pink dress that accentuated her femininity. The detectives couldn't help worrying about the girl. She was frail. When asked about his sudden demise, she was baffled. *No it made no sense. He had so much going for him. Why would he take his own life—it wasn't possible.* Her eyes filled with tears. She was truly worried about him. *Yes, they had decided to take time away from each other, and yes she was sure it was due to his depression, which was becoming increasingly worse since he dropped out of Columbia.*

"No way a girl that size can push a man out of a window." The detectives concurred. Suicide, despite the missing farewell note, had become his obvious fate.

The detectives measured and swabbed every inch of the prewar building—including the marble stairwell and concrete shaft way. Nothing. There was nothing. Well, almost nothing—they found black canvas fibers. The deceased clothes were typical of most army navy stores, and when they were finished with the boyfriend's wardrobe, they in fact found several jackets and pants made with the same black fibers.

So the suicide angle was looking better and better. A white boy takes a dive in a white, Jewish neighborhood and no one sees anything—typical. Case closed.

III

"Now approaching Block Island", the captain announced. "Five years ago". Lilith whispered as she exhaled. She gathered her duffle and exited the back of the boat along with the others. The first and last time she disembarked the vessel, her eyes were washed with muted pastels, the colors of summer on Block Island. He held her hand like a little girl. And she obliged, relishing the strength and love she believed came from the gesture.

*

Then, not now—now he was dead and she'd killed him. She hadn't meant to. In fact she had only gone to his home to demand the Grace Paley anthology she had lent him. That way he could see that she was in fact bright, and that intelligence meant more to her than he did.

"Give me back my Paley book". She demanded, when he opened the apartment door.

"Lilith, what are you doing here"?

"The BOOK!" She shouted. He ushered her in, fearful the neighbors would hear the commotion. Thank god he'd heard the old lady from 8B leave for the butchers.

"Ok, settle down. I'll get it. But you should have called first".

"Why"? She asked pacing back and forth." Is your new girlfriend visiting? I must have been really repugnant. You could have picked any one; anyone would be better than me." Then she started to laugh, until she was screaming. He didn't move.

"Lilith, calm down, this is insane." He went into the bedroom to get the book. He needed to get her out of his home, away from his life. She followed him. One of the walls was lined with white, chipped shelves, bowing from the weight of books. There must have been hundreds. He pulled her Paley anthology out and cradled it in the crook of his arm.

"Lilith, I'm really sorry." He rubbed his bare foot back and forth, a child in confession.

"I should have ended the relationship months before".

He stood in front of the large bedroom windows, double pained and opened wide. At one time they had screens, but now they stood unobstructed. The large windows had been installed to allow light to enter the bedroom from the shaft way.

He came toward her with the book stretched out in a gesture of remorse. In a sudden rush of agony and loss, she shoved him aside and raced toward the open windows.

"I hate grace Paley. I always have. Keep the goddamn book". Then she mouthed silently,

I can't do this. I need you. I don't have a life without you. She moved to the window and stood with her arms held above her head open in supplication. He panicked.

"Lilith don't, Lilith I'm dying. I'm HIV positive. I needed to— no I wanted to tell you. I was such a coward. I found out a few days before the Block Island trip. I...I...couldn't find the words to tell you. I couldn't look in your eyes. I couldn't stand the guilt. Oh my god, Lilith I might have infected you. So I left you. I left you and ruined your life". Lilith turned her face void of color and covered her ears shaking her head back and forth like an angry child. When she was able, she opened her eyes and spoke,

"When, how did you?... Was it that degenerate old professor—that Svengali? No don't tell me I can't stand it"? Her shoulders began shaking. Tears and mucous smeared the surface of her face. She turned to look out the window overwhelmed with questions, but he misread her movement and thought she was going to jump. He panicked and raced toward her. Lilith turned around and stepped aside. He came sailing toward he but was rerouted by a stray shoe, sending his body air-born, arms flailing. When his body reached the window, he dropped the book and reached out for the sill, the glass, anything, but his grip was clammy from nerves and guilt and he slipped out the window like a piece of paper.

Lilith wanted to scream, but nothing came out except a gasp. She covered her eyes while his body sailed out the window. She would have plugged her ears too, but she wasn't able to do both, besides, he never made a sound. Eight floors into the twilight of a dusty shaft way and not a sound.

"Oh god what a nightmare". She was breathing hard. Then as if she were being watched, she glanced around the room. She was looking for evidence that what just happened was real. But all was quiet. No frightful scream, no moaning from his broken body.

"Call 911 she whispered to the room. Call the police. No, no. He's dead I know it. Run Lilith run." And she did. She stopped momentarily to gather a couple of black jujitsu wrap tops, two pairs of cargo pants and the Grace Paly book. The clothes hung off her frail frame, but with a trapunto belt she could knot them fairly tight around her waist. Besides, she needed to feel the clothes against her skin. She needed them like she needed an explanation—any explanation. But none would ever come.

IV

Brought back into the present, no longer trapped by the tragedy, Lilith forgot how simple and quiet the island was. This was the place where he had loved her. But had he? He knew he was HIV positive when they arrived yet he kept it to himself—pretending everything was perfect.

"Lies. All Lies," she moaned.

"Lies," she whispered, "hurt more than truth".

She was alone now, wearing a white, shift cotton blouse and tan linen pants. She knelt where the deserted beach met the beach grass. The summer season had not yet begun, she was without company. She began to dig. At first she scooped mounds of sand in gentle piles, then she began to dig faster and faster in a fury, panting and sweating. When the grave was sufficient, she laid the clothes and the book inside the hole, and then gently patted them like a dead child in a coffin. More tears followed the garments into their resting place as she covered them with sand she buried the lies that her love had once been built on—love that never was. Her aimless wandering had finally come to an end.

Sitting next to the grave it occurred to her it wasn't him, but her that she had mourned all these years. She rose up on her knees and howled at the make-shift grave.

She settled down into the sand again regaining her composure. After all this time, all this despair—this homelessness: friend's couches, housesitting, a stint as a live-in nanny, anywhere, anywhere that could not be called home. Finally it was time to start over.

LISA ROTH-GULVIN

"No, I don't hate you. But I don't love you either. I feel nothing. Five years to get to nothing. Five years of fear and five years of sadness—five fucking years!" Lilith was numb.

She brushed the sand off of her clothes and made her way back to the ferry. Turning around, she took her last look at the island. There in the breeze with her face tilted toward the sky, she filled her lungs with cool clean air. When she exhaled she released her prison. The labyrinth that had been her life, finally dissolved.

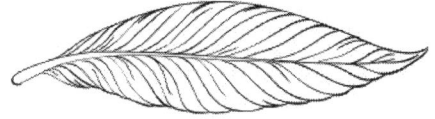

THE WASTE OF SPIRITS by A.C. Russell

Demetria gritted her teeth unconsciously as she pulled the ancient mail truck up to the apartment building. This stop was going to be a bear today. She was running about fifteen minutes behind schedule; long enough for the tenants to be impatient, but not long enough for them to give up and go back to their daytime TV. She backed her truck up to the little alley behind the main office where the mailboxes were. In the rear view, she could see them circling like vultures. Her regulars were there, lurking within the brick structure, plus a few kids from the pool now that it was getting warm enough to swim.

"We have arrived at the Willow Brook complex. We are currently seventeen minutes behind schedule. Diagnostics indicate that there is a problem with the starter—calling in now." Demetria frowned listening to the soft contralto of the onboard computer, wondering what could be wrong with the mail truck this time. She also wondered why she had one of the oldest vehicles in the fleet. Then again, maybe it was her; had she not plugged it in last night? Sometimes she was tired and wasn't too careful about dragging the heavy cord around the truck and plugging it into the outlet. Maybe it was just out of juice, but the vehicle's computer would have known that and the low charge warning would have sounded. Maybe the diagnostics were faulty. Maybe it needed gas. She scanned the rear view again.

The kids were flocking around a small motorized chair

occupied by Hank Delacourt from apartment 113. He lived in the first building and was always there waiting for her; he never failed to invite her in for a quick visit, an offer she had never accepted. He kept his patio door open year round, which was not such a bad thing half the year; Louisiana winters were relatively mild. However, Demetria could not understand how he could have the door open all summer too, when most days the humidity and temperature were above ninety. Demetria had never seen Hank out of his electric scooter in all the years she had been on this route. He was a grizzled, middle-aged white man with hair and eyes the color of cigarette ash; gray with flecks of white and black. He was always smiling in a determined way that made the skin of his face tight and smooth on his ruddy cheeks but crinkly around his eyes. Now he had half an eye on her as he bantered with the wet children. She knew another invitation was inevitable; at least she had a different excuse to refuse it today.

Hovering at the edge of the crowd was Lacey Fritch, a withered old woman whose consistently negative attitude made Demetria avoid even routine pleasantries with her. Her head seemed to jut forward, lips pursed and chin leading; Lacey's appearance always made Demetria think of the turtles in the lake behind her childhood home. Rouge made little red splotches on her pale cheeks, and her face was framed by tight, gray curls. Demetria noticed that there was always a flat spot in the back of the old woman's head where her arthritic arms probably could not reach. Lacey's clothes were always neatly pressed pastel prints which matched perfectly. Her white tennis shoes never had a sign of dirt or wear. The crease running up the front of each polyester-blend leg made Demetria wonder if Lacey had once been in the military. She guessed that the old lady did not get out much; she had observed it to be a common trait among mailbox-hoverers.

Today Lacey and Hank were joined not only by the dripping kids, but also a few of the other tenants. They were unfamiliar to her but she knew their type. They were unwilling to give up on the possibility of fresh mail and had probably gotten snagged in conversation against their wills. Hank was the person who normally did the snagging. Over the months that she had been on this route, Demetria had noticed that Hank did not discriminate.

He talked to everyone. He was always gruff and abrupt like his neighbor Lacey, but unlike her, he was always in a good mood and seemed willing to talk to anyone. People also seemed willing to reciprocate. Maybe it was because of his tendency to break into a lopsided, leering smile as he made lame jokes about people's names or activities. Demetria herself had been forced into many more conversations with him than she desired. It was through those lengthy, one-sided conversations that she had learned of his career in space, his various addictions, his political views, and many other things about which she did not require knowledge. She had learned early on in her career as a mail carrier how to smile and nod and pretend to be friendly without investing too much energy in the professional relationships that sprung up with her customers. Today was a day when those skills would be useful.

She felt sorry for these, the people who still waited for their daily paper mail with such regularity. The kids she could understand, they were just messing around. But the adults, especially the ones who looked like they had normal lives, just seemed pitiable to her. Didn't they get enough junk email to satisfy them? Why were they still eagerly checking their mail at all when just about everything from paychecks to coupons was transmitted online? It just seemed stupid, the whole mail system. She often wondered how long before the rest of the world wised up and she was out on her ass again, in her fifties, looking for a job. She jerked the rearview mirror toward her and could see the contempt on her face as she tucked a gray curl under her red bandanna: contempt for the people waiting for their useless pieces of paper, contempt for herself for having a crappy job that she hated, contempt for her entire wasted life.

Putting both the truck and her face in neutral, Demetria took a deep breath and forced her mind to emptiness before sliding the door back. It made its usual squeak and she wondered out of habit when she would be given one of the new mail trucks. Maybe if there was a real problem with the truck they would junk it and give her one with A/C at least. The thought slid from her mind as she waved at the crowd of faces in the alley. Turning her back to them, she slid open the equally squeaky rear door to get a tub of mail.

177

"Get on back in the pool and quit dripping on everything. Y'all'a get Miz Demetria's mail all wet. Go on now, GIT!" She heard Hank's rough voice and the giggles and slapping bare feet sounds of the kids as they made their way back to the pool. She silently blessed him for getting at least some of the obstacles out of her way. *Now if he would only take Lacey for a ride to the back of the complex...* Demetria thought longingly.

"Howdy, Miz Demetria! Anything good today? Maybe an extra check somebody don't want?" Hank haw-hawed at his usual stale joke.

"Ain't gon' be nothin' but bills and circulars, as usual," grumbled Lacey, who, despite her misgivings, had nevertheless stationed herself right by her box so as not to waste a second of precious time with her junk mail. Demetria nodded to them both as well as the other, more normal tenants who were standing nervously by, trying not to look too eager. She pulled out her keys by the first panel, the boxes for buildings 1-4. Hank's box was in this one and he made his way over to her.

"How 'bout this weather, eh? Warmin' up. Never seen a day this hot in April. Them kids got the right idea." Demetria nodded without turning her head as Hank continued. "I like to take me a dip in the pool, reminds me of the old days when I worked in zero-G. Best job ever! Outta this world!" As he haw-hawed loudly, Demetria marveled at the man's ability to amuse himself. She noticed that though Lacey had not moved from her spot, she had pointedly faced her body away from Hank. He now maneuvered his chair around Demetria so he could see her face better. "I sure do miss being up there. I been watching on the space channel how they got Phase Eleven of the lunar base under construction now. See, I started in on Phase Two, and that was fifteen years ago! Construction is pretty slow, but the moon ain't goin' nowhere I guess!" He chuckled again as Demetria handed him his small bundle of envelopes and sales papers. He shuffled through them absently but made no move to go. Demetria knew he was thinking up his next comment and she hoped, despite all her previous experiences with him that he would refrain from his usual offer of hospitality. She closed and locked the panel of boxes then moved on to the next; Lacey was standing there, pretending to be oblivious.

Fascinating as some people found stories of working in space, Demetria had long ago stopped listening. She had many ex-spacers on her route, she was an ex-spacer herself and could pick them out easily. With the training facility right there on the river some of them married locals and others settled their families in Baton Rouge or across the river in Port Allen; many more stayed on after retirement. Spacers in general had no close family and therefore nowhere special to go home to. Baton Rouge had some amenities that made it particularly attractive; there were good hospitals and cancer treatment centers, as well as college football, if you were into that. It was as good a place as any to stay after a career in space had ended; she herself had no urge to return to her hometown down the river. And as if through a sixth sense, the ex-spacers always seemed to find her, the female of the species. The mother/sister/wife substitute who also understood the lingo.

"Yep, that was the greatest job ever. It was just too bad I had to go and get injured. I coulda stay till retirement and got that fat package and everything. I woulda been sittin' pretty too. Probably woulda got in one of them retirement communities they're building up there now. You know that's what Phase Ten was all about, permanent livin' quarters." Hank launched into a brief description of the different building phases on the moon.

It was common knowledge that any reasonably intelligent person knew. Apart from what he termed the 'space channel' there were several TV programs that followed lunar celebrities and politics and anyone who watched any general news program was bound to see at least one or two articles a week on the project. The knowledge was mainstream; every country on Earth was contributing in some way to the lunar base. Hank had no special knowledge; he had no special line in to what was going on up there just because he had once been one of the legions of construction grunts. Two of Demetria's exes had been spacers too. Hank was no different from either of them, or any of the others that she had run into over the years. She finished the second panel and moved on to the third, just as Hank moved on from Phase Five to Phase Six.

Finally it was time to get back into the antique mail truck and head to the next complex. It was the second to last one on her route and with luck, maybe she would be delayed enough that the tenants there would be too impatient and hot to wait on their mail. Hank was certainly doing his best to make it so. She had not yet slid her door shut and he was perched on the sidewalk near her still rattling on about Phase Eight. With half an ear listening to him she turned the key absently. Nothing changed; the truck didn't start and Hank's narrative scratched on as if he were a recording. She tried again and heard the engine make a noise, but it still would not start.

"Diagnostics indicate a problem with the starter. Calling in now. I'm sorry Demetria, please wait while I get an ETA from the garage." Demetria listened to the gentle voice of the computer, bewildered. Out of her peripheral vision she saw motion. Hank had heard the onboard and sat there staring at her, something like a satisfied smile on his face.

"Looks like the feds are spending our tax dollars elsewhere," he smiled wolfishly at her, as if he had wanted this to happen. "Let me get Tico, he knows something about these old hybrids." He wheeled around and hailed the handyman of the complex as he was getting his mail."Mr. Dwayne! Where's Tico at today? Miz Demetria's jeep ain't startin'." He rotated his chair back toward Demetria, who was still sitting in the driver's seat with her hand on the ignition. "C'mon Miz Demetria, let's go on in my com-partment and have us some cold electrolytes while Tico does his magic." He laughed as he always did when he substituted spacer lingo for terrestrial words. "I made lemonade fresh this mornin'."

Demetria was tired and she had to admit that lemonade sounded good, but it would take more than that to get her into Hank's apartment. She was sure his overly affected use of space terminology was not his only annoying trait. She forced herself to be polite.

"Please excuse me while I call this in." She was relieved to see Hank nod, smiling, and turn his chair back toward his place. After waiting five minutes for Gigi in dispatch, she waited another five for the garage to answer. It was hot now, really hot and not just pleasantly warm. The flat screen of her phone was sweaty on her ear. She was still waiting for an answer when Tico appeared, loping along the sidewalk like a cartoon character. His

180

blue work shirt was coming out of his belt on one side and its top three buttons were open to reveal the sharp contrast of white undershirt and dark brown skin. He smiled at her as he approached, happy to have a diversion from his normal duties. She was happy to see him as well; young men like Tico made her think of the son she might have had if she had married instead of going into space. Anyway, it was another way to stay out of Hank's apartment.

"Hey Miz Demetria, Mistah Hank done tol' me come over here and take a look at yo' jeep." She did not stop him, but pulled the hood release, wondering how long it would take for Hank to get bored and remember to come back. At least Lacey had gone back to her air conditioned apartment as soon as she had gotten her mail. Sure enough, before she had even finished the though, there he was. His chair scootied spastically down the sidewalk toward her, and a big grin was plastered on his face. Just as he got in earshot, a sleek new fully-electric postal truck pulled up next to her. Had she not been facing in the direction of the drive, Demetria would not have known it was there, it was so quiet. It had a postal logo on the side but no words. Demetria recognized it as a one of the new vehicles they kept to show off to VIPs and field trips of school kids. Brows knit, she waited to see who would emerge from the no-doubt air-conditioned interior. Tico's rear remained where it was; sticking out of the front of her jeep.

"Hi Demetria. Wanna give me a hand with the trays?" It was Gene, a supervisor who had recently stopped delivering as he crawled toward retirement. Gene had bright blue eyes and dark hair that grayed dramatically at the temples. His uniform was sharp and crisp. This was probably his first time being out of air conditioning for the entire day. Demetria was keenly aware of the contrast they made. His pale skin made her deep brown skin seem even darker, and his middle-aged but muscular frame made her look old and scrawny rather than petite. The old red bandana on her head along with the sweat stains and untucked tails of her faded uniform made her look like a vagrant next to Gene. She met him at the back of the jeep and together they started transferring the rest of her deliveries to his truck, where there were thin shelves of metal mounted to shiny brackets on the walls. This truck could carry twice, maybe three times the amount of mail the old jeeps did, in about the same amount of space. She lingered at the open hatch, gazing at the interior and enjoying the cool air within.

"Pretty sweet, ain't it?" Gene chuckled as he hefted a tray onto a shelf. "Not everybody gets to drive this little honey around. In fact, I don't even have to do much driving, it practically drives itself. Just tells me when to get out!" Demetria grunted in reply and made her way around to the passenger side but as she made to get in, the car spoke.

"Unauthorized rider. Please do not attempt to enter. Federal law prohibits passengers in postal vehicles. Please do not attempt to enter." All the onboards had the same voice, and hearing the familiar tones of her daily companion sound so hostile filled Demetria with an irrational sense of betrayal and anger.

"Gene! Shut that thing up, will ya?" Demetria tried again to enter the truck.

"Oh no ma'am, I can't bring you with me." He grinned at her from the driver's seat. "I don't really need you anyway. It's got your route all mapped out in here," he patted the dash happily. "You got to stay with the dinosaur 'til Tiny gets here with the tow truck. He wasn't in when I left, but he'll probably be here before five or so." Demetria hated Gene at that moment; she stood there next to the passenger side of the truck, numb. The truck silently pulled away to reveal Hank, in all his battery powered glory, on the sidewalk opposite her. His right hand was on the control box while the other dangled off an armrest into his lap, and he was grinning at her with that crooked face. Demetria was still not that desperate for company and began to make her way through the gate to the front office, where she could be in air-conditioning and get water. Sometimes they even had cookies.

"They ain't in there, Ms. Demetria. Mackenzie showin' 'spective tenants 'round, and Ms. Karyn off today. It's locked up tight." Tico spoke from the hood of the jeep; she turned to see his dark black face peering out for just a second before he dove back in. Something moved in her peripheral vision. Hank.

"How 'bout dat lemonade then, hunh?" he winked at her and turning his chair, wobbled toward his building. He didn't look back to see if she would take him up on his invitation. Demetria looked past Tico as two squirrels ran across the bottom of the fence at the edge of the parking lot. The movement of their bodies and big, bushy tails made perfect wave formations as they jumped along. She wondered suddenly how they survived the heat in their fur coats. A car drove past and sent them scurrying up the fence, onto an overhanging branch and up into the cool heights of an oak. She saw the branches stirred by a mild breeze, unfelt in the heat of the asphalt and concrete parking lot. As if to cement the argument, a drop of sweat rolled into her eye, stinging briefly as she blinked it away. She sighed and followed Hank, admitting defeat.

*

"Ha, well, looks like I finally got ya in here! Don't worry; I'll be leaving the door open." Hank gave an exaggerated wink and Demetria rolled her eyes. She looked around for a place to sit, not sure yet if she wanted to touch anything. The room was not as bad as she had expected, she had to be honest with herself. In fact, it was much neater and more clean-looking than her previous boyfriend's place. He had been an electrician, life-long single just like her, and obviously in need of a woman in his life. Once the glow had worn off, he had become less interested in her body and more interested in her domestic abilities. And then the hitting started. Somehow she always let them get to that point, feeling like she deserved it.

But looking around at Hank's place, Demetria saw the same neat-as-a-pin quality she practiced in her own home. The couch had an afghan slung over the back, a bit nappy but neatly folded. Olive green, tan, white, goldenrod, and a skinny vibrant stripe of red zigzagged throughout; it looked like it was made with the scrap yarn left over from a dozen other projects and ugly as it was, it lent a certain coziness to the place. A smell of cigarettes lightly permeated the room and there was a clean ashtray on the coffee table. She saw no sign of alcohol beyond some dusty souvenir shot glasses on a shelf above an antique flat screen TV mounted on the wall.

Books were stacked neatly on the ubiquitous brick and board bookshelf, spines lined up so that they were flush with the front edge of each shelf. She had something similar at home. Scanning the titles she saw a typical spacer library: sci fi, physics, astronomy, general reference books, a few tattered graphic novels. Lots of stuff about the moon, of course. Suddenly alert, she looked around the room, paying more attention to the book titles and other items, knick knacks and framed items on the walls. Demetria had just realized something about Hank Delacourt, something that suddenly made her a little nervous. She flinched when he came back into the room.

"Here you go, ma'am." Demetria took the cold glass from Hank and sipped. It wasn't bad, and there was even a lemon wedge shoved onto the edge, an unexpectedly civilized detail. Demetria sipped again and placed the glass on the small, battered coffee table, unconsciously avoiding the rings already present in the woodwork.

"When exactly did you say you were you in space, Mr. Delacourt?" The question took him by surprise, she could tell, as if he were not used to people actually wanting to hear about it.

"Call me Hank, darlin'. And I'll tell you, but you gotta tell me when you were there too." He looked at her meaningfully. "Once a spacer, always a spacer. It ain't something you can hide."

Demetria could not help herself. She allowed a small smile, and then laughed outright. She couldn't stop in fact; it was a hysterical reaction to the stress of the day she'd had and she sat on the afghan-covered couch, too weary to care about being found out. Whatever else he might be, this man was a spacer, and they therefore shared a kinship.

"Deal." She wiped her eyes and took a deep breath. "But leave out all the stuff I already know from the mailbox." She nodded toward him, one eyebrow raised.

"That's fair." Hank put his drink on the coffee table and clasped his hands across his lap, elbows still on the armrests of his chair. "I was in the second or third construction wave that went up there to build the first lunar labs. Young too, right outta school. I had wanted to be an astronaut when I was little, but I never liked school enough. I think my folks knew that about me and never pushed me to go to college."

"Yeah, I hear ya. My thing was that my mom thought girls should not be interested in engineering and math. I had the smarts, but we didn't have a ton of money, and mama thought I should just get married and have babies like a good girl."

"Old fashioned sounds like. That's funny. Was she from one o' them old, rich families or somethin'?"

"Nah, but she wished she was! Always pushing me to marry a doctor or a lawyer or something, somebody with money. I guess she wanted to make up for my dad; he pretty much always lived paycheck to paycheck."

Their conversation continued. She learned that Hank went to the moon mainly because his family thought it was a good job for a young man, something with benefits and opportunities. She told him about her job as a flight tech and later as a mission specialist, much more than she ever thought she would've told him or anybody. In fact, it was much more than anyone had wanted to hear about her for a long time. They shared stories about the details of living and working in space that made her start to remember that part of her life in a new way.

"Here, let me refill." Hank grabbed their glasses and scooted jerkily toward the kitchen. "Damn it, gonna have to change my battery. Gimme a second." Demetria heard Hank open the pantry door and begin making noises and cursing. She decided not to offer help and instead pulled out her phone. She looked to see if she had somehow missed a call from Gigi or Tiny but there were no new notifications. She glanced out the door and saw Tico's rear still hanging out of the front of her jeep. She looked again at Hank's books.

He liked Asimov from the looks of it, but there were some other names that she recognized and enjoyed—Niven, Clarke, Stephenson. She already knew he had a sense of humor, so the comics were not surprising. Then she saw a book with a title that just didn't belong. It was a gardening reference, in perfect condition except for the spine, which was a bit faded but un-creased, as if the book had never been opened. Flipping through it, she saw delicate pencil drawings of seedlings and fruit trees and rows of plants on supports. Nice art work, but she had never been interested in gardening. She was about to put it back when the pages flipped down to reveal three greeting cards stuck under the front flap of the dust jacket. Curious, she took them out.

The cards were comical, funny pictures meant to convey emotion in a light-hearted way. Two were written to children, maybe teenagers, and the third was written to a wife. An inscription inside the cover was also to her, a woman named Callie. It was signed *yours forever, Henry.*

Demetria closed the book and gently replaced it on the shelf. She sat down again, not knowing what to make of this new information about Hank. There were no pictures on the wall indicating he had any family at all, but there obviously had been a wife and children. Judging by the dates she estimated that the kids had to be at least in their twenties now.

"Well here you go, ma'am. Got us some chips too, I'm gettin' hungry." He put a bag down between them on the table, along with the two refilled glasses.

"You have any family, Hank?" In all his ramblings he had never mentioned them, and Demetria was curious to see what he would say. He had been smiling, and the smile remained on his face, but somehow changed from jaunty to grim.

"Useta. Didn't work out." She nodded and they were silent a moment, both thinking about their failed relationships. Finally Hank snapped out of it, sniffing loudly and unnecessarily as people do when they call attention to the fact that they are about to speak.

"Anyway, I still talk to my kids, they're both in college, thank goodness. They got more smarts than me and their mom put together. My boy is twenty-two, about to graduate from LSU. And my baby girl is nineteen, just started at Vandy. Got herself a scholarship! Her ma was pissed that she went outta state; I told her to be glad she just went to Tennessee and not to the damn moon! Or worse, Alabama!" He threw his head back and guffawed in genuine amusement. Again Demetria marveled at this man's ability to amuse himself, but this time, she was laughing along with him. They subsided and Hank brought the conversation back to where they had interrupted themselves.

"So why'd you get outta space then, if you enjoyed the flights so much?" Hank waited for an answer as Demetria picked up the glass of lemonade and considered it, stalling. He noticed her hesitation. "I'm sorry, ma'am, if you don't want to talk about it—something bad happen?"

"No, that's ok; it's unpleasant, and I'm just not used to talking about it. I haven't talked about it in a long time." She took a deep breath. "Do you remember in late '26, there was an accident?"

She continued without waiting for a reply. "I was on that flight. I wasn't supposed to be, but I was. I was not in the best condition to fly; I was almost at the end of a sixteen week stint, ferrying grunts back and forth. I had a six hour flight every eighteen hours at first, and then we had them every twelve hours. None of us were getting a lot of sleep. We'd been sleeping anywhere we could, and getting woken up a lot that last week. I don't think I brushed my teeth for about three days at one point, and if we hadn't'a had the 24 hour clock, I wouldn't have even known whether it was morning or night."

"That was the last big push to finish Phase Four, when they were gonna bring up the Secretary General and all them," Hank said quietly. "I remember."

"Yeah, that's right, something like that." Demetria pushed on, anxious now to tell the story she had tried not to think about in so long. "Everything became automatic, we just pushed buttons. That's why it happened; we got careless in our fatigue. We made mistakes." She set down her glass and scrubbed at the short, grey curls under her bandanna. "I didn't know what was happening until after the alarms went off." She took a breath. "See, they had given us the codes to override the fail-safes. It made things go faster if we did it all manually. The grunts, they were in the airlock and out, in and out, in and out..." her voice trailed off. "It had been going on for hours, for days. Those poor grunts weren't human to us anymore, just another component in the machine. I just...got mixed up. It was all so repetitive, and I was so tired. I thought they were inside, but they were—" Demetria stopped. All the years of self-recrimination and regret choked her and she couldn't speak. There in a stranger's living room with satellite weather on the vid and her broken mail truck out in the parking lot, she was actually talking about it. Now she realized why she had avoided people to a large degree all these years. She took a deep breath.

"Where were they?" Hank prompted quietly.

"Well, they weren't inside."

Hank eased himself up from the chair of his scooter and, bent slightly at the waist, shuffled slowly around the coffee table to sit beside her. He put one arm around her shoulders, patting her knee with his free hand. In one corner of her mind Demetria

187

thought she should be annoyed with the physical proximity, but after sharing their spacer experiences, there was a familiar bond there, though they did not really know each other. It was like the housekeeping; living in space was about communal living, always, not by choice. Even if you loathed the guy you were bunking with, you still had to follow the regs to protect his life as much as your own. Once they had figured out that they were both spacers, they were automatically in a group together, apart from people around them. Lacey Fritch, Tico, Gene, the other tenants and all those dripping wet kids—none of them could ever be included. No matter if she sat and talked to those people for hours and got to be best friends with any of them, none of them would ever be able to get her in the fundamental way that another spacer would. There was something there, a very specific kind of trust and respect, which you just did not find with people who had never left the planet.

"You need to stop worrying about that, darlin'. It wasn't your fault. No ma'am, none o' that was your fault. That's the kinda shit happens when you're in space. It's a dangerous profession no matter if you're driving the rocket or scrubbin' the head. But that wasn't your fault. And them guys that got spaced that day, that wasn't your fault either. Trust me."

It took a minute or so for Hank's words to get through to her conscious mind; suddenly Demetria understood them and jerked her head toward him.

"What the hell do you mean? How would you know that? You weren't there. It was awful. If I had just realized a second sooner...."

"You couldn't have." Now Hank was looking down. "And I *was* there." Demetria was staring at him now, wondering what Hank could possibly know about this old story. "They covered it up because of the big wigs. They let you and the rest of the crew take the fall because it was the easiest thing to do, not because it was right. It was just less messy that way. What really happened was that we were just as tired as y'all, but the big difference was that we had been on Earth the night before, at the commissary on the base, and we were still drunk when we donned our suits and got on that damn elevator. By the time we got to the shuttle, we weren't drunk maybe, but we was definitely still buzzin'.

"There was this one guy on the crew, real nasty sombitch, name of Dumas. I guess he had been called 'dumb-ass' so much in his life that it actually stuck. He was the one who started it. He's the one shoulda lost his job, not all o' y'all on the crew."

"I don't remember that name, I just remember Jacques and Lerner. And Lerner's pregnant widow, with her other little kid standing there with her at the memorial service..." Demetria choked again. The little boy had been brown, brown like Tico, brown like she had always thought her babies would be.

"Yeah. I remember. Olivia. The kid was Evan Junior, and they had already agreed to name the baby Luna if it was a girl, since he worked up there. Turned out to be a boy." They both sat quietly for a minute and then Demetria remembered what Hank had said.

"So, Dumas? Who was that?"

"Larry Dumas. Well, he was a bully, real tough dude. He hated the guys like Lerner who were just doing seasonal or add on help. He was a lifer; probably still up there tightening bolts on the domes, if he ain't in the brig.

"Dumas didn't have many real friends, but he was popular, you know, charismatic. If he had wanted, he coulda had a lot of friends. But he had this mean streak, just couldn't be nice to people. Hated nice, friendly folks. Contempt, that's the word I want. They was like his prey, like how a cat sees a mouse, y'know? He liked to bait nice guys like Lerner and then blow them off, at the least, or beat 'em up if he thought he could get away with it. He preferred the latter." Hank paused to sniff and then took a swig of lemonade. "F'some reason I hung out with him a lot, especially when we went drinkin'. Kept him outta fights when I could; I guess I felt like he needed somebody to keep him outta trouble. We were still buzzed that morning, like I said, but Lerner and some of the other guys hadn't gone drinkin' with us. That was what Dumas used to start the fight.

"Dumas started making cracks about earthworms, about fancy college boys, anything he could think of to get a rise. Lerner ignored him, just smiled all serene and shit, like an angel or somethin'. Didn't even look up at him, even when Dumas was standing right over him. Usually that would be enough for him to give up on a guy. But the outer lock had closed and the inner lock was open, and Dumas wasn't givin' up for nothin'. He wanted Lerner to take his hat off.

"We shoulda all had our helmets still on, we shoulda all been following procedure. You ain't s'posed to take your hat off till you're through both locks. But Dumas had unlocked his helmet a little early to keep on razzin' Lerner. I took mine off to try to quiet him down. He wanted Lerner to break regs and get in trouble.

"So by this time, everybody else had got on in, and I tried grabbing him by the arm. That's when he knocked me silly. Out like a light. I heard later from Shinobi that that's when Jacques got involved, for which I will always bless his memory. He dragged my worthless carcass to the in-lock and let Shinobi pull me in, then went back because Dumas wouldn't let Lerner by. Shinobi saw the whole thing—he was still by the hatch—Lerner tried to get in when Jacques distracted Dumas. They had their backs to the out-lock. They shoulda been in by that time, and the in-lock closed on us and even then Dumb-ass wouldn't give it up. He could see the out-lock about to open and put his hat back on before Lerner and Jacques could react. He also grabbed on to somethin' and when the doors opened…well you know what happened. He bragged about it afterward. Shinobi had been trying to get me to the in-lock or he said the two of us woulda been spaced too. As it was, he managed to hit the emergency closure button just in time to keep me from going out the hatch. But I slammed pretty hard up against the doors; that's what scrambled my back. Keeps me in the chair most of the time now that I'm gettin' old. Anyway, long story short: weren't your fault."

Hank patted her knee in a clinical sort of way, conveying empathy and nothing more. Then he heaved himself up from the couch to amble back to his motorized chair. Demetria was silent, dredging up the memories of that day, worn and polished like a good luck fetish carried in a pocket. But here was something new; hearing Hank's story gave her the same feeling she had gotten at age six when she found the golden egg with the $2 bill in it at the family Easter egg hunt. For the first time in years she had an opportunity to let go of some of guilt she had assumed. She tested the feeling, *what if it really wasn't my fault?* She found that she liked it.

"So you got a husband? A boyfriend? I don't see a ring." It was a fair question but took her by surprise; her mind was elsewhere. An hour ago she would've refused to answer such a question, especially from him, but now she now felt comfortable enough with the man not to be offended. Hank was not aware of the change in her of course, how could he be?

"Flying solo at the moment." Demetria then switched to the exaggerated dialect of her aunts. "Tired o' all them mens fightin' ovah me down at the post office. Decided it would be better for all involved if I just went celibate." She leaned back deliberately on the couch, idly gazing at her nails and then polishing them on her shirt in an exaggerated manner. "Gotta beat 'em off with a stick now." Hank looked at her for a moment then chuckled. She smiled self-consciously and then laughed at her own antics. She was still laughing when her phone buzzed. She looked at it to see Tiny's face in the incoming call window.

"Well I'm glad you're havin' a good time while I'm out here in this heat wonderin' where the hell you are!"

"I'm sittin' here in the first building, Tiny, simmer down. If you just look you can see me waving from the door." Demetria leaned forward on the couch and waved. She could see Tiny, a huge figure on the sidewalk behind the truck, swivel slowly. It was bright out, and hard to see inside the relatively darker apartments. Tiny squinted and evidently spied her. He hung up without saying anything and went around to the front of the truck, out of Demetria's line of vision. She sat back, still smiling, unfazed by Tiny's gruffness. She knew that on a normal day he would be the first to tell a joke or give her a hug in greeting. Demetria reflected that she was not really alone. Maybe she never had been, except by choice.

"Well, looks like you gotta git. Nice talkin' to ya though. I'll wheel out witcha." Hank's eyes crinkled as he smiled at her. They made their way down the sidewalk toward the parking lot, a sidewalk that felt a bit different to Demetria now. Tico and Tiny were both under the hood of her jeep, arguing loudly about what might be wrong with the engine. They were an odd couple; the small but well-built, extremely dark young man almost disappeared next the pink-skinned, potbellied older mechanic with his bushy, dirty blonde hair pulled back in a ponytail. She thought of how she felt about the picture she and Gene presented an hour ago, and decided that Tiny looked like a vagrant now.

"Listen kid, whatever you think, this here jeep is gummint property and you need to get yer hands off! And anyway, these old hybrids had a different kind of chip in 'em than what you're talkin' about."

"I know dat, mister, dat's what I'm tryin' to tell you! Now if you look at dese here connections..." Tico burrowed back into the engine.

"I sure hope that young'un ain't got himself in trouble wit' your boy there. He really does know a lot about them old cars." Demetria could see that Hank was genuinely concerned.

"Oh don't worry 'bout him. Tiny's probably gonna offer him a job, he always hates dealing with the hybrids. He's more of a tech head." She chuckled. They watched the argument for a moment more, then Hank turned to go.

"Well, I'ma get on back inside. Hotter'n hell out here this late in the day. Nice talkin' to ya," he said again. "Hope we can do it again sometime."

"Yeah, you know, it was nice having that little break..." Demetria was thinking about how much she enjoyed talking with another spacer. "Thank you."

"My door's always open, ma'am, drop by any time." He winked and executed a tight 180. Demetria watched the chair scoot away. Just as he disappeared into his apartment, she recognized the stiff gait of a figure coming down the sidewalk between the buildings. Lacey Fritch hurried toward her, waving an envelope.

"Glad you're still here. This needs to go out today." The old lady was puffing and panting and Demetria even saw a bead of sweat on her temple.

"Sure thing, Miss Fritch." Surprising them both by using her name, Demetria took the letter from her and placed it in a tray in the back of the truck. "Why don't you go on in now, ma'am, it's awful hot out here."

"Yes, I think I will," the older woman paused, as if thinking of something to say to return Demetria's unexpected friendliness. "Well, uh, you take care now." She hurried off. Demetria smiled at the old woman's retreating back, and her confusion at this unaccustomed kindness. Demetria herself was unaccustomed to it, but she thought she might could get used to it.

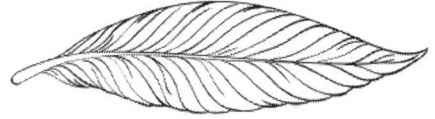

THE CALLING SONG by Heather M. Walker

Though her very first memory still burned hot and raw in her mind, Selena could not remember any of her childhood, nor did she know exactly how old she was. It was as if she had been dropped from the sky, newly born and wounded, into the middle of a clearing in the woods. There in the clearing, through tears of excruciating pain and confusion, everywhere she looked there were feathers. And blood. So much blood. Her back was a symphony of pain, bright notes of agony pounding like drums into her flesh, lacerating her mind with torment. The pain began at her shoulder blades and continued its torture down to her tailbone.

She reached her hand back to touch her shoulder in an effort to gauge the depths of her wounds. Her hand came back hot and wet with blood, deepening her panic and bewilderment. She could barely see through her tears and confusion, and the wind added to her disorientation as it whipped her long black hair and stung her eyes. As she pulled her hair back into submission, more pain blossomed in her back and shoulders as her hair separated from her flesh and came away matted with dried blood.

"Hello?" Selena called out, desperate for help. She heard nothing in return but the sound of the wind and her own choked sobs. Why were there so many feathers, and was all this blood her own? She tried to calm herself and let her mind grow

disassociated and distanced from her pain. She watched the
feathers dancing on the ground and in the air around her, turned
by the wind into pirouetting canvases painted in her blood. As
her panic began to ebb, waves of deep sorrow came to fill its
place. A sense of loss and utter dejection washed over her along
with the sudden knowledge that she was lost, alone and naked in
the woods; abandoned. She looked up at the sky with an
unforeseen flash of longing for its calm, azure zenith, an action
with reasons she couldn't begin to contemplate.

"What's happening!?" She screamed, her head thrown back to
the sky. It seemed to pulse in response, an undulation of barely
perceptible light moving quickly from the belly of the Heavens.
Was it a trick of the light, or the veil of tears obscuring her
vision? The air around her thrummed, its energy so tangible that
Selena thought she could reach out and touch it. The air held an
awareness as if someone was watching her, a sense of another's
pain and sorrow mixed in with her own. The atmosphere around
her became dense and heavy with the vibrations it carried within
it.

Blackness smudged at the edges of Selena's vision and
threatened to overtake her at any moment. She felt the last dregs
of her strength as it left her, but was able to summon her voice
by the force of her will.

"Who's there? Please, show yourself! Help me!" She called
out to whoever it was that she felt was watching her, her voice
coming out just above a whisper. The trees vibrated almost
imperceptibly, shivering in a cryptic reply. A new wave of
anguish and remorse hit her, but she was uncertain if it was her
own, or coming from the unknown observer she sensed watching
her in the woods. If someone was there, why were they not
helping her? Could they not see how desperate she was for help,
how wounded, how terrified?

The blackness moved in to fill her vision, and Selena knew
she was losing her battle with consciousness. In one last
desperate plea, she called one more time, her voice a tiny,
throaty whisper.

"Please..."

Then darkness claimed her as its own.

*

When she awoke, it was in a hospital bed, the room around her brightly lit and sparsely decorated. Her pain was subtly muted, though her confusion and panic rushed back to her the moment she opened her eyes. She could hear a beeping noise and the muffled sound of people speaking from far away. How had she gotten here?

As Selena opened her mouth to call out, a woman dressed in white entered her room looking at a clipboard. When Selena's voice didn't come, she lifted her hand out to the woman, who rushed to her side.

"Don't try to strain yourself," the woman said, "You've hurt yourself pretty badly. Blink once for yes, and twice for no. Do you understand?" Selena blinked once. "Very good. Do you remember what happened to you?" Selena blinked twice in response, upset that she couldn't recall anything before the woods. "That's alright, I'm sure it will come back to you. Do you know your name?" Again, two blinks, which were instantly followed by tears. Delirious with puzzlement, her tears turned into racking sobs. Her chest heaved with the force of her weeping.

The nurse sedated her, and she spent several weeks in the hospital letting her back heal. No matter how the doctors and police tried, no one could find any information as to who she was, where she was from or how old she was. No paperwork existed. There was no birth certificate or social security number. She overheard a doctor speaking to the police through her medicine induced haze saying, "It's as if she came from nowhere. We can't find anything at all, so I am making her a ward of the state. We are guessing her to be anywhere from fourteen to sixteen years old, and will be placing her into foster care as soon as she recovers."

"Well, what do we call her, officer? She has no name," asked the nurse. Selena watched through her clouded vision as the officer walked to her side and placed his hand over hers.

"Yes, it's a pity, that. She reminds me of my granddaughter, Selena. It seems a fitting name for her."

Selena came to find out all about what foster care meant in the years to come. Placed from home to home, as soon as she got used to one she was shuffled to the next, often for reasons she didn't understand. Sometimes she was glad to move on, her skin decorated with bruises and her heart covered in scars. The other children were just as cruel as the adults she was placed with. They teased her for the scars that covered her back. They called her crazy because she didn't know where she had come from, or anything else before the horror in the woods. She suffered their hate filled gazes, never truly making friends with any of them, too scared and timid to place herself in the vulnerable position of opening up to anyone. She had accepted that she would always be misunderstood, an outcast, and utterly alone. She belonged nowhere, and to no one. Forever lost.

At the last home, it had been particularly terrible. Her foster father had begun to be kind to her, and the moment she let a tiny stone out of the wall that protected her, he had taken that small piece of trust and thrust it into the deepest, most unreachable abyss. "I've never seen eyes like yours before," he had said, his voice slurred by alcohol. "What a deep cobalt blue they are, it's almost unnatural." She smiled politely at him and said nothing, not accustomed to any form of kindness. He kept feeding her compliments, and it felt so good to hear them.

He had then led her to the basement, luring her with his fawning and pretty words. No one had ever been so nice to her before. At first, she welcomed it, her soul desperate to hear anything affectionate after so much misery. It wasn't long, however before his flattery became physical and intrusive. His hand slid up her leg and under her skirt, his fingertips digging into her flesh. When she cried out and tried to move away, he slapped her hard across the face. Her lower lip split, filling her mouth with blood.

She had undergone many forms of abuse in foster care, but this was something new. No one had ever shown her any form of tenderness, and she wondered why it was taken from her so quickly. Why had he placed his hand on her like that? It felt far worse than the slap that had split her lip. What had she done to make him touch her so intrusively? She only had a moment to consider this, her heart breaking for the lost affection she would never have from him again. What had she done wrong? Before she had time to form another thought, his hand went across her face again, this time in a fist to her right eye.

"That'll teach you to bat those damned blue eyes of yours at me," he swore at her. "You go around sauntering yourself, tempting me, don't act like you don't know what I'm talking about Selena, you damned whore!" His voice was hot with anger, his eyes bulging from their sockets like blisters about to burst from rage.

Selena didn't know what a whore was, but she felt instantly sorry for angering this man. She tried to say she was sorry, but before she could part her blood stained lips, his hands were hammering into her, over and over. She had been hit before, but never like this. It never occurred to her to become angry or to think that it was his fault for what he had done to her. In her mind, she was the wretched, the debauched, though the reason as to why this was eluded her. Even as his fist struck her in the ribs with a sickening crunch, she only thought of what wrong she had committed.

It was only when consciousness threatened to abandon her again that she thought to ask him to stop. With blood dripping from her face in thick ribbons of crimson, she raised her hand to defend herself against another blow, and quietly called out, "Please stop."

He paused then, his hand poised to backhand her across the face. His breathing was labored and his eyes were white circles of fury. He lowered his hand slowly, and said, "It serves you right you know, tempting a good Christian man like me. I have a wife and kids of my own to look after. I took you into my home out of the kindness of my heart, and this is how you repay me?" He spat on the floor beside her, his contempt palpable.

The police had taken her from that foster home, committing her to a psychiatric ward, which was where she found herself now. The man told them that she was crazy, and had thrown herself down the stairs in a psychotic fit.

"She threw herself at me, I guess she was desperate for some attention," he told the police. "When I told her no she got upset and started to act crazy and hit herself in the face. I didn't know what to do, and before I knew it, she had thrown herself down the stairs. I guess she was trying to kill herself."

It didn't matter what she told the police, they wouldn't listen. They had become familiar with her over the years, placing her from one home to the next, often with bruises the foster parents claimed were self-inflicted. Most said that she was mentally imbalanced, that she was unable to interact socially and was overly emotional. One had theorized that she suffered from PTSD from what had happened to her in the woods. Whatever had happened had not only forever scarred her back, but her very soul as well.

It didn't help that she couldn't recall anything. She was seen as an anomaly to humanity, viewed with either animosity or pity for being insane. It had only been a matter of time before they committed her.

As she sat and stared out of the barred window to the ground three stories beneath her, tears once again streamed down her cheeks. She was sure no one could ever love her, certain that she was beyond anyone ever treating her with any act of kindness or compassion again. She was damaged beyond repair, unlovable, broken, and from what everyone told her, demented too. She was ashamed of herself, of her scars, of her lack of recollection of what had happened to her. She must be crazy she reasoned, to not know who she was.

She no longer wished to live this way, suffering the looks and acts of hatred from everyone around her. For every glance towards her filled with disdain, for every cruel word spoken to her, she died a little inside. At first, she tried to be strong, even feeling pity for them because they refused to understand her. *How terrible it must be,* she thought, *to be so totally devoid of kindness or empathy.* She promised herself that no matter what happened to her, she would never be like them, that they couldn't take her innocence and what little sense of self she had. They would never break her enough to steal her wonder, her captivation at sunsets and all of nature, or corrupt her enough to hate them in return. They could beat her, tease her, and brandish their abhorrence at her, but they could never remove her spirit.

That had been before she came to reside at Brook Haven, home for the mentally wayward. Here something sacred in her was mangled beyond repair, and it threatened to die within her. Though she tried fervently to keep her hope it slipped from her grasp, spiraling into nothingness as she clasped for its dying remains. She remembered reading a quote somewhere in a book of poetry she often immersed herself in, "Never take a man's hope, it may be all he has left." It was as if she was in Hell itself, and "Abandon all hope all ye who enter here" was written above the door of Brook Haven.

Summoning hope would take a great effort, as resurrecting it from the dead was close to impossible. If she could not, in this last act of desperation, invoke it forth, she had resolved herself to the dark embrace of Death. With all objects removed from her room that she could injure herself with, she decided she would break open the veins on each of her wrists with her teeth. Exsanguination seemed fitting, having been bled of any dreams of redemption. But she had to try one last time.

She had once read about something called a soul tribe, and that everyone belonged to one. That no matter what, everyone who was born had first existed in the ether of the other side with souls that were a family unit, belonging to each other and loved beyond measure. What if this was true? That meant that she too had a family of souls somewhere on this Earth, perhaps lonely like her, abandoned and ruined. Maybe they were looking for her but didn't know where or how to look.

Tonight she would call to them in one last act of wild hope. If no one came, then that meant she truly was alone in this world. Perhaps in the afterlife, someone would come to claim her.

As she silenced the steady flow of tears, Selena began to breathe slowly in an effort to become calm. She knew about meditation, and she opened herself up to the rhythm of her breath, to the beating of her broken heart, and to the cadence of her life's force. She was going to summon her soul tribe forth, with the energy signature of her soul's intentions and the power of her emotions, in a calling song. She didn't know which words she would sing, nor the tune that would come with it, but she trusted that the intensity of her sentiments and the passion of her purpose would bring forth exactly what was needed. She had meditated before, to close off the torture of this world, to silence the pain that had become a tattoo on her soul. It has been the only reprieve she had ever known.

Calmed and centered now, Selena sent out what would be her last prayer. "Please," she prayed, "Help me find the right words to call forth my soul's tribe. If I have earned any favors at all, let it be now that I receive it."

A strange, foreign energy began to course through her, a
soothing oscillation surging throughout her being. She harnessed
it and felt it blossom in her chest, opening her heart. It felt warm
and calming, as though she were being bathed in light.

"Now," it seemed to urge her, "Sing now." She took a deep
breath, the light in her heart pulsing with the force of her
intentions and the power of her emotion.

She began to sing. The beauty of her voice surprised her, and
the words she sang were strange and alien to her ears. With each
utterance, the luminescence in her heart grew. The potency of
her sentiments and desperation burned white fire in her soul. The
air around her began to stir, responding to her in steady
palpitations, as though it were listening to her and lifting up the
song from within her and sending it scintillating out into the
aether. She felt her song gain in strength, hope now returned to
her, feeding her voice with the jewels of its promise.

With each note, her hope grew, and her voice filled the room
with its potency and resonance. She sang, letting every pain,
every scar on her spirit, every tear she shed fuel her song. She
fed to it her loneliness, her need for empathy and understanding,
her fervent desire to be loved and held. The words flowed easily,
even though they were words that made little sense to her. The
beauty of the language seemed effortless, a steady stream of
incantations that poured from her with a growing ease.

Around her, the air carried her energy, condensing it into
pulses of dense waves and rocketing her song in intense
undulations to the very firmaments of the cosmos. Never had
Selena felt more in control. She was now more aware of herself
and the unknown potentials she held within.

And then, with a soft and drawn out utterance, her song was
done. She opened her eyes languidly, her heart pounding within
her chest, the sound like thunder in her ears. The echo of her
sacred words resonated off the walls in her chamber, vibrating in
the air around her. An ethereal luminescence pulsed subtly
throughout the room, reminding her of the day she had been
abandoned in the woods when she called out for help. The sky,
hadn't it done something similar?

Before she had time to consider the light further, she was

startled by the appearance of a palm pressed gently, soundlessly against the outside of her window. Her surprise abated quickly, replaced with a resounding hope filling her so completely that she thought perhaps she too, were sending off waves of thrumming light.

A whisper then, followed by warm breath against her right ear. "Indeed my dear, you shimmer with angelic luminance," it said. At hearing the words, she began to tremble, not with fear but with a longing oddly familiar to her. The voice was low and gentle, a man that spoke with obvious affection for her. Turning her head slowly, she saw who had spoken, albeit briefly. The room was still gently pulsing with light, and in the cadence of its heartbeat, she saw him.

He looked as though he were illuminated by candlelight, the shadows accentuating his noble, handsome features. His beauty was so intense it seemed instantly otherworldly, sending an unexpected surge of desire through her.

His face was like carved marble, pale with high cheekbones, suggesting aristocratic lineage. His hair was long and flowed down his back, the deep scarlet color of blood. It was full and lush, catching the light around him in a magnificent sheen. His lips were full and plush, a pale shade of pink that seemed to invite her to kiss them as he smiled at her. It was his eyes, however, that had the most impact on her. Like hers, they were an intense midnight blue.

His deep, beautiful voice came again, this time at her left ear. "Yes, you see something of yourself in my eyes, don't you?" She turned to see him, again bathed in a brief pulse of light. He smiled gently at her, becoming obscured as the light faded once more.

"What's happening?" Selena asked him, "Who are you?"

This time, he appeared in front of her. The light was no longer pulsing, but steady on him. The subtle glowing was having a slightly hypnotic effect on her.

"You sang in Enochian, my dear, the language of the angels. You sang with such passion that I could no longer deny you. Your calling song was the most beautiful I have ever heard, and the most moving." He took her hand gently, squeezing it softly. His hand was warm and soft, and the feeling of it over her own moved Selena almost to the point of tears. Never had she been touched like this, with such concern and tenderness.

As a tear made its way down her cheek, he took the pad of his thumb and ever so softly, wiped it away. She sighed and closed her eyes as he gently touched her skin, pleasantly overwhelmed by her emotions.

"My name is Nesaphael," he told her, looking deep into her eyes. In them, Selena saw her reflection, her face no longer bruised and swollen. How was any of what was happening possible? Before she could ask, his eyes seemed to change. They were transformed for a heartbeats length of time, from the radiant indigo to a strange, red-rimmed amber.

"Don't be scared," he said, "What you see in my eyes is my transformation. I won't be what you see before you much longer. I have disobeyed our Creator, knowing full well what my punishment would be. I was not to contact you ever again, though I never left you. All I could do was watch from the shadows as you were tormented and abused, torn apart by this world. I wanted to come to you so many times, but I was reminded constantly of what would happen if I did.

"I know you want to be told of your past, to understand who you are and where you came from, but knowledge comes with a price," His eyes shimmered as he spoke this, full of warning. "Once you know something, you cannot go back to not knowing again, back to innocence. Knowledge is a powerful thing, and sometimes it carries danger with it. I can tell you what happened, or I can show it to you, if you wish it."

Selena never took her eyes off his, watching with wonder as their color changed back and forth between the deep cobalt to the red rimmed amber. His pupils were changing too, from round to elliptical.

"You said you wanted to come to me before," She said, "Why would you come now, and not when I was scared and wounded in the woods? Why not come when I was in foster homes, alienated from everyone, confused, alone, desperate. Why now?"

His eyes left hers then, his lips drawn tight in a frown.

"It was your song, my love. I could not bear your suffering any longer. You moved me so that I could no longer be without you. I could not stand for you to be in such anguish any longer.

You have suffered terribly, and for far too long," His words were laden with sorrow, his remorse etched into the expression on his face.

"I can show you what happened, but you must understand the risk." He warned again. "Once I show you, there is no going back. Your innocence will be lost. There will be no more chance of redemption for you, as there is now none left for me," His voice dropped in timber, the sadness it carried thick. "I was willing to make the sacrifice to come to you, to show you what happened, but I am afraid it will be incredibly painful, confusing and overwhelming for you. Are you certain that you want to know?"

Whatever the risk was, Selena was willing to take it. She had so many questions, and this was her one chance to know them. What could be worse than not knowing who you were or where you had come from?

"Yes," Selena answered him, "A thousand times yes! Please, I have been tormented my whole life, unable to remember even the slightest thing. I have waited for you for so long, and finally, you have come. Please, don't leave me without knowing."

A deep sadness filled his face, and the sorrow in his eyes that made Selena wonder if she had made the right choice. Once more, his eyes changed from blue to amber, and this time, they did not change back to blue.

"What's happening to you Nesaphael?" she asked, concerned and confused.

"I am changing into something I never wanted to be. The punishment, though severe, is worth seeing you again." His amber eyes pierced her, as if to ask one final time if she was sure this was what she wanted. "You still have a chance now, if you go on without knowing, you can still achieve redemption. You can remain human as you now are, able to be cleansed of your sins. Once you know who and what you are, all innocence will be lost. You will change into what I am becoming as well."

Selena paused for a moment. Innocence, the one thing she had tried to protect her whole life, to never let anyone steal from her, taken from her forever. In exchange, she would finally know everything she had wanted to know for so long. What was Nesaphael, and what was he becoming? How could it be more wretched than what she was now? She had to know.

She nodded her head, now fully sure it was worth the risk. Everyone had to lose their innocence at some point. If she had to lose hers, she wanted it to be with him.

With tears brimming in his eyes, Nesaphael opened his arms to her. "Come to me then," he said, "I will show you."

Selena embraced him, aware of his heartbeat against her, feeling safe and loved for the first time in her life. He ran his hand over her hair, and kissed the top of her head tenderly.

"Promise me," he said, struggling against tears, "that when you return to me from your vision, that you will remember me as I am now, before I change into what I am fated to become. I don't want you to be afraid or repelled. I promise you that in return, when you come back to me and your own transformation is complete, I shall love you still, with the wholeness of my being, and that I will always love you. I will remember you as you were before you fell, and I will remember you as the beautiful human you are now."

"I promise," Selena replied, certain she could not forget his beauty even if she tried, no matter what happened from here on out.

Nesaphael sighed deeply, tilting her face up to his. "One last kiss," he said, and bent down to press his lips to her mouth.

Suddenly, Selena felt as though her soul had been torn from her body. She went rocketing out of herself, through space and time to a place she recognized at once. All around her was the presence of light, filled with love, glorious in its graceful, eminent power. It flowed to and from all things, from the towering heights of the trees, to the flowers that did not crush when she stepped upon them. She felt instantly at peace, her troubled soul calm and serene. Here, she had been happy. Here, she had been whole.

Selena turned and saw an image of what looked like herself only far taller, with snowy white wings, astounding in their immensity, growing from her back. Beside her stood Nesaphael. He too, with silvery, powerful wings folded neatly behind him. She watched, a ghost in a vision, as the two of them held hands, laughing, obviously in love.

Then she was spinning, once more torn from where she had

been, sent spiraling to another time and place. She instantly wished she was anywhere but where she was transported to, this scene nothing like the one before it.

Tall beings with enormous wings that blocked out the sky were all around her, each engaged in a fierce battle. The coppery scent of blood was pungent in the air, cloying and repugnant. Screams and the clashing of swords filled her ears, thunder rolling throughout the darkened sky. The ground beneath her specter like feet was torn and muddied with spilt blood, a desecration to the light that had filled this place not so long ago.

To her surprise, she saw herself again in the midst of the battle, sword raised and dripping blood in fat, red drops that fell to the war-ravaged earth. Her expression was fierce, determined to slaughter all that opposed her. Here she fought with her brothers and sisters of the light, against the army of darkness that had invaded the most sacred realms of Heaven. Her enemy had claimed to be as powerful and gifted as God Himself, and had sent evil forth into the world. She had fought together with Nesaphael with all her might and dedication. She saw the expression of ferocity that spread across her face as she slashed and stabbed at the monstrous demons that charged her, felling each one, but not before she received some grievous wounds of her own.

Was all of this real? Even as her memory came back to her while she watched what unfolded around her, she wondered, how could any of this possibly be?

Her pensive ruminations were quickly snuffed out by a scream that rose, louder and more distinct from the rest. It echoed against the skies of Heaven, and Selena watched herself lift her head in response, looking for the source of the scream. As she did so, her attention was taken away from her enemy, and in that split second, a grievous blow was dealt to her. One of her wings was sliced from her back, falling in a mess of blood and feathers, soiled by the bloody ground beneath.

A phantom pain radiated from her shoulder, her memory of the event filling her with its solemn truth. No wonder she had never been accepted by anyone, she was not of their kind. Perhaps they could feel it, unaware of how they knew she was not like them. *How like humans,* she thought, *to not welcome anyone unless they were the same as themselves.* Any difference meant an instant disliking, and an effort to conform the other into an image of themselves. Selena had been unable to do so, and thusly ostracized.

Again, the spinning and ripping of her spirit into another portal, to another point in her lost memories.

Here she knelt, wounded, in supplication, at a gilded altar with Nesaphael at her side. Her wounded wing pained her to look upon, the remains of the stump mangled and twisted. Blood still dripped from having been severed. Tears welled up and spilled down her cheeks, her voice a sob of despair as she petitioned the Creator.

"Please," she begged, "heal my wound, give me back my wing. I fought for Your cause, I have done my duty to You, oh powerful, all knowing God. I beg of You, hear me and grant my request."

Though in her current form, Selena could not hear the response, she knew at once that she had been refused. She watched as her form at the altar crumpled to the ground, all hope lost; defeated. Tears poured down her face, the dejection in her cries sending the memory of it back to her in a rush of heightened emotion.

"How can You do this to me?" She wailed to the Creator, her agony ripe and raw. "I have done as You have asked, why will You not grant me this? I fought in a war I was against since the beginning, I have slain my fallen brothers and sisters, all for Your glory, all to uphold You. It is not much that I ask of You. Please God," she cried, "I beg this of You."

There was a pause as she waited for a reply, and this time her sobbing turned to wails. Her fists pounded at the ground beneath her. Nesaphael held her, weeping with her. There was no going back, no healing granted.

"Why do you deny me? Is it because I was against the war? Is it because I didn't want to kill the fallen who were once Your beloved?" Selena watched her own ghost, the pain in her eyes strong as the light of God shimmered within them. All too soon, the light went out, and the light was replaced with the dim film of betrayal.

"You deny me for not wanting to fight in the war? For my

hearts burden that I would have to kill the brothers and sisters I once loved?" There was a sharp anger in her voice, and in that moment she knew her innocence had been slaughtered.

Her memory of this event came flooding back to her, overpowering her with the intensity of its weight. Anger flashed hot in her, overflowing into rage, seeded with despair. God had refused her, had betrayed her, and wounded her much deeper than the pain of losing her wing.

She heard Nesaphael's handsome voice whisper in her ear, "Perhaps there is another way."

The now familiar dizziness returned, sucking her out of that scene and into the next.

She recognized the face of the angel that stood before her and Nesaphael. Dressed in a green robe with a golden rope tied around his waist stood the archangel, Raphael, in all his beautiful, angelic splendor.

"I cannot stay here in Heaven, with such betrayal against me," Selena told him. "My heart is heavy with the loss of my innocence, with the knowledge that I have killed my fellow angels. I am burdened with the heaviness of the war that has come, stealing my peace, invading my soul with its brutality. I never wanted to fight in this war, I never wanted any part of it, but I did as I was asked and God has now refused me. I cannot have my wing back, but I beg of you to heal my heart instead. Return to me my innocence, my hope, my wonder and marveling at the glory of God."

Raphael's face was serious, contemplation furrowing his brow. "There is something I can do, but I don't think it will be any better for you than where you are now." Raphael folded his hands together, looking solemn. "Here, you have made your sacrifice to God, but you will not be rewarded for it the way that your heart longs for. I can grant your favor if you wish it, but it comes at a price. Your innocence will be returned to you, all knowledge of Heaven taken from your memories," He paused to look at Selena, his eyes holding the same warning expression that Nasaphael's had moments ago. "However, you will no longer be permitted through these gates that that have always been your home. You can start again, wounded terribly but pure. I can give you the life of a human, in a human body, one that is much more easily wounded and fragile than the spiritual body you now possess. You will suffer as a human suffers, but you will have a chance, as all humans have, of redemption, and thusly, admittance to the gates of Heaven with a human soul." He walked a step closer to her, lowering his face to hers, his voice hushed and serious. "You will have to make another sacrifice, this time for yourself. You must give up your wings, or what is left of them, in order to become human."

Selena looked back at her remaining wing, horrified at the pain, both emotional and physical, that would come with its removal.

"It will be much more painful than the slicing of your other wing, for I must pull it from your back, with my bare hands. This is your sacrifice, and the way it must be done."

"This is the only way she can have her innocence back?" asked Nesaphael, visibly shaken at the horrific revelation.

"Yes, but there is more." Raphael answered Nesaphael as he straightened himself and closed his wings tighter against his back. "Should the weight of not knowing who she is come to be more than she can bear, should she petition the Heavens to reveal her true nature to her once more, not only will she lose her innocence, but she will forever lose her place in Heaven, irredeemably. There can only be so many petitions to us, so many favors asked. She will fall from grace eternally, and become one of the Fallen."

Here Raphael turned his full attention to Nesaphael. "You must make a promise, and potentially a grave sacrifice as well. The favor she asks is a great one, and requires more than she can give." The angels looked at one another, the energy between them heavy and poignant. "You must promise never to contact her, never to comfort her in her pain, in her terror, in her confusion," Raphael's voice became softer as he continued, the gravity of his words clearly paining him. "You are forbidden to see her in any manner, no matter her tears and calls for help. It will be more than you can bear at times, Nesaphael, as the torments of humanity is at times insufferable. If you do go to her at any time, for any reason, you will sacrifice your Grace, and you too, will become one of the Damned."

Selena hung her head, unable to look either of them in the

eye. She was willing to suffer the removal of her wings, to always wonder who she was, and bear the weight of knowing she would always try to fill in the holes in her memory, forever unable to do so. If she became human then her pain would be washed from her, and she had the chance to have a pure, human soul. With it, she could be washed of all sin and wrong doing in the eyes of God. She could have her innocence returned to her, and have a chance at returning to Heaven, whole and pure. Perhaps, if she became a good enough human and suffered humbly she could even earn back her wings.

Selena faced Nesaphael, her eyes wide and her heart broken, unable to ask him to do this for her. How could she? It was more than anyone could ever ask of another. It was one thing for her to make a sacrifice on her own behalf, but to ask the angel that she loved more than herself to sacrifice for her was more than she could do.

"Your sacrifice is too great, Hanielle," spoke Nasaphael.

Selena heard her true name for the first time since her fall, the effect of which sent a lightning strike to her heart. The full knowledge of who and what she was now complete.

"But, if you desire it so desperately, I will promise to you never to come to your side, never to betray you, no matter your throes of agony, no matter your tears of suffering," He stepped closer to her, his voice heavy with sincerity. "I promise that I will never leave you though, that I will follow you, so that even though you may feel dejected and alone, you never will be. This is for my own conscience as well. Though the temptation to touch you, to hold you and feel your love returned will be great, I shall not damn us both with my weakness. If this is your true heart's desire, then I will not hold you back. Only be certain that this is what you want, there is no going back."

Nesaphael's last words echoed against Selena's damaged soul, now fully aware of what she had done. She had damned them both, with her selfish desires. She deserved every tear she had shed, every moment of turmoil. The weight of her transgression threatened to crush her as she watched herself as Hanielle speak her decision to Raphael.

"Yes, this is what I want, do it now, before I change my mind."

"As you will it, so it will be done," Said Raphael solemnly.

"Wait!" cried Nasaphael. He grabbed Hannielle and kissed her desperately, deeply, with all his passion, believing that he would never kiss her again. They fell into each other, their tears intermingling.

"I will return to you some day, when my mortal body dies," Hannielle told him, "I will come to you, virtuous and whole, redeemed. I will never know that God has betrayed me."

With one last embrace, Nasaphael stepped apart from her.

"Are you ready?" asked Raphael, pity thick in his voice.

"Yes," she answered.

Selena took the full, anguishing gravity of her deed with her as she felt her soul slam back into her body. She jolted upright with the force of her soul having returned. As she opened her eyes, she took in a deep, strangled breath.

She looked for Nasaphael, finding him curled up in the corner of her room, his back turned to her, his wings transforming from the beautiful silvery wings he once had into something monstrous. After a moment of uncertainty, she called out to him. He didn't respond, and that is when she heard his sobbing.

"I have betrayed you, Hannielle," He said after a long pause. "I have condemned us both," His voice was choked as he struggled to talk through his tears.

She went to him and knelt down behind him, and placed her hand on his back, between his transforming wings. He flinched when she did so, surprising her. His recoiling from her touch brought on fresh tears of her own, the pain coalescing with that of Nasaphael's to form an oubliette of despair in her soul.

"I don't want you to see me like this," he said between sobs, his voice deepening into a voice that sounded much lower and somewhat fierce. Selena looked down at her hand on his back, horrified to see that her own skin was turning from a healthy pink to the rotten color of diseased flesh.

Hearing her cry out in alarm, Nasaphael turned his head slightly in her direction. Gone was his angelic beauty, replaced with a darkness that stole the light of his purity, replacing it with the contortions of the Damned.

"You're transforming now too. It's all because of me, because I couldn't stay away from you. I'm so sorry," He threw his head back and wailed, a horrifying sound of despondency and torment, laced with a growl so horrifying it froze Selena's heart for several beats.

"No, it isn't your fault, Nasaphael, my love," She said after she had taken a moment to let his wails fade. "It is I who have condemned us both with my selfish longing for what should have stayed unobtainable." Selena bent her head in shame, doing her best not to sob uncontrollably. "I risked damnation for us both. I promised you that I would remember you how you were, but I will love you no matter what form you take. You have my heart; you have not betrayed me. You came when I called for you, in my most desperate moment. If you had not come, I would have killed myself, damning myself all the same. At least now I have you, and you will always have me."

He turned towards her, hope in his amber, elliptical eyes. His once smooth skin was marred by flesh colored scales, his once beautiful mouth now a thinly lipped slash in his face. His ears curved into points, the ends tufted with black hair.

Selena placed her now greyed hand to his cheek, her love for him not deterred by his transformation. Here was a being that had risked his very soul to make her happy, willing to be cast into the bowels of Hell come the time when Gabriel sounded his trumpet. If ever there was love, was it not this? How could he think she would forsake him, the only one who had ever loved her?

"All is not lost, my love," She told Nasaphael,"For you and I still have each other. We have an eternity together now, whether it is on this Earth, or in the caverns of Hell. That is more than I ever had in this cruel world, and a more honest love than I had with our Creator. As long as we are together, we will be alright."

Nesaphael opened his arms to her, and she fell into them, once more feeling safe within his embrace. They stayed in each other's arms as their transformations continued, leaving all hope of redemption behind them, certain that their love would see them through any man made or celestial form of Hell. They would be together forever, no longer alienated and alone, and that was worth all innocence lost.

12 GRAINS by Michael Young

...8...9...10...11...12.

The grains of rice dropped from their dispenser, collecting like a pile of tiny pearls in the center of the dish. Minnie took a deep breath and brought the hollow plastic chopsticks onto the dish, and counted each grain again. She counted them a third time to be absolutely sure. There were exactly twelve. A month ago she'd gotten careless and allowed another grain to sneak into the pile stuck to another. It didn't do any permanent damage, but it was excruciatingly painful and had thrown her metabolism out of whack. Her body had just started to settle down again, and she wasn't taking chances.

Minnie stood just under five feet tall and weighed barely enough to keep the Earth's gravity working on her. Her skin draped over her bones like a loose coat thrown over a coat rack. Hardly a cell of fat showed on her whole body, and her stringy muscles barely managed the job of moving her slight frame. She wore a thin, white lab coat, and her head was topped with a circular cap, under which sprouted a stringy crop of mousy brown hair.

Like most people, she kept a canister of medical nanites on her person to act as a first response against broken bones. Unfortunately for her, this was almost an everyday occurrence.

What she lacked in physical prowess, she made up in spirit. She always rose before sunrise, and only retired when her body gave out. The meticulous, unending work anchored her, giving her little time to dwell on her weakness or the bleakness of her predicament.

She gingerly picked the grains up one by one and placed them on the tip of her tongue. She held each one in her mouth for a moment, savoring the bland taste. It was all she had.

Once the last grain had disappeared into her mouth, she glanced down at her wrist and pressed a button on the plastic watch. The timer reset so that the luminous numbers once again read 12 hours and began their march down to 0. She nodded in resignation. It was just another round of the Rule of Twelve: twelve grains every twelve hours.

Their research station, designated Station Topaz, stood in the middle of the vast desert that had once been the Midwestern United States, and conducted essential research into getting plants to grow in radiation-contaminated soil. For years, Minnie's labors produced few results, until just this week. A bed of roses she had been cultivating in the station's greenhouse bloomed, giving her a much-needed glimpse of hope. Expectantly, she had minced some of the roses and created a solution which she applied to the rest of greenhouse, earnestly hoping that this success was not just a lucky fluke.

She and Dr. Avery, a brilliant scientist and her sole human companion at the station, had nearly danced around all week. He had smiled more than Minnie had seen him do in years, and they had filled the long hours with happy conversation of what this breakthrough could mean for them and for the other stations scattered throughout the world.

Minnie frowned at an obnoxious beeping sound trying to grab her attention.

What now?

"Excuse me, ma'am," a synthesized human voice asked, interrupting her thoughts. "I think there is something on the display that you should see."

Minnie turned around to face the voice and saw her slender assistant robot ABE standing nearby. He stood about her height with a humanoid body, but a thin, square screen where the head should be. He was fond of changing the face on the display to reflect his moods. Right now, the display showed the face of a worried old woman with deep wrinkles and dark bags under her eyes.

"ABE, I wasn't expecting you. You don't usually leave the lower levels." ABE nodded and changed his face to a young boy instead. "That's true, but I think you need to see this. It's about Adam."

Minnie wrinkled her brow, "Jones or Zimmerman?"

"Jones. We're not getting any vital signs." Minnie's heart froze. In all her years here, she had feared this would happen. Her voice rose slightly, and she tried to hide the hint of panic there. "Why didn't the alarms sound?"

ABE adopted a thoughtful look. "It is uncertain, ma'am. It's possible that the sensors have experienced a malfunction. I discovered a discrepancy in our power usage when I ran my daily tests, and figured it must mean that a system had gone offline." ABE paused for only a moment before continuing, his voice earnest. "Ma'am, you need to get down there right now. I am not permitted to open the capsule."

Minnie wrinkled her eyebrows ,"Why can't Dr. Avery do it? He has clearance too."

"He is away on business and will not return for some time. Do you have reservations about going down there?" the robot asked.

"Well, it's just…just—" She stopped, regained her composure and continued, "It's just that I've never been down there. I don't know what to expect. It's not my job to that sort of thing anyway. Wouldn't Dr. Avery really be better? I mean, it's probably nothing."

The robot's face changed to the face of a serious looking principal with jowled cheeks and a bad comb over.

"Miss Minnie, I hardly need to remind you what's at stake here. Dr. Avery has not yet returned from visiting Ruby Station. He is attempting to duplicate the results of the formula you concocted from the roses at another station."

Minnie gritted her teeth and struggled for another suitable excuse. She had been so engrossed in her success that morning, that she had forgotten the doctor was not due to return until late that evening. Finding herself without ammunition, she gave in. The robot was right.

She glided over to the far wall, opened a panel and stared at the elevator compartment with narrowed eyes before stepping inside. She fastened straps across her chest, shaking her head, and the door closed automatically. She pressed her hand against the wall, which lit up at her touch. She cleared her throat and forced herself to give the command. "Adam's Chamber, sub-basement five."

The compartment shot down the tower at dizzying speed, whisking her into the basement levels. The tower was nearly as large below the surface as above, and though it had once been brimming with workers and scientists, she now had only Dr. Avery and the robots for company. Though some of them had fallen prey to the harsh living conditions and disease, many people had simply left for what they had deemed more important or promising projects.

The elevator slid to a halt and the door swung open, revealing a darkened corridor. She stepped out, and a line of dim overhead lights flicked on. She walked down the hall as quickly as her brittle legs could take her, and when she reached the end, she found it opened into an enclosed alcove.

In the room lay two coffin-sized metal capsules encased in glass. Between them sat a computer terminal and a collection of medical monitoring equipment. Minnie approached the screen and scanned it. Nothing appeared to be amiss. She pressed a few more buttons and the glass coverings retracted. The capsules were completely smooth except for a label. "Jones" and "Zimmerman."

She knelt beside the capsule marked Jones and checked the smaller display which monitored the vital signs of the man inside. Her heart caught in her throat. All of the displays were completely blank. She paused for a moment and craned her head to one side. A muffled sound like a man talking came from within the capsule. She called out in shock, "Hello, is anyone in there? Can you hear me?"

When no one answered and the noise continued, she whirled about to the terminal, frantically giving the command to open the capsule. It did not budge. She pressed the key again and again, her fragile fingers bruising from the strain.

"Come on," she willed. "Why doesn't anything work around

here?"

Minnie clamped her eyes shut and imagined the consequences of her failure. Dr. Avery had spoken to her at length about how important the Adams were to the survival of their race. She would not be the one responsible for letting their last hope slip away just because she was too weak to do what was necessary.

Grunting, she pushed with both arms against the lid of the capsule. Her spindly arms stood no chance against the heavy lid. She took a deep breath and threw her entire body weight against the lid. A sickening crack as a stab of pain shot through her hand. Probably broken again. With a moan, she worked at her belt to free a canister that kept the nanites she could use to triage the break. With her good hand, she pressed her thumb against sensor strip and the cap of the canister flipped back to reveal an injection device. With a well-rehearsed motion, she stabbed it into her hand near the break, gritting her teeth against the pain as sweat beaded on her brow.

As she felt the nanites begin to work, she replaced the canister, sure she would need it again before the day was out. Tears forming in her eyes, she grappled with her free arm to bring herself upright. She pressed her ear against the side of the capsule and finally started to understand the mysterious sounds coming from within.

"I am Adam number 10, designation Jones. I was placed here during the final years of the 21st century when scientists discovered a moon-sized object on a direct trajectory with Earth. Plans were made to destroy the mass or move it with the aid of spacecraft. However, it was quickly determined that it was not going to collide with the Earth. Instead, the object fell into orbit around the earth, becoming a second moon."

The story brought back the stories her parents had told her before they had died during a mercenary raid. They had called it "The Emerald Moon" because of its strange green coloring. Its effect, however, was anything but beautiful. The moon showered the earth with lethal doses of radiation, effectively ending her parents' way of life and leaving their children with a tainted legacy.

Minnie's pained expression turned to one of surprise. It was the video that was supposed to run when Adam came out of his hibernation state to make sure those bringing him out were current on Adam's mission. But with no vitals, there was no reason it should be playing. The recording continued.

"Billions died across the globe from radiation sickness, starvation, and the resulting civil unrest. The nations of the world scrambled again to deal with the problem. An international squadron of spacecraft launched a massive attack on the moon, blasting it apart with hundreds of nuclear missiles. They planned to then use other ships to tow away the debris into space but failed at the attempt. The moon's destruction released an immense wave of radiation from the moon's core that incinerated the entire fleet in seconds. The debris fell to the Earth, causing rampant destruction."

Minnie winced. Vivid scenes of the wreckage that had served as her childhood home flashed through her mind. The Spartan quarters had barely kept out the cold and the predators.

"The explosion also released a message in an alien tongue picked up by receptors all across the world. The message, however, faded in importance in the following days as the world situation declined. Faced with the fact that the radiation would remain, scientist and governments then turned their efforts to the preservation of those left. They constructed massive facilities where the inhabitants would be safe from the radiation's effects. Unfortunately, by this time, the world's food supply had been irreversibly tainted, and the soil rendered unable to produce new crops. Extinction appeared certain, until a brilliant scientist, Dr. Laura Brightman, of Oxford University discovered a radical solution. Through genetic manipulation, she created a strain of rice plant that could produce a limited supply of food even in the contaminated soil. In addition, her research team discovered a process through which the human metabolism could be altered so that a person could survive by eating only a small amount of rice. Together, the discoveries promised a fledgling hope for survival."

Minnie smiled in spite of herself. Her mother had talked of Dr. Brightman almost as much and as highly as her own grandmother.

"The human race divided itself from that time forward. Some

accepted the treatment and entered the safe havens. Other refused it and most of them perished in the barren wasteland of the outside world. Still others salvaged what they could and took to the stars in colony ships in the hope of founding another settlement."

"In anticipation of a day in which mankind might return to its original state, each facility was entrusted with two 'Adams', people harboring the antidote to bring human metabolism back to normal, who would be kept in hibernation until the proper time. You are one of these people, and if you have been awoken, then that time has, at last, arrived."

A sudden beeping noise from behind her broke her attention. Startled, she spun around to see that the overhead screen displayed ABE's face.

Minnie exhaled in exasperation. Apparently part of ABE's programming led him to butt in at the worst times. He now looked like a mortician with a drab, sorrowful expression on his face." Miss Minnie, I am anxiously awaiting your report. What is happening?"

Scarcely able to catch her breath, she rambled out an explanation of what she had found and added. "The recording's playing now, and I can't detect any vitals. We need to contact Dr. Avery. He would want to know about this."

ABE bobbed his head." Yes, I think this warrants a legitimate emergency. I will send a communication to Ruby Station and route it down to you. Standby."

The screen went blank and then flashed a logo of a green crescent on a background of blue coupled with the words Ruby Station. The word "standby" flashed briefly across the screen, followed by a man's face. His face had the same gaunt appearance as Minnie's. He had identical sunken cheeks, eyes, and pallid skin. His limp hair had long since turned gray and hung in tufts about his wrinkled head. He wore a thin lab coat and carried a handheld computer into which he was entering information. "This is Doctor Menze. With whom am I speaking?"

"This is Minnie from Topaz Station. I need to speak to Dr. Avery right away. It's an emergency."

The wrinkles on Dr. Menze's brow sunk even deeper, "Dr.

Avery? I have not seen him for some time. To my knowledge, he isn't here."

"What?" Minnie gasped, "Are you sure? ABE told me he was going to visit you. He had a formula I developed that he was going to test with you." Minnie felt her already high heart rate spiraling to a dangerous staccato.

Dr. Menze shrugged." I'm sure I would have noticed if he had been here. He promised me a couple months ago that he would make a trip out here some time to assist in our analysis of a meteorite from the Emerald Moon, but I haven't heard back from him since. It's a shame because the meteorite contains strange, alien writing on the surface and is embedded with circuitry. We are even thinking that it's possible that the moon was manufactured by intelligent beings, though how and why—"

As fascinating as this prospect was, Minnie had more immediate problems. "Dr. Menze," she interrupted, her voice rising in pitch. "I think at least one of our Adams has been compromised. He's not showing any vital signs and I cannot open the capsule. What should I do?"

Her brows came down over the bridge of her nose as she pushed her index finger against her pursed lips, waiting for his response.

Dr. Menze looked like he had just been punched hard in the stomach, "Oh, this is terrible. You've got to get that capsule open. Have you checked the other capsule?"

Minnie shook her head." No, but you're right, I should check to see if he's okay. What do I do if they don't open? I think I broke my hand trying to budge the first one. I've got the nanites working on it, but I probably shouldn't try again. There's only so much they can do."

Dr. Menze groaned. "Oh, I can't believe this is happening again," he muttered. "It can't be a coincidence."

Minnie arched her thin eyebrows, and snaked her good arm around her stomach, clutching it tightly."What do you mean? Has this happened before?"

Dr. Menze nodded gravely. "I'm surprised Dr. Avery hasn't told you. I let him know about it myself. I think people would start to panic if the word got out, but it is happening across the world. Most of the Adams have gone missing, one by one. Yours may be the last ones we have."

"Missing?" Minnie asked, the twelve grains in her stomach churning menacingly. "Not dead, but missing? How can that be?"

Dr. Menze shook his head sadly. "I don't know, but I it might not make any difference. There has been no positive news in some time now. I'm afraid Dr. Brightman's program, inspired as it is, is headed toward disaster. We must simply make do with what time we have left." His voice trailed off, and his eyes lowered in resignation. He paused, and then looked up again. "I will make some calls of my own to see if I can locate Dr. Avery. In the meantime, see if you can secure the other Adam. Extra security precautions might be in order."

She thanked him and closed the communication. Darkness clouded around her vision, a sinister anxiety that threatened to drown the little hope she had fostered for so long.

She shot up and waved her arm as if shooing a wasp. "No. There's an explanation, and we still have another Adam." If Dr. Avery hadn't arrived, it probably just meant trouble with his aircraft, which happened often enough. She sighed and turned towards the other capsule. "Extra security precautions, huh?" she muttered. "Why couldn't they have told us about those before this happened?"

She turned and pressed the button to operate the other capsule. It creaked and groaned, but did not open. She winced as pain lanced through her arm. She tried, again and again, to convince the stubborn capsule to open, and finally raised her good hand to strike it. She stopped herself at the last moment, thinking that the last thing she needed was another broken hand.

She turned back to the communication unit and dialed up to the observation deck where ABE would be waiting. The robot's face filled the screen. "Miss Minnie, what have you found?"

"Oh, it's dreadful," Minnie blurted. "The capsules won't open and Dr. Menze said that Dr. Avery—" She stopped suddenly as a wave of static washed over the screen. She caught only snatches of ABE's response, and she continued calling to the screen as it flickered and died. The already dim lights dimmed even further, and the air in the room took on a sudden chill.

A violent shudder ripped through her body, and suddenly, all she could think about was getting out of the basement. She scrambled back down the hall, feeling the room press down in on her. The elevator loomed before her, but before she could reach it, the doors swung open and a dark figure strode out. Minnie let out a screech and instinctively backed away. The figure stepped into the light and Minnie sighed with relief. "Oh, ABE, it's you. How did you get here so...?"

She stopped as she noticed ABE's face. Blank. Goosebumps stood up on the back of her neck. He had never gone without a face.

Suddenly, two bright, narrow eyes flashed on ABE's face screen. They hovered in the darkness like twin match flames, casting an eerie glow down the corridor. Minnie stood frozen as ABE raised his arm, revealing a wicked, spiked club in his hand. "I'm sorry Miss Minnie. I can't let you leave."

"What do you mean, ABE? You're scaring me!"

"He needs the blood," the robot droned. "He's waiting for it now." ABE advanced, the creaking of his joints echoing ominously off the smooth walls.

He's gone crazy! How did this happen? There's nowhere to hide—nowhere to go!

Minnie turned and ran. ABE lumbered in pursuit, swinging his bludgeon behind her. Sweat dripped down over Minnie's eye and her hand throbbed as she bolted back, quickly reaching the dead end that housed the capsules.

She ducked behind a capsule, trying to provide some defense from her attacker's blows. ABE's strikes flew to both sides of her, landing much too close to be avoided for long.

She feinted left, waited for the next blow to land, and then propelled herself right in a desperate attempt for the exit. After only a few steps, she tripped and fell hard in front of the computer terminal. She cried out and raised her hands to ward off the killing blow, which in her condition, would be anyone that landed. The bulk of the robot loomed in her vision, its arm poised to strike. Minnie tried to close her eyes but found that she couldn't wrest her gaze away from the weapon.

The club whistled through the air but suddenly flew off course as a massive form tackled the robot from behind. Sounds of a struggle ensued, grinding metal and flying sparks, and then silence. A minute later, Minnie sensed a figure huddling over her.

"Are you okay?" her rescuer asked. "Don't worry. That thing won't be bothering you anymore." He held up one hand, displaying the severed screen that had once been ABE's head. Minnie stared up through blurred vision.

"Who are you?" she whispered.

"My real name is Paul Newburg, but I guess I've been going by Adam Jones lately." Minnie's eyes began to clear and she saw a brown haired man with blue eyes and a slight smile. A single one of him amounted to at least three of Minnie. His arms and legs appeared like barrels in comparison to hers, and his face radiated health and energy. He wore a dark blue jumpsuit that hugged his muscular body, "Can you stand?" he asked.

"No," she managed, "I don't think so." He leaned down and lifted her up. She could feel the blood on his hands from where he had been wounded fighting ABE. It seeped through her lab coat and onto her skin. Strangely, the blood tingled on contact, sending a feeling of warmth throughout her body. He carried her down the hallway and she could feel his warm, rapid breath against her face. They reached the elevator, and Minnie groaned, feeling more uncomfortable than she could ever remember.

Adam lay Minnie down, stood and opened a hatch on the wall next to the elevator. Without a word, he extracted a roll of bandages and a tube of salve and set to work dressing Minnie's wounds.

"How did you know how to do that that?" Minnie asked in surprise, "You've been hibernating for…"

"…Two hundred twenty-three years and fifty-five days? I know. We weren't just sleeping in there. The device sent us information through dreams almost every day. I actually know quite a bit more than I did before I went to sleep, including how to treat a variety of injuries. It was like being force-fed facts for 200 years."

A sudden new sensation gripped Minnie. She wrenched and writhed in Adam's arms, clutching her stomach. "My stomach…oh, I'm so…hungry!"

Adam wrinkled his brow. "How long has it been since you ate?" She gestured at the timer on her arm, "I ate only an hour ago. I shouldn't need to eat for 11 hours."

"Hang in there," Adam said. "We'll find you something."

She groaned pitifully as a new round of pain gripped her. "Go to the observation deck. There's food there."

Handling the controls like a natural, he navigated the elevator to the correct floor. The door slid open and they returned to Minnie's familiar territory. "Take me to the rice dispenser...there against the left wall."

He took her over and placed her mouth directly under the opening. He cradled her in one arm and dispensed rice into her mouth with the other. He started with the twelve grains, but she gestured for him to continue. He pressed the button again and again, dropping grain after gleaming grain into her mouth where she swallowed them greedily. She nodded, spurring him on for several minutes, and Adam could hardly press the button fast enough to satisfy her ravenous appetite.

When at last she signaled for a stop, she had nearly depleted the entire store of the container. She sighed in contentment.

"You've really never had a cheeseburger, have you?" Adam asked. She looked puzzled, and Adam waved the comment aside. "Never mind. Just tell me one thing. What's it like out there? Have things really gotten better?"

Unable to open her eyes, she simply gestured towards the far wall. "Open the shades. You'll see. It's the blue lever over there."

Adam set Minnie down on a bench and walked over to the lever. He rested his hand on it, hesitating. "I'm not sure I'm ready to see this."

"Just do it," she urged him. "You wouldn't be here if you weren't supposed to be."

He took a deep breath and thrust the lever down. The shutters flew off the windows that formed the walls of the room. Dusty, sickly sunlight streamed in, revealing a vast, lifeless landscape in every direction. Adam sank to his knees. "Why did they wake me? How did this happen! The world isn't ready yet!" He stared off dejectedly into the distance. "Guess I better learn to like rice," he muttered.

Minnie joined him and noticed a tiny black speck on the horizon. Minnie blinked and rubbed her eyes, thinking that it might be a mirage. The speck continued to grow, however, forming into the sleek shape of a black aircraft. As it continued to approach, Adam turned to Minnie, "They're headed towards us. Who that might be?"

He described the craft and Minnie's eyes lit up. "That's Dr. Avery's craft! He'll know what to do." She smiled weakly and Adam grimaced at the gnawing feeling of doubt forming at the pit of his stomach.

"I don't know if he'll be happy to see me," Adam said. "Why don't you explain to him first?"

Minnie nodded. "I'll do that. Don't worry. But maybe close that and let me explain before he sees you."

Adam shut the blinds and retreated to a dark corner of the room to remain hidden. As Minnie walked toward the center of the room, she tripped and fell on her side, landing up against a long shelf. She tried to rise but found her stomach cramping so violently she could barely breathe.

The ship approached and landed, and the elevator opened a few minutes later. A willowy man, all angular bones and billowing white hair, stepped out. Thick spectacles covered the top part of his face, and a subtle, satisfied smile peeked out through a voluminous beard. Minnie tried to call out but was unable to speak loud enough to catch Dr. Avery's attention.

The doctor clutched a small parcel under his arm. He stepped directly to a communication port and keyed in a rapid succession of digits. A man with a rotund, ruddy face appeared on the screen. The man on the screen laughed jovially."Dr. Avery, you look terrible. Are you ready to join us?"

The doctor nodded enthusiastically. "Oh, yes, sir. I tire of this base existence. I have enjoyed the morsels you sent me, and I am ready for more. I have just returned from completing the tasks you gave me." The doctor pressed a button and a larger screen dropped from the ceiling, revealing a large group of portly men and women, draped in flowing dark robes of various colors.

"Do you have the blood?" a woman in a scarlet robe asked. "It's becoming rarer these days. You know we can't let you in without it."

Dr. Avery averted his gaze, and ran a hand over the back of his neck, "Well, I have some of it. One of the Adams's. I am going to check on the other one right now. My robot should have taken care of him and the remainder of my staff."

The members of the group nodded to each other. "You had better," the woman said. "We will have a transport there in 15 minutes. If you do not have it in time, we will leave you behind permanently. Is that clear?"

Dr. Avery nodded, swallowing hard. "Clear."

He ended the transmission and stroked his long beard. before reaching up to punch in a command into the computer terminal. Nothing happened. He punched it in again. Still nothing. He stamped his foot and slapped his palm against the screen. "Where is that cursed robot?"

Silent tears ran down Minnie's face. The man who had cared for her and worked with her for so many years had ordered her to be killed. She attempted to bring herself upright and nearly fell forward as she was blindsided by a wave of dizziness. She steadied herself and then attempted to stand. The dizziness rushed back in force, and she fell hard to one knee. She braced for the pain, but felt only a momentary discomfort, though her stomach cramps remained. The sound altered Dr. Avery, who wheeled on her, his face contorted. "Minnie, you're here…I mean, of course, you're here."

Minnie scowled. "Where are you going, Dr. Avery? Who are those people?"

Dr. Avery adopted a placating smile. "My dear Minnie, they are simply new friends. They have discovered a cache of untainted food and a way to restart the human metabolism. They live a higher form of life, and they've invited us to join their paradise."

Minnie's gaze remained level. "You're lying! You sent ABE to kill me! Why?"

Dr. Avery pursed his lips in thought. "You're a clever girl, Minnie, always have been. The problem is, you're a bit too clever."

He set down the parcel he had been carrying under his arm, slid his hand into his lab coat, and filled a slender syringe with amber liquid from a vial in his coat. He advanced on Minnie will a sad smile. "Don't worry, Minnie, you won't be forgotten. My time here with you was quite enjoyable and I'll think of you every time I sit down to a succulent feast."

Minnie's blood rushed fast through her veins, and she could feel a new energy flowing into her muscles. She struggled and managed to rise to her feet. She glanced around frantically and found a heavy book lying on a table to her left. She reached for it and Dr. Avery laughed. "Come now. Don't be ridiculous. We both know you can't lift it."

It had probably never been lifted in her lifetime. She grasped it anyway. Dr. Avery advanced and Minnie's fingers tightened around the book, knowing that throwing it might either save her life or break her shoulder. With all her might, she flung the book at Dr. Avery. It soared through the air and hit him square in the chest, sending him sailing backward. Dr. Avery crumpled with a sickening crack, clutching his ribs.

At the same instant, Adam leaped from the shadows, hurling himself at the wounded doctor. The doctor lay sprawled out on his back, still wielding the syringe. He struck up with it and caught Adam squarely in the arm. Adam grunted in pain, clasped his arm and fell sideways to the floor.

Weakly, Dr. Avery reached back into his lab coat and withdrew another syringe. This he injected into his own arm. A shudder rippled through his body, and he rose to his feet, wheezing and clutching his chest. "I'll get you for that, you little worm!" he snarled. "Where I'm going, we'll use people like you for toothpicks."

Minnie, meanwhile, had ducked behind a counter, fumbling for a familiar drawer. She found it and felt an unexpected smile cross her face. Within a moment, a plan sprang into her mind, fully formed. "Please, Dr. Avery, do you really think I'm a threat to you? We've worked together for years—I-I thought you were my friend! Doesn't that mean something to you? My muscles may be weak, but my mind is razor sharp. I can help you. We can still find a cure for the land."

Dr. Avery scoffed, inching his way towards the sound of her voice. "I'm done looking for a cure you foolish child. Look around! There isn't one!"

"That's not true! Think of the formula from the roses. They're still alive. They're the most beautiful thing I've ever seen!"

"A fluke, nothing more," Dr. Avery said. "Face it. It's every man for himself now. If the world's going to end, why don't we make the best of what we have left? Too bad for you, I don't feel inclined to share. There'd be less to go around."

She had led Dr. Avery into the darkest part of the room, while scooting her way towards Adam and the doctor's parcel, which lay on a nearby table. Her eyes locked on the parcel, and she crept toward it. Suddenly, she heard Dr. Avery's voice directly behind her, and she panicked, sprinting forward and snatching the lightweight parcel, clasping it to her chest with her good arm. Dr. Avery emerged out of the darkness behind her, his eyes wild and hateful. She raised the parcel with both hands over her head, and Dr. Avery halted in his tracks. "Take another step and I'll smash it."

Dr. Avery's lips curled back in a snarl. "Don't even think about it. Minnie. I've worked too hard for that case. Put it down and I might just let you live."

Minnie shook her head defiantly. "You need this case don't you? When did they say they were going to be here? Ten minutes? Five? I bet they won't be pleased if don't have the— what was it? Ah, yes, blood. Adam Zimmerman's blood I'm guessing."

Dr. Avery's face softened, the color draining from it like water pressed out of a sponge. "Give me the case," he said calmly. "And I will let you go. We can forget this all happened. I'll give you all my research and you can take over the station. Isn't that what you always wanted? Just set it down, and I will be on my way to feast, and you can continue groping around in the dark, day after day toward a hopeless destination. We both get what we want."

Minnie considered this for a moment. "What about Adam Jones?" she asked. "What will you do to him?"

Dr. Avery glanced down at the fallen man between them. "I'm afraid he'll have to come with me. The dose of the drug I gave him would have killed you, but should only render him unconscious. The others were very insistent. We need all the blood we can possibly get."

Minnie winced and nodded her head. "Can I say goodbye to him first? He saved my life, and I at least want to thank him."

Dr. Avery pondered and then displayed his crooked teeth. "For the affection I still bear for you, I will allow it. I will prepare the docking station for the arrival of our guests. Make it quick."

His tongue ran over his lips as he picked up his case. "Oh, and don't try to run, Minnie. I've engaged all the security systems. You won't get very far."

Minnie followed him with her eyes as he disappeared into the elevator.

Taking advantage of Dr. Avery's absence, she stumbled to her desk and withdrew several vials she had filled that morning when sampling the roses. She then turned her attention to Adam. She bent down over him, still lying on the floor, and pressed the vials into his hands.

Her stomach knotting, she placed a wispy hand on his forehead and felt its heat before leaning down to whisper in his ear, letting him in on a little secret she had not wished to discuss in front of Dr. Avery. He barely moved but offered a subtle wink and a slight smile.

She walked over and met Dr. Avery when the elevator doors opened again. Two robots similar to ABE flanked him, both bulkier and better suited to hard labor. They trudged silently into the room and picked up Adam, hoisting him between them. "They are here," he announced. And they will not be kept waiting. The case, if you please."

Slowly, she reached out and offered it to Dr. Avery. He snatched the case and turned his back on Minnie. "Goodbye, Minnie. Enjoy your rice."

The elevator shut behind him and it shot down towards the docking station. A minute later, she walked over to the elevator and found the doors jammed. With a barely audible sigh, she turned around and walked over to open the shutters. Once sunlight spilled back into the room, she approached the observation windows to watch the ship's departure.

She sat calmly in a chair and stared out into the distance, watching the ship take off and disappear. She waited for hours, staring at the same spot. She did not rise to eat, though she could feel the hunger pains returning. She knew that she was trapped, but this did not concern her. Though she had not known him long, she felt instinctively that she could trust Adam.

As the day passed into twilight, a distant speck appeared on the horizon. It shot towards the tower at a surprising speed, followed quickly by another speck. Slowly she rose and approached the window. She squinted at the shape, not daring to hope that things had actually gone according to plan. As the shape drew nearer, however, she confirmed her suspicions. It was the same ship that had picked up Dr. Avery hours before.

The communication screen next to her flared to life, revealing Adam's frantic face. "Minnie, you don't happen to have anything that could...you know...take care of my uninvited guest?"

Minnie's eyes frantically scanned the rows of levers, buttons, and screens, wracking her brain for anything that could help. "No, there's nothing here! This is a science station, not a military base."

Adam's image flickered and shook as a round of weapon fire rocked the ship. "Well, keep looking. This little rust bucket won't stand up much longer."

Minnie bit her lip as she choked down her fear. Her vision swam and her hands shuddered like brittle leaves clinging to dead branches. She scanned the control panels again: the lights, the weather sensors, the crane...

The crane! She looked at the display and saw that its rusty jaws still grasped a derelict aircraft. Quickly, she switched off all the lights in the tower except for one. She then took over the crane's controls and coaxed the neglected machine to life. "Adam, can you lure your pursuer towards that light? I'll take care of it."

"Can do!" he replied. Minnie watched tensely as Adam lured the enemy ship towards the lighted floor. His pursuers launched a volley of missiles at Adam's craft, forcing him to take evasive action away from the intended area.

Minnie clenched her jaw and tested the lever that controlled the rotation of the crane. The crane groaned in protest but finally budged as Minnie coaxed the lever even further forward. She held her breath, as Adam activated the ship's decoy flares. The missiles swerved wide and exploded in mid-air.

Adam's voice crackled over the line. "Sorry about that, Minnie! A little turbulent out here, but let's try that again."

Adam brought the ship through a tight vertical loop and released a volley of his own weapon's fire. The nimble enemy ship fled and regrouped in a matter of seconds. Adam wove back and forth, narrowly avoiding his enemy's renewed assault.

In a terrible second, Adam's ship took a direct hit on its left wing, sending his craft careening off course. Minnie gasped and nearly let go of the lever.

"Adam! Pull up! You're right in their sights!"

Either the communications had been fried by the last shot, or Adam had chosen to ignore the warning. He maintained a wobbly course, leading the enemy ship closer and closer to the appointed zone.

Minnie gripped the lever, her fingernails digging painfully into her skin. She wanted to clench her eyes shut to block out the scene of destruction that she was sure loomed only seconds away.

She blinked hard once, steadied her nerves, and focused on the approaching ships. The enemy ship unleashed another volley, and Minnie knew she had only once chance to save her newfound friend.

She jammed the lever forward and swung the crane around from the other side of the tower. The crane's arm flew, carting the wreck with it towards the enemy ship. An instant before impact, the enemy pilot dove sharply to avoid a collision. The pilot scrambled to level himself, but overcorrected and slammed into the side of the tower, vanishing in a magnificent explosion.

Adam's voice crackled back on the line. "Minnie, that was incredible! It's people like you who've kept this race alive." He stayed silent a moment and then continued, "I'll be there in five minutes if this old clunker holds together."

A few minutes later, Adam stumbled from the elevator, looking a bit worse for wear, but breathing. "Well, that was a bit of bumpy ride, but it worked. They took the bait. I played dead until we arrived, and then put a well-deserved fist in each of their faces. They were a bit sturdier than you, but nothing that I couldn't handle. After that, I threw them out, commandeered the ship and high-tailed it back here. Thank goodness for that sleep training. This thing has more buttons than an officer's uniform."

"And the case?" Minnie asked.

Adam grinned in satisfaction. "As I said, they took the bait. I'm sure they'll find out soon that I switched out my blood samples for the rose samples you gave me."

Minnie's eyes perked up at the mention of her roses. "Which reminds me—I need to go check on their progress. Come with me!"

Together, they took the larger elevator down to the greenhouse. Nervously, they opened the door to reveal a room full of flowers: roses, daisies, carnations and a glorious assortment of others. Minnie gasped, her hand flying to her gaping mouth. "They...they grew! They all grew!"

Adam smiled and placed a careful arm around Minnie's slim shoulders, "Perhaps the menu doesn't look so bland after all. Do you think we could figure out how to grow potatoes?"

Minnie shot him a confused look. "Potatoes?"

Adam sighed, "Trust me, they're incredible. Come on; let's see what we can scrounge up from storage." The together they left for the storeroom and could hardly wait to see what they could encourage to grow.

Adam placed an arm around Minnie and led her into the elevator. The doors slid closed and the elevator shot downwards. In the greenhouse, new sprouts pushed through the soil, emerging into a world of new-found promise.

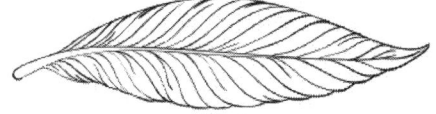

ˈRESSURECTION GIRL by Mira Domsky

We're all zombies, really. At least, that's what I tell myself as I set up my folding chair against the wall of the cemetery. We're all just going through the motions of our lives without actually living them, swimming through the ache of surviving each day. And when someone asks, 'how are you?' You give them the acceptable, expected response: 'I'm fine. Doing better, actually.' Maybe it's just me.

I step onto the folding chair. It gives me the height I need to vault the wall, carefully setting my hands between the vertical spikes designed to discourage the exact thing I'm doing. Well, maybe not exactly what I'm doing. I land on the grass on the other side of the wall with a thump that I feel in all of my joints, all the way up the scar on my arm. Then I stand and begin walking. Even in the dark, I know where I'm going. I've been there more times than I can count in the last 3 years. "Don't do this to yourself. It won't work. And even if it does, it won't be what you want. It's time to move on, Steph. To really move on." That was what my mother said when she caught me with my great grandmother's book of home remedies. She snatched the book out of my hands and went to pack it up with the rest of Grammy's things. That was what everyone was always saying. 'It's time to move on.' 'It's time to start dating.' 'He's dead.' 'It's time, it's time.' Whatever. It's like they think I can just flip a switch, just decide to get over it. 'Just stop loving Harry.' But I

can't. It doesn't matter that he's dead. It doesn't matter if
Grammy's recipe works. He's still the one who holds me in my
dreams, still the one whose name I taste on my lips in the dark.
How can I not try?
It's dark in the cemetery. They lock the iron gates at night,
and there aren't any lamps. The ambient glow from the city and
the cold starlight above me is all I have to see with, but it's
enough for me to find the paved road that winds through the
plots. Everything is a light gilded shadow. But the moon will
rise soon. A crescent moon, waxing towards full. I must do this
in the moonlight, as it rises, and grows.
I don't have any trouble finding Harry's grave. I can't read
the headstone, but I know which one is his as much by feel as by
following the road and counting stones. He was 27 when our car
crashed, and he will never be another day older. I woke up in the
hospital with a deep gash in my arm. He never woke up. We
were arguing in those final moments, and I can't even remember
what it was about. I never got to say I was sorry. I never got to
hold him again. I couldn't live with it then, and I can't now. He's
still sleeping here, under the ground, and I intend to wake him.
I kneel in the middle of his grave and glance up at the sky.
The moon is rising. It's time.
I pull the little pouch and the knife from my pocket. Inside
the pouch is the powder I prepared according to my
grandmother's "cookbook." I dip my hand in and begin
sprinkling the powder into the grass. I'm supposed to sing as I do
this, but it's as if I've forgotten every song I ever heard. I grope
through my brain and begin singing the first song I can hold
onto: "Happy Birthday." Perhaps it's appropriate, though my
voice is weak and uneven with emotion.
When the powder is gone I pick up the knife in one hand
and hold my palm open with the other. Then I remember, and
pull an alcohol wipe from my pocket. I swab my hand and the
knife, looking over my hand and trying to decide what the easiest
place to bandage will be. I can't believe I didn't think of this
beforehand. I'd thought of everything else. I decide on my left
index finger and press it to the blade before I can hesitate any
longer. My blood wells black and glittering in the moonlight and
drips into the grass. A shiver runs down my spine.

"Come home, Harry. Come home to me," I whisper. And then I wait.

\#

I wake up cold, soaked in winter dew, with my face in the grass. I'm curled up in a ball on Harry's grave, and the gray light of dawn feels bright. I sit up, stiff and sore, and touch the indentations the grass left on my cheeks. I turn to the grave searching for something, anything that might be different, but there's nothing. The grass is undisturbed except for where I was sleeping, and the headstone is unmoved. Nothing remains of my spell on the grass; no powder, not even a drop of blood. Silent tears drip down my face and as I push myself to standing I feel a sharp pain in my finger. I lift it to look, and see the cut I made last night. At least there's proof I tried to do something. I stand up and begin to trudge back to the wall.

I go home and go through the motions of showering and dressing for work automatically. The day passes in a blur, and I sleepwalk through it. At the end of my day, I don't even remember driving home. I sit in front of the TV, but I don't turn it on. I feel a gurgle in my stomach and wonder if I'm hungry. Why did I think it would work? Why?

A chill runs up my spine, and I grab a blanket from the arm of the couch. I look out the window at the deepening twilight and realize that the sun has set and the temperature must be dropping.

I wake up to the sound of knocking on my door. It's constant, one dull thud after another, and I have no idea what time it is. I wrap the blanket around myself, colder than ever, and go to the peephole. I can see the silhouette of the person outside, but not their face.

"Who is it?"

There's no answer.

"Who are you?" I ask again, my voice growing shriller.

"I... It's Harry." The voice is rough, barely recognizable, but I unlock the door and throw it open anyway. Harry is slouching in his muddy and torn burial suit. There's dirt on his gaunt and sunken face, and mud in his shaggy blonde hair too, but I can tell it's him. He's paler than he was, and his blue eyes are shot through with angry red and black veins, but it's him. It's him. I throw my arms around him and begin to sob.

"I'm so sorry! I'm so sorry about everything! I've needed you so much, and now you're here! Oh, thank God!" I wail into his shoulder. He stinks of rot and dirt and sulfur, but I don't care. He puts his arms around me hesitantly.

"God had nothing to do with this," he says. "It hurts."

I cry harder, but I don't let go, even when he peels back the blanket and bites my shoulder. It hurts, but not as much as losing him did so I grit my teeth against my screams. I feel the blood run down my shoulder as he tears at me. I feel him sucking on the blood, and hear him swallow. I gasp at the pain, but he holds me up, and tightens his arms around me.

"Thank you. That's what I think I needed," he says. "Can we go inside?"

Still crying, I let him in. I close the door behind him, and press a hand to my bleeding shoulder. He turns around.

"I don't know what's going on," he says.

"I brought you back," I say, running my eyes over him greedily. He's dirty, his face smeared with blood, and his hair disheveled. His eyes are sunk deep into the sockets, and they are much too dark.

"Let's go get cleaned up," I say heading for the bathroom. I draw a steaming bath, as I clean up the wound on my shoulder.

"I'm sorry," Harry says as he watches me disinfect the jagged bite. "I don't know why I did that. I just... I needed... I needed... Blood. I think. Your blood. Will you turn into a zombie now too? That's what happens in movies..."

"I don't think so," I say. "It's not like you have rabies, or got bitten by a rage infected monkey. You didn't get bitten by a monkey, did you?"

He smiles at that, and there's blood between his teeth.

"I don't think so."

"Good then. Come on, let's take a bath," I say. He smiles his bloody smile again.

In the tub, I clean him carefully. He's unearthly pale, a little leathery, and his skin is dried out. The left side of his chest is still a little caved in from the car accident, and I can feel the broken ribs as I help him wash. I find the head wound that killed him before the internal bleeding could when I wash his hair. Seeing him broken like this hurts, but it's a good hurt. At least he's here. I can touch him, talk to him. I tell him what has happened in the three years he's been dead. I think he looks pretty good for a three-year-old corpse.

As I dry him off, I start to shiver.

"You're cold," he says, and he pulls me into his arms to warm me. But he's not warm. I let him hold me, anyway. Tears sting my eyes.

"I don't think I can stay," he whispers into my hair.

"You have to," I reply, my face pressed against his broken ribs. "I brought you back because I needed you."

"But I'm getting hungry again," he says.

"I don't care," I say.

"I do. I don't want to."

I pull away from him and lead him by the hand back to the bedroom. For the first time in three years, I fall asleep in his arms. In the morning, as the sun filters through the blinds, I wake up next to a cold corpse. I try to shake him awake, but he's as stiff and unyielding as carved wood. He doesn't wake up.

I call in sick to work, and curl up next him again, molding my body against his. When I wake, it's late afternoon. I stare at the body in my bed. It still looks pretty good for a corpse, but there's a faint odor of death. I climb out of bed, silent tears running down my face. I grab a bag of pretzels and a half empty bottle of cake flavored vodka from the cabinet and proceed to finish both. I turn on the TV just to hear another human voice. My phone rings a few times, but I ignore it.

As darkness gathers outside I stare at the television, but everything is alcohol blurred and I don't know what I'm watching. Something with a laugh track I think. Who's the zombie now?

And then he sits down next to me on the couch like it's nothing. Like he hasn't been dead again all day. I wonder if I'm dreaming.

"Did you save any of that bottle for me? I could use a drink too," he says. I gape at him.

"You were dead all day..."

"And now it's night and I'm alive again. You mean you don't know how this works?"

"I don't know how it works. I skimmed the 'recipe,' but I

only got a picture of one page before my mother caught me." I squeeze my eyes shut. I'm too drunk to remember, or to be very reasonable. I feel him take the bottle from my hand.

"Damn," he says upon discovering that it's empty. I open my eyes and look up at him. His eyes are brilliantly blue in contrast with the red and black veins. I smile and lean forward for a kiss. He gives me a light, dry-lipped peck then leans to the side. He pulls the bandage off my arm and sinks his teeth into my shoulder again. It doesn't hurt as much this time, probably thanks to all the vodka. Vodka, making cannibalism easier for humans and zombies since 18-who-gives-a-fuck. I giggle.

Harry pulls away and looks at me with concern.

"What's so funny? I'm hurting you. I can't stop myself, and I wish I could. How is this funny?"

"Alcohol."

He nods.

"I'm glad I can be here with you. But I don't want to hurt you," he says.

"It's worth it," I say. And I mean it. As much as my arm hurts, living without him hurt more.

I let him take a few more bites, then go to the bathroom to clean up the blood and disinfect. I make popcorn and switch to drinking water. Eventually I fall asleep on the couch with him, watching late night sci-fi movies. At about 4 in the morning, I wake up and raise my head to look at him. In the dark, he looks almost as he did when he was alive.

"It's almost morning," he says.

"I know." I hug him all the harder for it. He still feels dry and stiff with none of the pliability of living flesh, but I don't care. I kiss him. His mouth tastes of my blood. He picks me up and carries me to the bedroom, where we kiss but do nothing more, until the sun rises. He fades away gradually, as if he's falling asleep, and I don't look at him once he stops moving.

My arm throbs horribly, as does my head, so I down a handful of ibuprofen and get in the shower. Today, I dress and go to work. My body protests, tired and aching from a hangover and the arm wound, but I'm too happy to let that keep me down. I feel whole again, despite the missing flesh on my arm.

Several of my coworkers comment that I look like death,

and maybe I should stay home and not share whatever disease I've contracted.

"I'm fine," I say and sit down in my cubicle to answer phones. Everything is fine until one of my co-workers catches me checking my bandages in the bathroom.

"Oh my god! What happened to you?"

"Oh, I... dog bite," I fumble for words, having nothing prepared.

"Did they get the dog?" she asks, stepping closer with her face screwed up in concern. Her name tag reads Rachel.

"I'm fine, really," I say. "It'll heal." Suddenly, I wonder how it's supposed to heal if Harry needs to chew on it every night. I wonder if I can buy him some raw hamburger or something.

"What does the doctor say?" Rachel asks.

"Um, he says that it looks worse than it is," I say, but I sound unsure even to myself. Rachel continues to look at me. I can see the wheels turning in her head.

"That doesn't look like a dog bite. . ." she says.

I shrug, pulling my jacket gingerly over my arm. Then I brush past the stunned woman back to my cubicle.

My supervisor catches me sleeping on my keyboard after lunch and writes me up. I down two cups of black, acrid coffee and another handful of ibuprofen and power through the end of my shift. On the way home I stop at the grocery store and buy a nice bloody steak, two potatoes, and green bean casserole supplies, hoping to be home in time to surprise Harry. Unfortunately, as I leave the grocery store I see the sun sink behind the mountains. I drive home in the red light of the dying sunset, and throw open the door to my apartment.

"Honey, I'm home!" I say. I set the groceries down. The apartment is silent. Cold fear grips my stomach and I search the apartment. He's gone. Where could he go? Why? Why would he leave! I realize I'm starting to hyperventilate but I can't stop, and then the tears start to burn in my eyes. The panic oozes out my pores. I run to the bathroom and vomit. I'm curled up in a ball trying to squeeze my body out of existence on the bathroom tile when I hear the front door close. I'm shocked out of my panic attack, and I lay still. Harry comes into the bathroom and finds me.

"Hey, what's wrong? What happened?" he asks.

"You... You... Left," I manage, sounding soggy. I blink. He looks... Bad. His cheeks look hollower, and there's a greenish tinge to his pale, leathery skin. Yet somehow his mouth looks almost pink.

"Only for about an hour. I'm here now," he says, kneeling beside me and reaching for me. He puts his arms around me, and he feels bonier than last night. I grip one of his hands, and notice how the blue veins stands out on the back. That's when I see the rust colored stain under his nails. ...And notice the smell of blood.

"Where did you go?" I ask, my voice low and quiet. I look up into his face.

"Just out. On an errand," he replies, looking away. His lips aren't pink; there's red dried in the cracks of his skin.

"You don't have errands. You're dead," I say. Now when he looks at me his eyes look like a windshield about to shatter there are so many red and black veins. They stand out against the dark blue irises, and shine with hurt. I've hurt the zombie's feelings. How odd.

"What errand?" I ask. He looks away again. Oh God. I did this. I called a man out of his grave because I couldn't live without him, but everyone knows how zombies work, even if the details are a little different in reality than in fiction.

"I was hungry."

"And what did you eat? Or maybe I should ask who?" I feel cold fear knot in my stomach, and hot jealousy knife through my chest. The logical part of my brain detaches itself from these reactions, telling me that they make no sense.

"No one. No one!" He shakes his head violently, but I know him and I know when he's lying. I pull out of his arms. The fear and the jealousy stomp on my logic like a bug.

"Who! WHO!"

"No one! No one you know!"

"You've been dead for three years; how do you know I don't know them?"

"You called me back! You brought me here! Did you think there wouldn't be a price?"

I stare at him, and for the first time since he came back, I think I'm actually seeing him for what he is, not who he was. I did this. I was okay paying the price with my own blood. My life was pain without him. What was a little blood, a pound of flesh? But someone else's blood? No, I couldn't. And if he'd still been alive, he wouldn't have. But this was not the man I'd known. Not anymore. That man was dead. Really and truly dead. So, who was this man kneeling beside me?

"Steph?" he asks. I shake my head and scoot far enough away to stand up.

"I have to go," says an unfamiliar voice, though it's coming out of my mouth. Harry lurches towards me. I dart around him and into the hallway. I grab my car keys and run out the door without bothering to lock it. As I back out of the driveway, he steps outside and watches me pull away.

I drive. It's dark and I don't think about where I'm going, I just drive on autopilot and panic. Some part of my mind knows what I need to do, where I need to go, so I'm only a little surprised when I pull into the driveway.

I knock on my mother's door and wait. It's only 8p.m., so she's still awake. My mother opens the door and looks me up and down. She presses her lips into a thin line, glances behind me, then pulls me inside.

"What happened?" she asks. She's afraid, but I can hear the blade-like edge of anger in her tone. I don't answer. I don't look at her.

"I need to see the cookbook," I mumble. Thirty years old, and I'm still afraid of my mother. Afraid to admit I did something wrong.

"Grammy's cookbook," she says, and it's not a question. I nod anyway.

"You knew better," she says. I nod again. She doesn't say another word, just turns her back on me and walks down the hall. I hear the attic trapdoor open, and slump over to a kitchen chair to wait. She comes back with the book wrapped in brown paper and sealed with red wax. She sets it in front of me on the kitchen table, but I don't look up at her.

"Will you use it to do the right thing, now?" she asks.

"Yes," I whisper.

"I'm going to do dishes now," she says with all the warmth of a glacier, and steps away.

I tear the brown paper and open the book, leafing through to the page I'd snapped a quick photo of 2 weeks ago, hoping no one would catch me. Then I turn to the page behind it. My eyes scan over the faded text, and the smeared hand-written notes in the margin. Phrases like "corpse will require several ounces of your blood daily," and "Under no circumstance should corpse be allowed the blood of others" stand out. The gist of it is this: My blood had been used to raise Harry. As long as he was allowed to slowly eat me to death, he would remain in this half-life. If I starved him, he would turn to eating others, and decay into a rabid animal madness not unlike the zombies seen in horror films. The book recommends putting all corpses back in their graves within a few days of raising them to prevent long term bodily damage. Oh joy. And at the bottom of the page is what I need: the way to send him back to his grave. Even now, the thought sends a sharp pain through my stomach and squeezes the air from my lungs, but then I remember the nameless person he most likely killed. The haunted look in his bleeding eyes. It is only a shadow of him that remains. He's gone, and has been for a long time. This thought is cold and heavy, but it settles in gently. He is gone. I take a deep breath, re-read the instructions, and close the book. Then I stand and grab my car keys. I hug my mother quickly and head out the door. She calls something after me, but my mind is elsewhere, already generating a list of the things I need to buy.

\#

My errands completed, I return to the cemetery and pull the folding chairs out of my trunk. I haul myself over the cemetery wall, wincing at the dull ache in my shoulder. There's no wincing away from the ache in my chest, though. Wending my way through the dark graves is familiar, but this time there is no fear, and no excitement. Just the realization that some things are beyond fixing or changing, even with magic. My mother was right.

I hate that she was right.

I kneel over Harry's grave. The dirt is turned up, clods of grass pressed back into the upset earth. I pull a sandwich bag full of kosher salt out of the 99 cent store bag I've brought with me, sprinkle a handful onto the earth, and say the words I need to say. I dig my hand into the dirt and make a fist around a clump of soil and salt. I pull a water bottle out of the bag and stuff the handful of dirt and salt into it. I shake the bottle hard, then pull the last item out of the plastic bag. The tiny water gun from the 99 cent store is neon green, but it looks sickening rather than cheerful in the moonlight. I unplug the bottom and squeeze the muddy water from the bottle into the toy. Then I stand. I need Harry for the last part. I wonder if I will have to go fetch him.

I don't. He's homed in on me again, just as he did the first night he came back. Just as he did in life. I swallow the painful lump in my throat and straighten my back, waiting for him to arrive. He stumbles a little now as he walks, and for the first time, I truly see him as a zombie. Dead. Lost. I can't make out his face in the dark, but I hear him moan as he shuffles toward me.

"Steph... Please don't run from me..."

I shudder and raise the water pistol, full of dirt and salt and water to remind his body of what it is supposed to be: dust. Undoing a spell and restoring the natural order is apparently much easier than upsetting the natural order in the first place. Who knew?

"I'm sorry. I'll miss you. Always," I whisper, and press the trigger. Nothing happens.

"Shit! Stupid 99 cent piece of crap!" I say, shaking the water pistol hard and trying again. Nothing.

Then I feel Harry's hands on me. They're strong, and ropey with tendons. I look up into his glazed, bloody eyes and they cut right through me. Behind the blood and the greenish, rotting skin and through the red and black cracks of veins his eyes still look like his: blue as the sky at noon.

I pull the plug from the back of the water gun and splash the water directly into Harry's face. He freezes, looking stunned and betrayed, even as his eyes sink into his rotting face. The light fades from them, and his hands grow limp on my shoulders. He sinks to the ground, and a sulfurous stench wafts up to me. My eyes run with tears, and I don't know if it's the smell, or losing him again which prompts them. The worst part is it's not over yet.

I kneel, and begin pushing back the loose earth of his grave with my hands. The dirt is soft and churned up from when he climbed out three days ago. A sob bubbles up from my throat and breaks, sharp as glass, from my lips. I keep digging.

By the time I've made a hole deep enough to conceal Harry's body and covered him up, the sky is growing gray with dawn. I'm covered in mud from my tears, snot and sweat mixing with the grave dirt. I probably look like some kind of swamp monster. I pat the grave dirt down and trudge back to the wall. I crawl over and drive home. Once I'm home I lock the door, lay down on the living room floor, and sleep like the dead.

When I wake I have no idea what time it is, but it's dark out again. I feel sticky all over, including inside my mouth, and I stink. I've never felt more disgusting as I peel my clothes off. In the shower, I watch the mud slough off and swirl down the drain. I wash everything three times to be sure I get all the dirt off, taking extra care for the wound on my shoulder. Somehow, I still don't feel clean. When I get out of the shower, I swipe my hand through the steam in the mirror and grab my toothbrush. As I brush my teeth with a wad of toothpaste the size Texas, I look at the girl reflected in the slash of clear mirror. She looks like hell. I rinse and spit, then look up at that girl again. She is pale and drawn, more dead than alive. But... She is alive. And if she can live through all of that, then she can live through the next thing, and the next. Maybe this is what resurrection is meant to be.

ABOUT THE AUTHORS

Stephanie Barr (Second Slavery)

Stephanie Barr is a part time novelist, full time rocket scientist, mother of three children and slave to many cats. She has three blogs, which are sporadically updated: Rocket Scientist, Rockets and Dragons, and The Unlikely Otaku. Anything else even vaguely interesting about her can be found in her writing since she puts a little bit of herself in everything she writes . . . just not the same piece. Stephanie Barr has published five novels, two anthologies of her own stories, and a book of poetry and has had stories published in multiple anthologies and ezines. She also has a bit of a manga obsession. Keep up with new releases and events by signing up for her newsletter on any of her blogs or check out her author page on Facebook (https://www.facebook.com/stephanieebarr/).

Timothy Callahan (Fade)

Born and raised in Philadelphia, PA, Timothy has been writing since the early age of 11.

He's a computer technician by day, doggie daddy at night and writer on the weekends and at lunch.

You can check him out at www.timothypcallahan.com

Eli Dawson (Lady Marie)
Has not provided a biography.

J.Z. Belexes (Favors)

J. Z. Belexes lives with his elderly grandmother as her caretaker and has spent this past year working with the rest of his family to get her out of her own abusive situation. It has not been an easy road, but it has been one of personal growth. He loves the music of Kansas and costumes as superheroes for charity events. He has a tendency to retreat into elaborate fantasy worlds, which he will share with you if you're not careful. He hopes to one day profit from this trait by becoming a professional novelist; this seems like a good start.

Karen Janowsky (Steps)

Karen lives in Maryland with her husband and son. When not writing, she teaches yoga. She has been writing and publishing poetry and fiction for most of her life. She earned her Master's Degree in Creative Writing at Florida State University, many many decades ago. https://theclothescollection.wordpress.com/issue-four-2/karen-janowsky/

R. C. Larlham (Ghost Out of Time)

R C Larlham is a retired environmental engineer living in southeast Michigan, "…south of the moon and north of Detroit." He began writing by writing tales of growing up in post-war America during the 1940s and 1950s to entertain his family and friends. That work grew into a two-volume memoir he called The Old Man and Me. Once that was finished, he began writing fiction, much of which, like this story, centered on a spirit who lived for centuries, animating the bodies of recently dead people.

When he's not writing, Mr Larlham spends his time with his grown children and his grandchildren.

Kaki Olsen (Just One Chance)

Kaki Olsen is known by many as the insatiable traveler, who will show you hundreds of pictures from her last trip or the itinerary for her next great adventure. Others know that her affinity for music leads her to attend the symphony often and play Beethoven sonatas for stress-relief. Many know well that for every novel she finishes, she is planning at least three more. It is most commonly known that she is a geek who has in-depth opinions on superhero allegory and writes papers on speculative fiction for fun. She currently makes her home far from her hometown of Boston, but occasionally mistakes her apartment for Fenway Park and aspires to be as well-stocked as the Boston

Public Library. Her blog and published works can be perused at www.kakiolsenbooks.com.

Kim Ross (The Evening Light)

Kim lives in Newcastle, Australia, with her husband, three sons, and family golden retriever. She writes as K.M.Ross, Kim Michelle Ross, Kim Ross but mostly answers to Mum. Formerly worked as a laboratory technician (biology, pathology), landscape gardener, Mail Officer, medieval re-en actor player. Hunter Writers' Centre member 2007-14, facilitator Women@theLockup writers 2009-11. 2010 Lit-Link Mentorship recipient with award winning speculative fiction poet-author, Jenny Blackford. Kim is also a belly dancer and performs professionally with Silk Caravan Belly Dance Troupe. Find out more at https://www.amazon.com/K.M.-Ross/e/B0742D36H8/ref=dp_byline_cont_pop_ebooks_6

Lisa Roth-Gulvin (The Tourist)

Lisa Roth-Gulvin holds and honor degree in English Literature with an emphasis in writing. Her work, both fiction and memoir, has been published on Literary Mama, the Anthology Three Minus Zero through She Writes press, "The Gift" in Quail Belle Magazine, "Confession" in OTV Magazine, "The Tourist" to be released in the Doves Project Anthology" October 2017, and "Tapestry" in Open Minds Quarterly. You can follow her blog at lisarothgulvin.wordpress.com.
Contact: lisarothgulvin@gmail.com

A. C. Russell (The Waste of Spirits)

Has not provided a biography.

Heather M. Walker (The Calling Song)

Heather M. Walker currently lives in LaGrange Georgia, with her partner of 16 years, Billy, her 8 year old daughter Makaylah, and her 4 cats. While writing is her main passion, she also enjoys crafting in every form, from paper crafts to working with glass. She considers herself a shy, introverted person, with a silly sense of humor and eclectic personality. She has been published by Balck Velvet Seductions with two books, "The Otherling," and "The Reclaiming Of Charlotte Moss." She would love to hear from her readers about her work. She can be reached at picassomoons@hotmail.com.

Michael Young (12 Grains)

Has not provided a biography.

Mira Domsky (Resurrection Girl)

Mira Domsky, is an undercover gothbrarian, injured ninja, vegetarian, writer, sometimes artist, and all the time geek. She puts together a homepage of collected images and links to all the stuff she likes to create: art, stories, sarcastic jokes, maybe some food, probably a mess...

You can read what she thinks about stuff on her blog: Vegetarian Ninja Librarian
It's mostly about books she likes, and whatever she decided to cook last week.

49669109R00154

Made in the USA
Middletown, DE
21 October 2017